Mac   MacBeth, George

          The Katana

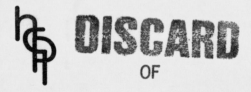

Books by George MacBeth

THE KATANA
POEMS OF LOVE & DEATH
THE SURVIVOR
THE SEVEN WITCHES
THE SAMURAI
SHRAPNEL & THE POET'S YEAR
COLLECTED POEMS 1958–1970

日本の刀

THE KATANA

A Novel

by George MacBeth

Based on the wartime
diaries of John Beeby

SIMON and SCHUSTER
New York

This novel is a work of historical fiction. Names, characters, places and incidents re-
lating to non-historical figures are either the product of the author's imagination or
are used fictitiously, and any resemblance of such non-historical figures, places or incidents to actual persons, living or dead, events or locales is entirely coincidental.

Copyright © 1981 by George MacBeth and John Beeby
All rights reserved
including the right of reproduction
in whole or in part in any form
Published by Simon and Schuster
A Division of Gulf & Western Corporation
Simon & Schuster Building
Rockefeller Center
1230 Avenue of the Americas
New York, New York 10020
SIMON AND SCHUSTER and colophon are trademarks of Simon & Schuster
Designed by C. Linda Dingler
Manufactured in the United States of America

10 9 8 7 6 5 4 3 2 1

Library of Congress Cataloging in Publication Data

MacBeth, George.
The Katana.
I. Beeby, John.   II.Title.
PR6063.A13K3 1981   823'.914   81-13550
                                   AACR2

ISBN 0-671-43245-1

For Peggy of beloved memory
and for
Ken and Diane

There are no villains, I presume, in a Democracy. He was only just as wrong as hell.

—ERNEST HEMINGWAY
Across the River and into the Trees

1

They say that every man has a book somewhere inside him, a sort of credo, or confession. And I suppose that's true. It's just that in most cases it never comes out. The mute, inglorious Miltons go on leading their quiet existences in the shires. Unless, of course, some strange crisis occurs, and the even tenor of their lives is shaken off the hook. In my own case, it was something more secondhand. But it triggered the underlying need, the years of frustrated silence that I'd kept locked up too long.

Mountbatten assassinated. The headline caught my eye as soon as I settled myself by the window, ready for a late breakfast. I remember looking up, and then for a moment I was completely gone.

I was back in my office at a baroque mahogany desk under Clapham Common in the spring of 1941. And a thin, spruce young Japanese officer in the uniform of an English major was coming to attention on my worn strip of Axminster.

"Name?"

"Major Strand, sir."

Then I was back in Shropshire, and the sun was shining, and my breakfast was going cold. I looked across the terrace towards the balustrade. The iron garden seats were flaking. It wasn't so easy as it used to be to keep things up. I read the date again on *The Gazette*. It seemed hard to believe it was 1979.

I'd served under Mountbatten in the Far East for three years. I'd seen him take an army that was a defeated rabble and weld it back into a fighting force that had thrown the Japanese out of Burma.

I thought of my old wartime leader there in his cabin cruiser, the boy beside him looking out toward the lobster pots, the assassin far away on the cliff top with his little transmitter. Eyes screwed into good binoculars, pulling the target to the identifying point of closeness. And then the finger turning the grooved knob to the right frequency, and the huge, remote fountain of neutral water.

So much for Lord Louis Mountbatten, the last of the great shoguns. Killed at the age of seventy-nine, still on the naval reserve, and by an unknown man with a toy for controlling model airplanes.

Mary had taken to laying my tray out beside the south window in the drawing room, and I felt the warmth of the sun on my face as I reached out for toast and marmalade. It was easier to absorb it all while I was eating. I poured coffee and leaned back in the armchair. I'm not so young as I was. It takes more energy to resist a sudden shock when you get to sixty-nine.

I read the story through again. Yes, two men had been arrested and were helping the police with their inquiries. But it was clear enough, reading between the lines, that they weren't the executive arm. Someone had turned that dial on top of a distant hill, and a boat out in a bay had been blown to smithereens. That someone was still at large, and might always be.

I thought how history repeats itself. The paper made no more than a brief mention of the earlier assassination attempt in 1944 when Mountbatten was nearly blown up by a bomb in a sacred casket at the Temple of the Tooth in Kandy. It was the Japanese then, they said, the IRA today. History repeats itself.

Perhaps, I thought. But only I knew how close the Japanese had come to success. I and a handful of others, mostly dead. There was a footnote to history now to be written, one with a fresh and terrible relevance, and I was the one man who could tell the inside story.

I took a turn by the window, and stood looking down the lawn with my hand on the shutters. I'd have to get the roller out and do something about the grass. Perhaps John would help when he came down from Trinity for the summer.

It had been a good life these last years. The war and all that it had meant had begun to seem like a kind of dream. I thought that I'd come to terms with the pain and the bitterness at last. I hadn't seen Clark and Brundall since the 1960s. And then there was Strand.

I'd remembered Strand almost every day of my life. But it seemed for a while I could let him lie in the back of my mind until I died. It was different now. I knew for certain as I stood there looking toward my little stream running through the hazel coppice that I should have to write the story down at last. There was no one else who could.

So I got the Daimler out, and drove to Ludlow, and took the train up from Shropshire to Euston. I had a comfortable empty carriage, and I read the other papers to pass the time. It was always the same story. Lord Louis Mountbatten had been assassinated by the Provisional IRA. Two men were being held for questioning. But the one who triggered off the bomb was still at large.

Only he knew the truth, I reflected. Only he could fill in the gaps of the newspaper reports. I closed the papers and spent the last part of the journey looking out of the train window. At least the record on the 1944 assassination attempt could be put straight. At least there was someone who could still spell Kandy left alive. It was pleasant walking weather, so I went on foot across the park to the Public Record Office. I'd telephoned to say I was coming, but it wasn't necessary.

When you wear your town coat neatly cut in England, and furl your umbrella properly, you can still usually get some service from the bureaucrats. The clerk was polite. He kept me waiting a few minutes, with a chance to study the Spy cartoons on the walls. But he got out the box.

All it needed was my wartime ID card, and a signature, and I had the files out on a four-week research pass. No doubt any young American graduate student could have done the same

9

with a note from his supervisor. If anyone had been interested.

"Writing your memoirs, Colonel."

He made it more of a statement than a question. I suppose he must have been handing out these green boxes to dozens of rigid old military birds like me since the expiry of the thirty-year embargo.

"Were you in the Army?" I asked.

It pays to make friends with them.

"After the war. I fought in Cyprus."

I nodded.

"Nasty business with EOKA," I said. "You must have seen some action."

"A bit," he said, preening himself.

He was flattered.

"Bloody shame about Mountbatten," I said. "I thought he'd live forever. I was there in 1944, you know, when the Japs tried to kill him."

The clerk nodded sympathetically.

"Take care, Colonel," he said.

He was warning me about the turn in the stone steps. He didn't want his precious file spewed over the floor. But I took his point another way.

Not many of those involved were still alive. Brundall, I'd heard, had had a heart attack, and died, of all places, at Benghazi. He'd become a writer of travel books. Molly might still be alive. I didn't know. But Clark was—for sure. He'd be near to retiring age, but he still had his regular column on that slushy provincial rag in Berkshire. And Vonnegut. Vonnegut with his filing cabinets. He was still there.

I thought about this on the train home, and I thought about it some more with the box unopened beside me later that evening in my study. But I had to go on. My mind was as firmly fixed on those distant events as if it had been rammed home with a pin. I had to write, and I had to tell the truth.

So I opened the box. Turning the little brass key once, and then again once, in the lock. It was all there. The letters, the confidential reports, the secret memoranda. And, of course, Strand's diary. I'd expected that. Without it there would have to have been gaps. But there was something else. Something that did surprise me.

I switched on the table lamp in the gathering dusk and lifted the object out of the box. I felt the skin prickle on my neck as I touched the ridged black lines of the *roiro* scabbard.

The mounts were silver. All *en suite*, as I remembered them. Waves of a stormy sea, curled back on themselves, and incised in the best *katakiri* engraving.

In a way, the short sword seemed to sum it up. I suppose that Clark must have decided to put it in when he closed the file in 1945. It would have seemed the right thing to do. All those cold pages of print made the story seem rather dead. It came alive in the mute, unspoken symbolism of the *tanto*.

I drew the blade a little way from the sheath. It was clean and shining, the bright wavy line of the temper opaquely gleaming under the light.

It made me remember. And as I remembered I felt something near to tears coming. Clark had been right to put the sword in. I slid the blade back in the sheath and locked the sword away. It was time to begin.

For a moment I sat with my hands clasped on the box. Then I began to put down the story of a very strange and a very brave man. It was my story, too, when it all started. And it still is, nearly forty years later.

So it seems best to tell it from my own point of view, even if that means losing richness. At least what I say will be true.

It's a complex story, with all its twists and turns, and it begins in Asia, before the war.

I entered Sandhurst in 1928, and passed out, I suppose, with some honor. I had lucky postings in the Far East, and saw some service in India, on the North-West Frontier. I was never wounded, but there were bullets flying, and I got a mention in dispatches. This, plus a natural talent for languages and an ambitious disposition, were the main sources of a rapid advancement.

I found myself in a staff job at Delhi, and I started reading the newspapers. I was no more keen on the death or glory stuff

11

than the next man, and a career in the higher echelons of administration rather appealed to me. So I paid some attention to what was going on in the world. And to what was *going* to go on.

I was convinced as early as 1936 that the Japanese wanted war. I was attached to the Embassy in Tokyo as military attaché at the time of the abortive right-wing coup, and I was clear that there were men of aggressive ambitions in both the imperial and the parliamentary parties. It made sense too. The Japanese needed oil to fuel their industrial expansion, and neither the Americans nor ourselves were going to sell it to them.

They knew that. So they were prepared to take what they needed by force of arms. Nowadays we make the same mistakes. It always makes me furious. We still think the Japanese islands are populated by stupid little men with buckteeth and round spectacles who spend their time giggling and drinking green tea. It's cost us the shipbuilding industry. Half of the Clyde has ground to a halt because the idiots in Whitehall can't take the Japanese seriously.

In 1941 it was worse. It cost us thousands and thousands of lives. I knew it would. I spent five years bombarding the Cabinet Office with detailed memoranda about what was plain as a pikestaff: the Japanese design to invade Malaya and capture Singapore. But no one listened. They were too busy with their own dreams of British invulnerability.

They set up Department M in Far Eastern Intelligence in 1939. The object was to study Japan. For all the attention paid to our reports we might just as well have concerned ourselves with *kabuki* prints and geisha girls. When I became head of the Department I had a staff of forty: officers, clerks, typists, even a porter for the suite of rooms we had in the old Foreign Office building. It was a luxurious operation, in keeping with the view that our potential enemy in the Far East would be Japan.

Unfortunately, in their self-satisfaction, the powers that be were quite unprepared to accept any revision of their preconceived notions. These were, very roughly, that the Japanese were about as dangerous, militarily speaking, as the Zulus had been in 1879. They might harass us a bit in the event of an outbreak of hostilities, but their culture was too backward to produce any surprising or threatening plan of campaign.

So what happened to our increasingly strongly worded reports about Japanese intentions? As far as I could see, they might have been flushed down the Prime Minister's lavatory for all the good they were doing. Finally my patience broke. I wrote a personal memo, in the most direct terms, demanding an immediate interview with the Director of Far Eastern Intelligence.

I got it. I can see him now standing there with his hands under the tails of his khaki jacket, warming his legs in front of his ancient gas fire. Pretending to be the bonny Earl of Moray home from a day's shooting on his grouse moor. He was a snobbish little bastard.

"Colonel," he said.

I knew I was in for trouble. He wouldn't have dropped my name unless the shit was going to hit the fan, as the Americans used to say.

"Sir," I said.

I was still young enough in those days to see the wisdom of licking a boot or two on occasion.

"Colonel," he said again, emphasizing my junior rank.

He wasn't impressed by my politeness. He had a nasty job to do, and he meant to get on with it. He straightened his shoulders as if for invisible cameras.

"I know what you want to see me about, and I know what you want to say. It's all in your—er—most carefully documented reports."

Those all-too-precisely-honed vowels of his were beginning to get up my nose. I was tired, and I could feel my sense of caution going.

"Not all, General," I said. "Not quite all."

He blinked and swallowed.

"Colonel," he said, in a whisper, closing his eyes.

He even spread his hands, as if cleaving his way through a sea of oppressive papers.

"There is nothing more I need to hear from you on the subject of Japanese military intentions. You have made your point. Unfortunately, your assessment of the situation is at complete variance with the appreciation of the General Staff, the Singapore authorities and, I may add, the Prime Minister."

This was news to me at the time, and bad news. I'd had hopes that there might be at least one ally left, right at the top. It seemed I was wrong.

"Then God help us," I said.

At this point I seem to remember him taking a turn around the room, as if he'd come to evaluate the pictures. But my recollection is vague. I stared down at the carpet through a puce fog. When I came to he was standing beside his rhinoceros of a desk with a slip of paper in his hand.

"I'm sorry," he was saying.

Perhaps he was, but he didn't sound it. I could see the firing squad leveling their rifles. It was a bright day, but I wasn't going to walk out into it with any illusions left.

"Winston," he said reverently. "I'm afraid Winston has urged me to purge my stables of alarmists."

He was gently smoothing the slip of paper flat on his blotter, as if it had been a holy relic. I suppose in a way it was, considering the authority Churchill wielded in those days.

"This means two things," he said thoughtfully. "First of all, I shall require that your future reports be researched more fully in the light of received wisdom before they are documented in their final form."

I watched the flicker of leaves on a little group of silver birch trees in the corner of the Foreign Office garden.

"I see," I said.

I did see. He wanted the stuff censored at source before it got posted off to Fort Canning in Singapore. I was being asked to become a rubber stamp for the local ostriches. It was a kind of treason.

"Second," he said, "I'm afraid I shall need to make some changes in the housing of your personnel."

So it was exile too. I took a deep breath. All right, I thought. Let them try to forget what's under their noses. Let them try to sweep the Department and General Tojo and the military ob-

14

jectives of the Japanese people under the carpet. Let's see how long they stay there.

"Winston has been rather generous," the Director was concluding. "His office tells me the reserve invasion bunker under Clapham Common is currently surplus to requirements. You and your brave lads are to be let camp out for a spell. You won't be as comfortable as you've been down the corridor here. But then you won't be as many either. I've decided to cut down your establishment here and there. After all," he was saying, rising to his feet with that prim smile he had, "it may be that some of the deadwood was causing the muzziness in your thinking. Goodbye, Colonel."

So in April 1941 I was squatting in the Prime Minister's reserve concrete HQ under Clapham Common, reduced, by the inexorable ax of military ineptitude, to a last-ditch staff of myself, my adjutant Major Clark, Captain Brundall, two corporals who did the filing, and a female typist, Molly Jenkins. I was bitter but I wasn't beaten. It was only a question of time. I had to wait, but I knew that my chance would come. Mercifully it came sooner than I might have expected. And the man who brought it, and laid it out for me on a plate, was Major Michael Strand of the Army School of Oriental Languages.

2

Nowadays you wouldn't notice the concrete air vents of my old HQ if you walked across Clapham Common. The only signs are occasional groups of low grassy mounds here and there. I remember once during the rubbish strike in 1978 seeing a couple of young blacks picking over the top of one for anything they could salvage out of the burst plastic bags. London isn't what it was. You wouldn't have seen scavengers in 1941.

What you *would* have seen, if you were out walking your dog or carrying your gas mask on your way to school, would have been several irregular groups of concrete mushrooms. They wouldn't have started you thinking about the hydrogen-bomb explosion—unless you were unusually prescient—or anything else very warlike, for that matter. They might just have seemed like the covers for some kind of static water tank. There were certainly plenty of those about.

In fact those rather ordinary and innocent-looking beige umbrellas had been erected under a top-secret specification by the War Office at the outbreak of hostilities in 1939. They were the only visible surface evidence of Neville Chamberlain's last-ditch line of defense. Underneath them nearly two hundred acres of solid London clay had been rabbit-warrened into a near-impregnable series of interconnected chambers.

In the event of the Prime Minister's Whitehall shelter being rendered inoperative by enemy action, the seat of government would shift to Clapham. That was the architect's dream, anyway. But he was evidently no Albert Speer. God help Winston Churchill and the British war effort if they'd ever had to survive and flourish in the way Department M was supposed to.

The Clapham Center, as it was rather self-contradictorily called, was powered by mains electricity, and there was a reserve supply deriving from an independent generating plant. We had all the power we needed. Unfortunately we were never allowed to use it. There was a strict system of bulb rationing both by number and by wattage from the day we moved in, so that most of our time was spent under the sort of watery, dim light more suitable for a chapel than an office.

The electricity supply was also supposed to provide us with heating and hot water, but we hadn't been more than two months there when I had a directive to moderate expenses by cutting down on radiators and use of the boiler. So we had to shiver through an icy spring on a miserable four hours a day allowance.

It wouldn't have been so bad if the rooms had been reasonably small and low-ceilinged. Unfortunately, in some bizarre fit of grandeur, Chamberlain or one of his lackeys had laid down instructions for the accommodation to be modeled as closely as possible on the overground Cabinet offices in central London. So my staff and I froze and peered in Victorian splendor.

The reception hall was a pillared extravaganza with a tiled floor occasionally covered by tiger skins with set-up heads. I was always tripping over them. The fittings in my own office were a touch more succinct.

There was the loaded-looking desk I've already mentioned. Wall maps, like blinds, on rollers. Even an imaginary fireplace, with a florid marble surround and an iron coal scuttle I kept files in. It all reminded me faintly, in its windowless way, of my childhood in India.

Perhaps they imagined that if the Center was ever captured by German invaders we would at least be seen to have gone down with the flag flying in appropriate imperial style. I never found out. One thing was certainly clear. When Churchill came to power he'd taken one look at the place and burst out laughing. It wasn't a headquarters, it was a museum.

So it was no doubt an apt touch of humor that the disgraced Department M should be put down here in its mothballs. I can savor their wit now with a better grace than I did in 1941. In those days I used to click down my echoing corridors with a firm determination to grind the Director and the War Cabinet into the ground at the earliest possible opportunity.

One of the particular irritants I smarted under was the War Cabinet's refusal to grant me the key to the front door. There was an efficient hydraulic lift system which led directly into the heart of the complex through a vertical shaft surfacing in a disused men's lavatory. The water tanks had been geared to a set of pulleys in such a way that the cages would rise and fall when water was displaced from one chamber to another by the pull of a rope. You could see the same sort of thing right up to the 1950s in the BBC Training School in Lexington Gardens.

It would have saved me and my staff a half-mile walk through sweating, dank concrete if we could have arrived and left through this central lift system. So I went to the Director and asked permission.

"Very sorry, Colonel," he said. "I sense your boredom, but we have to think of security. It would hardly do for a constant stream of uniformed men and women to be seen entering and leaving a closed urinal."

I'd gone back to Clapham with a flea in my ear. They had every intention of making me eat dirt. And of shoveling it onto my plate with a trowel. We continued, as we had been forced to commence, by entering and leaving through Clapham Common Underground Station.

This was exactly what I was doing on the morning my story effectively begins. It was a sharp, clear April day, and I'd walked along the side of the Common from my lodgings in Cavendish Gardens. You can still see the old block today, but there's a piece of postwar austerity across the road, and the usual population of our African friends. In those days the faces were all white, and the ones that weren't were in uniform.

I went down the steps under the little clock tower and

showed my pass to the porter at the gate. At the bottom of the elevator there was a door marked PRIVATE. I've no idea what was behind it. I never saw it opened then or since. Its usefulness to me was simply as a guide to where my secret entrance was. The keyhole was six feet from the doorknob, and today it was covered by a large Fougasse poster of two men gossiping on a tube train while a third, evidently listening in to their conversation, pretended to be absorbed in a newspaper. The third man was Adolf Hitler.

I liked Fougasse, but propaganda always made me wince. I could hardly believe that the British public was quite so simpleminded. Were people really influenced by this jokey nudging? I had my doubts. It struck me then, and it strikes me now, that the man in the street is a good deal more sensible when it comes to keeping his mouth shut than many of his supposed masters and betters.

At the top, people crack, and things get twisted. In Intelligence work you confront human nature at the point where ambition reveals its darkest strains. I've seen too many mouths opened by greed, and shut by fear.

My mind was running on this as I paused to look around. I was in a sort of enlarged broom cupboard. A sink stood against the far wall, and beside this, with its blue paint peeling, there was the door of what looked like a cupboard. Walking up to it I pressed a panel in the side. At once a whole section of the wall moved sideways on runners and I was free to pass through into a broad corridor.

The walk down this always took about five minutes. I won't bore you with the details. There weren't any. Simply bare concrete with naked bulbs in holders at ten-yard intervals. At the end there was another door, this time a steel one, with another lock.

I went through, and at once the contrast hit me. I tipped my furled umbrella—it had looked like rain, but the shower had held off—into an ornate wooden cylinder supported by a carved grizzly bear.

There was the sound of Molly typing, and it sounded incongruous through the chill mist from the chandeliers. I clattered my way over inlaid Moslem patterns toward my office. The Tiffany lamp was on, and Brundall was standing beside my mantelpiece with a steaming cup.

I sniffed.

"Ersatz again," I said.

Brundall smirked. He was one of those neat, toothbrush-moustached young men who all seemed to be imitating Anthony Eden and ended up looking like out-of-work car salesmen. The uniforms didn't really help. They never seemed to fit at the sleeves.

Even so, I quite liked Brundall. He was a glutton for work, or at least for promotion, and he managed to keep the files in order. He was talking now as I settled down behind my desk.

"There's Major Strand to see you," he said. "He's in the waiting room."

I looked at my watch. It was after ten. Strand was on time.

"He's been here since nine-thirty," said Brundall. "The House of Commons may have been hit last night, but the Germans didn't succeed in delaying Major Strand."

I nodded. They often did arrive ahead of time. Since the Department was formed we'd had a steady stream of visitors—cranks, experts, ambitious young officers wanting transfers, the lot. The stream had thinned to a mean trickle in the Clapham epoch, but the eagerness of most of the visitors hadn't.

They all had something to sell or something they thought we might want to buy. It was either their information or their invasion plans or their time. I'd learned from experience that they were all the same, and they were never much use. The occasions when an unsolicited request for an interview yielded anything of value were rare.

So I made it a regular if boring chore to lay aside an hour every morning to deal with anyone who phoned up to ask if he could see me. There was nothing about Strand's request that had made him sound any more interesting than the others—until he was there in front of me.

Sitting here now, with Clee Hill away in the distance to the right of my window, I can still see Strand as he looked when I first met him. It's hard to remember exactly, in the light of subsequent events, but the central impression is vivid and clear. This was a Japanese officer in the uniform of a British major.

He was perfect. He had the tight smile, the small, screwed-up eyes, the trim, erect, minute figure. The only thing that didn't fit was his very professional, and very British, military salute.

"Sit down, Major," I said.

He crossed his legs in the Eastlake armchair, and I watched the way his hands and his eyes moved. It was odd. Everything about him was English, the way he laced his knuckles, the glance he gave at the high polish on his boots. And yet his features and his physique were absolutely those of a Japanese.

I looked down at the file Brundall had laid ready for me. The explanation, of course, was all there in the background. But the background hadn't struck me as so interesting until I was faced with its results in the shape of this amazing chimera on the other side of my desk.

I took my time to absorb the details. I found that it wore my visitors down to keep them waiting. They grew afraid, and they talked less. I still didn't expect Strand to be anything out of the usual.

"Smoke if you like," I suggested.

This too I had found was a good idea. They got nervous lighting their match, or having to ask for an ashtray.

"Thank you," said Strand.

I watched him, but he made no move. He was going to bide his time. One mark to you, I thought. You're a cool customer. I cleared my throat and began to read aloud.

"You were born in Osaka. Your father managed an import and export business. Your mother was Chinese. You are an only child. You were educated at a Japanese school."

I paused. My last statement was a question.

"For a time," Strand said, answering the question. "It was good for business. My father believed in assimilation. We used to sit at home in kimonos and eat off low tables—you know the sort of thing."

His voice was precise, contained, ominous. There was all the masterful scornfulness of Wellington and Sandhurst in it. I was beginning to be interested in Major Strand.

"I was educated in England until I was fifteen. Then my father thought I should pick up the final graces at the Peers' School in Tokyo. I suppose it paid off well, for a time."

Strand smiled.

"There was plenty of business."

I listened as he told me his story. The years of childhood acquiring the veneer of Japanese culture essential to smooth the rise of a foreign merchant. The interim years at an English public school in Somerset. The years back in Osaka working in the firm. Traveling the length and breadth of Japan.

"I traveled abroad as well," he said. "I was all over the Far East. Dutch East Indies, Hong Kong, Malaya. We did business as far afield as Australia and the Middle East."

I was making notes in my mind as he spoke. One word had begun to drum like a refrain in my head. Malaya. He knew Malaya.

"You liked the Japanese?" I suggested casually.

I was looking down at my blotting pad as I spoke. There was dead silence. After a moment I looked up. I hadn't expected the fury my remark would arouse. Strand's face had gone white with rage.

"They murdered my mother," he said quietly. "She was staying with relatives in Shanghai. You may have heard of the massacre."

He was on his feet now, reaching into his pocket for a packet of Player's, rasping the wheel of his lighter, inhaling smoke.

"Look," he said. "You people who sit here in England are all the same. You don't know what the Japanese are like. You think they're all funny little fellows with long sleeves and nice lacquer boxes. You think that all they want is to be left alone to make pretty paper flowers and metal toys for you. Well, you're wrong. The Japanese are the most intelligently dedicated and cruel people on this earth."

I felt a great wave of excitement rising in me. I seemed to be listening to a tape recorder playing back my own opinions.

Only this time they were coming from the mouth of someone who looked just like a Japanese.

Strand sat down.

"Oh, yes," he was saying. "I suppose I did like them, for a time. I enjoyed their grace and their oddness. I admired their art and their traditions. I even had quite a good collection of prints. A Hiroshige. Some *shunga.*"

He was drawing smoke into his lungs, letting it out slowly.

"It wasn't just the massacre," he said. "There were lots of signs. I'd seen the way things were going for years. I just didn't want to notice, I suppose. Then one day it had all changed. I don't think my father could quite take it in. He can't now. But he knew that we had to get out. There was no way we could stay and work in Osaka when the authorities realized that my mother had family in China who were actively opposing their administration."

Strand shrugged.

"We had to get out fast. My mother was accused of having been a spy. Windows were broken in our main shop by an angry mob. There were fears for our own lives. So we took the first flight we could get to Hong Kong. From there we came on to England. I was helping my father to build up his business again until the war broke out. Then I enlisted to teach Oriental languages."

"Japanese, in fact," I said, referring to the file.

"But I speak fair Cantonese too. And some dialects."

I nodded.

"So why are you here?"

It was the crucial question. Usually they wanted a job on my staff. They pined for a flash of the bright lights of London, the heady breath of Intelligence work. In Strand's case I was already clear that I'd have liked to take him on. But I didn't have a post to put him in.

"You know why I'm here," said Strand surprisingly. "I'm sorry about the outburst just now. It's a touchy point with me. You must forgive me. I've done my research. I know that you know about what the Japanese have in mind. You did your time in Tokyo, Colonel."

I was flattered. The major had clearly briefed himself well before making his appointment.

"You see the danger as well as I do," Strand was continuing. "They need our oil, our rubber and our tin. The trade agreements are a farce. And they know that we won't negotiate a change. The military faction is bent on war."

So far, so good. It was exactly my own view.

"So what do you think they mean to do?" I asked.

"Invade Malaya."

Strand was on his feet again. He walked over to the map of Southeast Asia unrolled on the wall beside my desk. He pointed to Singapore.

"The guns are facing out to sea," he said. "They'd be blown to pieces if they tried to use their navy."

He tapped the map with his finger.

"They mean to come down from the north."

And for fifteen careful minutes Major Michael Strand of the Army School of Oriental Languages elaborated what sounded the most feasible plan for such an invasion that I'd so far heard. It made Hayley-Bell's analysis seem out of date. In all respects it coincided with what I believed but had failed to detail so exactly.

When Strand finished I drew in my breath.

"Major Strand," I said, "you have my admiration. I believe absolutely in the likelihood of what you predict. There's only one problem."

I paused.

"Apart from you and me, no one in Whitehall is going to accept it."

I sketched on my blotter with my pencil. The plan was already beginning to form in my mind. But it was too soon to put it to Strand openly.

"Look," I said. "All I can suggest is that you put this analysis on paper and have it sent round to me here for rerouting to my Director and the War Cabinet. I'll do my utmost to see that it's read by the Prime Minister in person."

I laid my pencil down.

"But I don't promise you anything."

Strand was rising to go. I motioned him to sit down.

"There's just one thing I *can* do," I said.

I went over to a grandiose 1840s sideboard and opened the door. It had been adapted as a filing cabinet, but I'd left the zinc-lined bottom drawer as it was. I took out a bottle of malt whiskey and two glasses. I held the bottle up.

"Have a drink," I suggested.

I watched Strand stub his cigarette out in the crystal ashtray on my desk. As he did so the hot ash momentarily burned his finger, and I saw him withdraw his hand and lift it to his earlobe. That was just the kind of thing a real Japanese would have done, since the Japanese regard the ear as the coldest part of the body. It was a tiny detail, but it made my pulses quicken.

It was too soon to tell him so, but Strand was my man. Between us we would plan a coup that would lift my Department back into favor at a single stroke. And in the process deliver a blow right at the heart of the enemy war machine. There were many details to be worked out, but the central shape of the idea was crystal-clear.

I let Strand talk for another ten minutes about his childhood and background, and then we parted with a handshake and a promise on my part to be in touch again. I waited until he'd had time to cross the tiled hall and go out into the corridor. Then I made my move. I was bursting to relieve my bladder, and at the same time I couldn't wait to perfect the details of my plan.

3

I walked stiff-legged to the sideboard, I remember, and I opened the swing door that sheltered my secret files. I ran my fingers quickly over the tops and drew out a thin beige folder with a number of loose papers inside it.

Then I stepped through my door, crossed the hall, nodded to Molly in her typing sanctum, and entered the lugubrious acanthus-leaf-shrouded portals of the cloakroom.

It was done up in the style of its counterpart at the Athenaeum, if you want a comparison, except that there wasn't a uniformed flunky shifting brushes and expecting a heavy tip.

I stepped into the right hand of the two inner cubicles and closed the door with its brass bolt. It took me only a few moments to relieve myself, and then I sat down on the closed mahogany panel of the closet and opened the folder.

The light was no dimmer in here than anywhere else, and it was the one place in my elaborate fortress where I could be certain of ten minutes' complete freedom from interference.

I fingered the porcelain handle on the end of its chain, and began to read.

The file I'd taken out was marked HAYLEY-BELL, and it had a red CLOSED sticker across the front. The contents of the file reminded me that a Colonel Hayley-Bell had been sent out to Singapore in 1936 to begin an investigation into Japanese espionage activities in Malaya. Hayley-Bell, like Strand, had been brought up as a boy in Japan, he spoke fluent Japanese and he understood the Japanese mentality.

Over two and a half years he had assembled the materials of a damning indictment. There was a Japanese population of nearly six thousand in Singapore, and several hundred of them, from evidence supplied by the local police and the British Intelligence services in the Far East, were involved in spying for the Japanese government.

The fact itself had never surprised me. I'd visited Singapore more than once in the course of my tour of duty in Tokyo, and I knew from my own sources that a fair amount of Intelligence work for Tojo was being done there. It was the extent of the network revealed by Hayley-Bell's report that amazed me.

Unfortunately this was the very factor that led to his downfall. I reread the file in my narrow cubicle with mounting sympathy. Exactly the same fate had befallen Hayley-Bell as my own Department M. He had presented a picture so disturbingly at variance with what the High Command wanted to know that he had had his reports permanently put on ice, and his organization was returned to the United Kingdom in May 1939, and very shortly thereafter disbanded.

I remember leaning back and playing with the marble toilet-roll holder as I reached the final memo transferring Hayley-Bell to other duties. I wondered where he was, and what he was doing. His luck had been even worse than mine.

You'll have your revenge, old lad, I remember thinking. I'll see to it that every word in these reports pays interest at a hundred percent.

I meant it, too. Colonel Hayley-Bell had laid the foundations for what was going to be the greatest Intelligence coup of the war. Major Michael Strand was the supplier of the necessary materials for the superstructure. The architect of the grand design was going to be myself.

One crucial detail in the Hayley-Bell reports was a contingency plan for the rounding up of all Japanese residents in Singapore in the event of an invasion. They were to be put aboard ships at Keppel Harbor and taken to prison camps in India. It was a carefully worked out scheme, and it seemed to me that it would have succeeded.

Of course the authorities would have to have accepted the prospect of invasion in the first place, and laid their plans. To do them justice at the local level, perhaps they had. There were signs that the police awareness of Japanese espionage was fairly acute. Regrettably, there was no evidence that the British government had the slightest intention of taking Hayley-Bell's prediction of a Japanese invasion any more seriously than mine or Strand's.

There was, in fact, a remarkable consensus. He too believed that the thrust would come from the north, through the jungle. He too had a similar view to ours about the number of troops likely to be involved, and the probable points of landing and lines of advance.

Strand's own predictions were more up-to-date and even more convincing. But the area of agreement was considerable. The Cabinet ought to accept his report as the clinching thesis in an argument maintained with great consistency by several proponents over many years.

They ought to; but they wouldn't. I had little doubt that the most likely consequence of my submitting Strand's paper to the Cabinet Office would be a speedy arrangement for his transfer to a front-line post in the desert. Their minds were closed, and this wasn't the way to open them.

I had a better plan for Major Michael Strand. For the purpose I had in mind, he had one vital advantage over Hayley-Bell or myself or anyone else I could think of with the same outlook on Japanese military intentions. In a word, he looked exactly like a Japanese.

There was a diffident knock on the door as I reached this point in my thinking.

"Sir," inquired a civilized, uncertain voice.

"I'm sorry, Brundall," I replied confidently. "I'm having some trouble with my bowels. Tell them," I added firmly, "whoever they are, that I'll telephone them back later in the afternoon."

Footsteps receded, and I was left in the dripping Victorian gloom with my thoughts. I glanced at my Ingersoll. It had only cost a few pounds, but it kept good time.

I smiled. I'd already been over forty minutes alone in here. No wonder poor Brundall had plucked up his courage to intervene.

I fumbled a pencil out of my pocket and began to make notes. I would have to do further extensive checks. How far would Strand's accent seem convincing to a native? How accurate would his behavior be, even under unusual or stressful circumstances? I remembered the way he had touched his earlobe when he burned himself with the cigarette. Major Strand was clearly very deeply imbued with the patterning he had received at the Peers' School in Tokyo.

I felt reassured. I would need to do psychological checks too. I had been impressed by Strand's vigilance and his contained energy. Did he have the essential secretiveness? Did he, also, have that final imponderable, the ruthlessness to be willing to go for the jugular in an emergency? Did he, in fact, have the killer instinct?

I remembered his face when he spoke of the death of his mother. I was pretty sure that Strand was just dying for a chance to get his hands on the enemy.

But it might not matter, even if I was wrong. The other characteristics were more important. So long as he could pass without question as a native Japanese the plan would work. And I thought that he could.

I stood up, stretched, and unbolted the door. I was feeling cramped, and I decided to enlarge the demesne of my privacy. I stepped out, crossed the checkerboard floor and bolted the door into the cloakroom itself.

They were bound to think I was committing suicide if they bothered to try the door, but for the moment I didn't really mind. I had to be alone. I sat down on the marble edge of one of the washbasins and continued with my reflections.

In a nutshell my idea was this. I now felt certain that the Japanese were intending to invade Malaya. Defeatist as it may sound, I also felt pretty certain that they would succeed in their main objective of reaching and capturing Singapore.

Prior to this, the local authorities, with a little pushing from London, would arrest and deport the whole Japanese population, spies and all. However, it might just be possible, or at any rate plausible, for a particularly clever local agent to escape the British net and emerge to greet his liberators. In that event, such a man would be received with open arms, and would enter into the full confidence of his countrymen. He would be in an excellent position to feed the arriving army with full details of the situation in the city just before the British defeat. And in return he could expect rapid promotion, and the full favor of the Kempei Tai, the Japanese Gestapo.

I intended that there should be such a local agent. And that his name would be Michael Strand. I felt the cold seeping up through my trousers, and I eased myself onto the floor, pacing to and fro in my excitement.

I would select, with local help, an agent at present working for the Japanese who had a fairly close physical resemblance to Strand. There were obviously plenty of agents to choose from. It shouldn't be impossible to find the right man.

Once the man was chosen, Strand would be furnished with a suitable alias and would begin to travel by sea from Rangoon to Singapore as a top-level businessman. There were still a few people doing this—enough, at any rate, to divert suspicion on the part of the local Japanese espionage network.

He would make a close study of the chosen agent and would be able, at the crucial moment, to step effectively into his shoes. Then, when the arrests began, Strand would go into hiding in Singapore and emerge as his double when the Japanese took over. Once the confidence of the liberators had been established, his career as a trusted agent of the Kempei Tai was assured.

There were dangers. I didn't let my mind dwell too closely on what might happen to Strand if his cover was blown. That was part of the risk of this kind of operation. Strand would know that before he undertook the job. If he agreed, he would be risking his life.

Of course, he might not agree. Most people might have bet

a lot of money that he never would. I could see the chances. But I remembered the look on his face when he spoke of his mother, and I felt convinced that I had my man.

There were numerous details still to work out. One of the most critical was how to make the choice of the right local Japanese agent in Singapore. I had no doubt in my mind that I could expect no help whatsoever through official channels. This operation had to be kept a strict secret from the word go.

If I so much as breathed a word of the idea to the Director it would mean the end of Department M then and there. I could just see his lips pursing and the look of controlled distaste on his face as he told me once again that he had already told me to mind my own business and lie low for a while. I was not being employed to come up with bright ideas about what to do in the event of contingencies that the War Office had decided were not going to occur. Like a Japanese invasion of Malaya.

No, I had to do this on my own. In the first stages the only people who must know anything about the plan had to be myself, Strand and the staff of Department M. The selection of the agent in Singapore would have to be made by ourselves, working quite outside the framework of Army Intelligence. I had an idea how to arrange this. But first of all I decided to brief my team.

I unlocked the door and walked out into the lofty grandeur of my subterranean hall.

I passed Molly's door and instructed her to invite Major Clark and Captain Brundall to come in to see me. Then I re-entered my office and prepared my mind. I leaned back in my leather throne behind the carved pedestals of the desk and considered what I was going to say.

Clark arrived first. He saluted in his slightly insolent fashion, then sat down in the Eastlake chair. I hadn't asked him to, but Clark was a past master in the art of going just a bit further than he ought to and getting away with it.

I studied the cigarette ash down the front of his uniform with a faint nausea. Clark would never make a soldier. But he was ambitious, and he had a native shrewdness. These qualities were going to be useful.

Brundall followed him in, and waited to be motioned to the sofa. He bolted for it like a rabbit as soon as I waved my hand. These were my troops, I thought. No wonder the war was going so badly. Nevertheless I needed their help. I had to excite their interest, and win their loyalty.

"You know the position of the Department here," I began, stroking my letter opener in my fingers. "Despite the high quality of the information prepared and processed by yourselves our work has not been properly appreciated. Our reports have been neglected, and we have been banished to the wilderness."

I paused.

"The situation has become intolerable," I continued. "I am no longer prepared to accept the humiliating conditions under which my staff have to operate."

I was laying it on a bit thick, but I could see it was going down well, particularly with Brundall. He was nodding seriously down at his knuckles. There was a signet ring on one, I noticed.

"Matters have reached a crisis," I went on. "Within the last few hours, information has reached me on the basis of which I regard all our predictions of a Japanese invasion of Malaya as confirmed."

This was far too steep, but I had their attention. They knew that it was something to do with Strand. I could sense Clark's sharp little brain ticking away like an alarm clock. He was sitting forward in his chair with his knees together.

"Major Strand," I said, "has left with me a detailed assessment of the situation with which I am in full sympathy, but which I am convinced will have no more effect on our superiors than our earlier memoranda. It would be a waste of time to pass it on as it stands. The time has come to achieve our objectives by alternative means."

"Excuse me, sir," said Clark, with a slight cough. "What exactly *are* our objectives?"

"The return of this unit to favor in the eyes of the High Command," I said crisply. "With one object," I added: "the frustration of the enemy war effort in Southeast Asia. Without us, without our expertise and acumen, the Malayan peninsula is as good as lost. With us, and with the secret weapon I am about to disclose to you, the fall of Singapore, which I believe now to be inevitable, will not be such a complete disaster as might be expected. Gentlemen, we can do nothing to stop the fall of Singapore. But we can snatch the coals of victory from the fire."

In those days the Churchill touch often had its effect. It's hard to remember nowadays how easily we were all swayed by a bit of flashy rhetoric. I'd come to be quite a dab-hand at it, in my day. And I could see that even the cynical Clark was caught by my enthusiasm.

I seized my advantage. I went rapidly on to outline the main heads of my plan.

When I had finished, Brundall drew in his breath and sighed. He seemed to be unsure whether or not I was joking. Clark was more thoughtful.

"You think it could work?" he said, fiddling with a button.

"Look," I said, putting my boot on the fender. "This is entirely between ourselves. As matters stand neither of you has the slightest chance of promotion or of receiving attention for the enormously important work you've been doing. You're in a backwater. I'm giving you both a choice. You can ask for a transfer to another department, and I'll see that no obstacles are put in your way. Or you can stay on my staff here and go through with this plan. But I'm warning you"—here I leaned forward and did my heavy father act—"if you remain you'll be committing yourselves to a venture full of risks, and with uncertain rewards. All that I can promise you is a real chance of contributing to the war effort and, in the process, an outside opportunity of some personal honor and distinction."

That last bit got them. I knew it would.

"Stay or go," I said. "Which will it be?" I paused. "Brundall?"

There was never really any question. I suppose they both knew even then that if anything went wrong the can would be carried by me. They would simply plead that they were carrying out my orders. But if they asked for a transfer, after I'd told them the bones of my plan, there was little doubt that they'd feel the full weight of my displeasure. And that could have meant some vicious underhand guiding in their postings.

So I rang the bell for Molly to arrange some corned-beef sandwiches and a pot of tea, and we got down to details.

"The first essential is this," I said, as we settled down to our lunch. "As from now we're going to operate entirely on our own. We'll continue to supply a thin flow of reports to the Cabinet, but we'll spend no time on research for them. Our whole effort is going to go into what I now propose to code-name Operation Chameleon: the recruitment, planting and servicing of a British agent in the Japanese Army. We'll need to keep our lines open to MI5 and the Foreign Office. The input of information is even more important than before. It's just that the output will be entirely related to our own project. In time, of course, we may disclose our whole plan. But only in the event of complete and continuing success."

Clark was smiling. He has a nasty, twisted little mouth, and the years haven't improved his smile.

"We'll teach them a lesson," he said, with his mouth full. "Something they'll never forget."

He might have meant the Japanese, but I hoped that he meant the Cabinet Office. The sentiments were very much my own. Nevertheless I felt that a proper reserve had to be maintained.

"The point is to win the war," I said. "The enemy must be identified and then neutralized. Nothing else is important. Now let's consider the problems. As far as I can see, there are three main areas to be explored."

I took them over the ground, and we drank our tea while the chiming clock on the mantel took us through the afternoon. The first problem, which was persuading Strand to take part in the scheme, was something I could have handled best in person. But I had excellent reasons for delegating this to Clark. To begin with, I felt quite sure Strand would agree. My doubts, insofar as they persisted, related much more to his suitability, and here I felt in some need of a second opinion.

Clark was more skeptical than I was that Strand would accept our offer, and this meant that he would approach the testing of Strand's qualifications with a severe and unprejudiced eye. I welcomed this. Moreover, I'd worked out a way of testing Strand that had a secondary usefulness to me. It was very much in the foreground of my mind.

Apart from all that, there were vital reasons for my handling in person the selection of the Japanese agent in Singapore whom Strand was to replace. This job would necessitate a trip to Singapore, and it would be easier at this stage to obtain the necessary pass for an officer of my own rank. For the moment, there would be quite enough to keep me fully occupied on that alone.

As for Brundall, I knew that he'd been on some kind of electrical engineering course before the war, and he seemed the obvious man to explore the third area of difficulty, which was how to set up the machinery for radio contact between Strand and his control in Singapore and our own base, wherever that was to be, in safe British territory.

"Take a look at the map," I said, with a jab of my thumb. "I want you to pick out the obvious place for our base to be. Bear in mind the likely extent of Japanese military conquest, as we've been predicting it, over the next eighteen months. You may choose Burma, or somewhere in China. See what you think."

"It may depend on the kind of radio transmitter we can get," said Brundall. "There are limits, you know, to how far these things can send a signal."

There were times when Brundall annoyed me.

"I know there are limits," I said. "So will you please check and report back. I want your proposals, in detail, on my desk within a week."

When Brundall had left I offered Clark the last of the corned-beef sandwiches. He took it. He was like that. A little nettled, I went over with him the details of arrangements to contact Strand near his base at Camberley.

"I've asked him to send up his report in writing," I said. "But I'm going to phone suggesting that he hand it over in person, for security reasons, to my second in command. I'll arrange for you to meet him in a local pub. You can form your own impressions with an informal chat over a glass of beer. If you're satisfied I want you to invite him to undergo the following test. . . ."

For a few moments I elaborated my plan. Clark looked surprised, but I think he'd already anticipated my reasons. I watched him brush his crumbs away.

"Grade Two expenses, I suppose," he said, swallowing the last of his corned beef. "In other words, The Saracen's Head."

"I'm afraid so," I confirmed.

He withdrew to his work, and I had leisure to reflect.

· The first steps had been taken. With Clark and Brundall on my side we already had the nucleus of our organization. The next stage hinged on Strand. Much would depend on how he reacted to Clark's approach in Camberley. I could only wait and see.

I went to the sideboard and poured myself another malt whiskey, a strong one. I raised my glass to the map on the wall.

"To you, Major Strand," I said.

4

In those days Camberley was a bustling, incisive town. It may have changed: I haven't been back since 1945. It used to have a special atmosphere created by the Free French. You'd see them in all the bars, drinking shorts instead of beer and stubbing out their endless Gauloises.

It had a Casablanca quality. You only needed Paul Henreid to walk into a crowded pub and say "Play the 'Marseillaise'" to the man at the piano and half the clientele would have stood to attention over their cognacs. I rather liked it myself. It was an antidote to the seedy, dedicated drinking of the British.

Clark seems to have thought otherwise. I really despise that little man every time I go through these desperate, pompous memoranda of his. I've got half a mind to heave the lot over into the wastepaper basket and have done with him.

Unfortunately, this is the point where I need his testimony. It was Clark I sent down to make the contact with Strand and it was Clark's report that set the whole thing going. It isn't difficult to reconstruct from the bare bones of Clark's notes the conversation they must have had in Jorrocks' Club.

Clark had put up at The Saracen's Head and eaten a dull dinner of rissoles and boiled potatoes. He'd rung up Strand earlier in the day and arranged the rendezvous for the delivery of Strand's report. Finding Jorrocks' Club in the blackout wasn't easy, but he'd fallen in with a group of officer cadets who led the way with a pencil torch.

Up the stairs, in the wooden loft, he'd obviously taken an instant dislike to the smell of the cigarettes, the sweetness of the drinks and the enthusiasm of the language. The French were in command: thirty or forty officers from their billets at St. Gregory's Roman Catholic School up the London road.

Clark felt like a fish out of water. There were British officers there too, but they were mostly young cadets from Sandhurst. He didn't like their voices, and he didn't like their confidence.

For twenty minutes he sat seething over his Guinness. He was lonely and irritated. The arrival of Strand must have cheered him considerably. Here at last was someone even more incongruous in these surroundings than himself. Exactly as he'd looked in Clapham—Japanese in British uniform.

"Another Guinness?" said Strand, as they shook hands.

It won over Clark immediately; but he was on his guard. He drained his earlier glass as Strand returned and sat down.

"Cheers," he said.

"I have the report in the inside pocket of my coat," said Strand quietly. "I don't quite see the need for this cloak-and-dagger stuff but I'll slip it over to you unobtrusively on the way out."

I don't think he liked Clark, even then. His diary doesn't start until the period in Singapore, but I can guess his first reactions. This dreary little idiot had better be put in his place.

Clark has his qualities, though. He was watching Strand, and he was deliberately overdoing the grammar-school-boy-out-with-his-betters bit. He wanted to test how sensitive Strand was to a disguise.

For a time they made idle conversation. Clark allowed himself to seem more of a fool than he is. Then he struck.

"Listen," he said, in Japanese. "I didn't come here simply to take custody of your report. I expect you've guessed that. There's something else."

It might not have been good security, but it was an effective psychological shock. There were some Frenchmen over at the bar starting to sing "There'll Always Be an England" in mock English. Strand looked across at them and smiled.

"You've got a nice accent," he said dismissively.

It was insulting, but it didn't put Clark off his stride. It put him more on his guard. Here was a cool one all right.

"They killed your mother," he said brutally, still in Japanese. "You hate the bastards."

He didn't like what he saw in Strand's eyes any more than I had, and it told him all he needed to know. He's a killer, he recorded.

"The colonel has a proposition," said Clark. "He may need your help for a special operation he's planning. The point is," he continued, leaning forward, "it's dangerous, it will damage the Japanese, and it's secret. So I need to know two things before I can tell you more."

Strand was silent. He was drinking Scotch, and he took another sip while he waited for Clark to go on. He drank like a Japanese, Clark thought, as if from a tiny lacquer cup. So far, so good.

"First," said Clark. "Are you interested?"

The Frenchmen were well into their parody now, and the young British officers were trying hard to look amused.

"You know I'm interested," said Strand. "Whether or not I'm sufficiently interested to cooperate will depend on what's involved. So tell me more."

"There's another thing," said Clark, in his element now. "I need to be sure that you're suitable. Your experience in the Army so far has been educational. The work we're concerned with in Clapham is Intelligence. There's a difference. I need to test your abilities. Another Scotch?"

This time it was Clark who gained the initiative by his trip to the bar. He set the double Haig down on the table and looked Strand in the eye.

"Will you take a test?"

Last orders were being called, and Strand looked down at his glass for a moment. He seemed to be thinking.

"Is it really necessary?" he began. Then, seeing Clark about to launch into a long rigmarole, he nodded, and lifted his drink. "All right," he said. "I'll take a test."

"You know the whereabouts of the Staff College," said Clark, making sure that he sounded suitably solemn. "I want you to break in there and photograph the confidential reports on senior Intelligence officers currently under consideration for promotion to the rank of general and above. There are seven files."

Strand was holding up his hand.

"You said a test," he said. "I thought you meant some kind of examination. Written papers. A psychological interview. What you're suggesting is totally different. I'd be court-martialed if I was caught."

There was a burst of laughter in the room, the energy of the evening's drinking rising to its final climax. Clark sat immobile over his Guinness.

"I may not have made myself clear," he said stonily. "We don't want to recruit another officer to work at a desk. We're looking for a field worker."

He paused.

"You could say a spy."

Strand stared at him over the little table. In the smoke-filled room Clark found his expression completely impassive, but he could make his guess at what was going on in Strand's mind. For a long second he thought he might have gone too far. Then he relaxed. The hook was already in the fish's gills.

"Go on," said Strand.

"There are seven files," continued Clark. "I happen to know that tonight you'll find them locked in the desk of Major Alan Saunders, in Room Forty-one on the second floor of the Admin Block. You'll have to work out your own means of entry and exit, and you ought to remember that the guard on the gate will have live ammunition."

"He wouldn't be much use if he didn't," said Strand.

He was fiddling with his empty glass.

"I have three questions," he said. "First of all, I assume that you'll supply me with a camera."

Clark slapped the pocket of his overcoat.

"I have an advanced form of subminiature for you," he said. "It will take accurate pictures down to a distance of eight inches. But you won't be given a tripod, and you'll have to keep your hand steady."

"Second," said Strand softly, running his fingers gently up and down the fluting of his glass. "I assume that, in the event of accident or capture, you'll wash your hands of me. I'll be on my own."

"Not entirely," said Clark. "We should naturally do everything in our power to bail you out. Soldier's friend at your trial, that sort of thing."

It was nonsense, of course, and Clark reports that he didn't think Strand believed him. In fact, it was one of the elements that most impressed him about Strand's suitability. He looked skeptical and professional.

"Third," said Strand, and then he paused. "This is England," he said. "I don't suppose that you'd want me to go in armed?"

It was, reports Clark, the detail that finally set his seal of approval on the choice of Strand. He recalls controlling his pleasure and making seriously reproving noises.

"We don't want anyone killed or hurt," he said. "You do this quietly or you don't do it at all."

"I understand," said Strand.

So that was that, a recruitment as straightforward as I'd already envisaged, although I wasn't to know the results until three days later. Clark's conversation with Strand took place on a Friday evening and I'd spent all that afternoon at my desk in Clapham working with Brundall.

The selection of a base turned out to be fairly easy. Brundall had spent the morning with Bartholomew's atlas laid out across his desk, and he'd boiled down the possible sites to three. After a plate of Molly's best Spam sandwiches and a glass of cider, we got down to the process of elimination.

Brundall had assumed his eager young subaltern manner. You could hear the clicking of imaginary heels at the end of every sentence. But he'd done his homework. I watched him point out the sites with a swagger stick on my unrolled wall map.

"Chungking was my first thought, sir," he said. "Alongside General Sir Carton de Wiart's Military Mission with Chiang Kai-shek. Here it is."

He tapped the map.

"In the foothills of the mountains. At the confluence of the Yangtze—"

I cut him short.

"I know where it is, Captain," I said. "And it's too far north. Besides, we'd be in Indian territory. Our presence up there is contingent on the Generalissimo's good will. I'd feel uneasy."

Brundall nodded keenly.

"So would I, sir," he said. "I'm glad you agree with my assessment."

He was already clearing his throat for his second site, oblivious to his impertinence. They were an insensitive lot of young cubs out of Sandhurst, even in those days.

"Rangoon," he was saying. "That was my second thought."

He spared me a reminder of where Rangoon was.

"Closer," he said. "And in British territory. In fact, in most respects the best site of the three."

"But you don't recommend it," I said.

I knew why, but I thought I'd let him have his moment. He was only young, after all.

"Frankly, sir," said Brundall seriously, "if the Japanese take Singapore from the north, as we all expect, they'll be ideally placed for a strike to their right into Burma. I doubt if Rangoon will last six months."

That might have been long enough, I thought. At any rate for the purpose of getting Strand safely planted in the Kempei Tai. But I had my private doubts about whether Rangoon would survive even as long as six weeks. And that would be useless.

"Go on," I said.

I watched Brundall's pointer travel over the Bay of Bengal and hover on the broken teardrop at the tip of India's nose.

He'd reached the same conclusion as myself. Good lad, I thought.

"Ceylon," said Brundall. "We would establish our base in Colombo. No matter how badly the war goes, Colombo will remain a last ditch. In my opinion, the headquarters of SEAC will be somewhere on the island of Ceylon within half a year of hostilities breaking out."

I nodded. He was right. This was May 1941, and we had made no declaration of war on Japan. For Brundall to be as clear as I was myself about the likely developments of the next year was an excellent sign. I knew he'd learned his lessons well from earlier analyses he'd done. But it was good to hear my own doctrine spoken aloud.

"We'll make it Ceylon," I said. "There's only one difficulty."

"The radio," he anticipated. "I know."

You're getting fast, I thought. Very fast, my boy. But Brundall was already thrusting forward with his assessment.

"We're going to need two portable sets, each with a range of seventeen hundred miles, transmitting on twenty meters. I'm already in touch with Marconi about the possibilities. I should have what we need by the end of next week."

I remember his confidence, and the precision with which the technical details came out. I suppose I ought to have questioned him more closely at the time, but I didn't. I took his assessment on trust. As you'll hear, this turned out to be an error. Not a fatal error, but a crucial one. It brought in another power, and that led to many of my troubles.

After Brundall had gone I turned my attention to the selection of a sleeper in Singapore. This was the trickiest part of the whole operation. Admittedly, if Hayley-Bell's research was accurate there was plenty to choose from. But I couldn't make direct use of his material.

I had to find an alternative source of information. Fortunately, there was one ready to hand. It would require personal contact, and it had its risks—not least to life and limb. But it had the merit of secrecy.

43

I would need a cover story for my visit to Singapore. But that shouldn't be too hard. It was more than a year since I'd been out in person, and I could easily justify a refresher trip. I smiled as I formulated my memo. The Director would probably be glad to have me out of London for a while.

"Molly," I said, leaning around the door of her office, "come in and take some dictation, would you?"

I pursed my lips beside my map, watching her cross her lisle stockings and poise her pencil.

"In view of the rapidly changing situation in the Malayan peninsula," I began, "I feel it would be appropriate to keep my antennae alert to the nuances of the local areas of sensitivity, as currently defined by the Singapore military authorities."

You could never lay it on too strong. They believed what they wanted to believe. The image of my contrite and repentant self going out in person to·eat dirt and apologize was exactly what would fit the Director's private fantasy.

There was more in the same strain. In due course I knew that he'd swallow it whole, and he did. I was busy signing the typed memo on Monday morning when Clark arrived. I screwed the cap back on my old Platignum and waved Molly away with the envelope.

"Sit down, Major," I said.

The door had hardly closed when Clark was reaching into his attaché case for the strips of film. I took one and held it up to the light. As I've said, the light was dim and the images were hard to decipher. But it was plain enough that the photographs were of lines of military names.

"I can set up a darkroom," Clark was saying. "One of the clerks can do the developing. Billington worked in a chemist's once, I believe."

I had the strip of film under a magnifying glass now. We weren't going to need a set of prints. I passed the glass to Clark.

"This looks like the real thing," I said. "I want someone to transcribe the strips before noon today. Use the glass and make only one copy. Then burn the film."

I was excited. There was no doubt in my mind that Strand had survived the test. The details were unimportant; we'd get them later, from his own lips. For the moment it was enough to know that he'd revealed the kind of nerve and ingenuity we needed. And got me the information I feared into the bargain.

I looked at Clark. He was smirking all over his face. I didn't blame him. By any standards, this was quite a coup.

"Well done, Major," I said. "It's a good job you're not working for the Germans."

That afternoon, at two o'clock, I had all I wanted to know. The names and information on the strips of film were without doubt from the Staff College files. I could have had the information evaluated by an expert in another department, but I didn't think that very wise. I was feeling pretty grim.

"Clark," I said, when I'd finished reading the transcript, "you will be aware of my reactions to this material. On the basis of it I intend to go forward with the recruitment of Major Strand as a field agent to be planted in the Japanese Army. See to it that he presents himself here for a full briefing on Thursday morning."

Clark was turning to go. I spoke very softly.

"Clark," I said, "you didn't keep a copy of any of this, did you?"

Clark looked shocked. Fake shocked.

"Sir," he said. "Of course not. Very unfair assessment," he added. "Of certain officers. In my opinion."

"Thank you, Major," I said. "You will keep that opinion to yourself. And you will see to it that Molly does the same. That's an order."

When he'd gone I lit the paper with the flame from my Ronson. Together with the film it burned into a fierce blaze for a second in my wastepaper basket. Then it faded to ash.

But the words I'd read on the fifth strip of film remained in my memory. They fueled my resolution and confirmed my plans.

First of all, there was my name and rank. Then the description of my current job, and the assessment of my career:

Successful if undistinguished early record in India. Skillfully unobtrusive in Tokyo, 1936–1939. Increasingly arrogant and undisciplined in reports on Japanese military preparedness. Pigheaded, loyal, crudely patriotic. He is unwilling or unable to correlate his own judgments with those of others. This officer is not promotable. Query, in certain circumstances, demotable.

I have a good memory, and I knew it all by heart. I watched the last edges of the film curl and die.

Pigheaded, I thought. Crudely patriotic. Unobtrusive. Well, I'd show them. The powers that be were going to regret that assessment. I held a weapon in my hand that would ensure me a full revenge. And on Thursday morning its blade would be unsheathed.

5

The arrangement of Strand's transfer presented no problems. Brundall's Japanese had never been *cordon bleu,* and I was able to sustain a case for an extra translator. It wouldn't have been so easy if I'd had to pay him, but the Army School of Oriental Languages had, as it turned out, a problem of accommodation. They were delighted to make a saving in office space.

In return for our housing Strand they were ready to go on paying his wages. At least on the basis of a six-month attachment, which in the first place was all I thought I needed. After all, at the end of six months he might be dead.

On that first Thursday morning, when Strand arrived for my special briefing, he was very much alive. It was a wet and cold day. At ten o'clock we were shivering over our early biscuits in the War Room. I'd had a particularly nasty tramp along the side of the Common, splashed up to the knees by a heavy convoy driving toward the coast on the old Brighton road.

It hadn't helped my temper to be soaked to the skin by a rabble of inefficient army drivers, and the coffee was doing its usual best to make matters worse. I looked down along my pine skirting boards with their fancy ogival molding, and it nearly made me sick. They could have paid for a brigade of Matilda tanks with the money they'd wasted on this folly of Chamberlain's.

I was sitting in an upholstered armchair at the center of the raised platform, facing out and up the tiers of curved leather benches toward the doors at the back of the room. They were solid mahogany, torn out of some dilapidated mansion in the Cotswolds and embedded here into rough ash-colored concrete. They seemed to me then the conclusive ridicule.

I looked at my watch. It was nearly time. I was sure that today Strand wouldn't be early. He'd arrive precisely on the hour. I took a last sip at my coffee. The idea in my mind was to make a bit of a performance of the briefing. Not so much for Strand's sake: I could already guess at his cynical smile when he came through those tomblike doors into this mausoleum. It was the home team I was anxious to impress.

Clark and Brundall were already looking slightly overawed by the boardroom atmosphere. Billington and Walpole, the two clerks, were frankly daunted. Molly had her normal glum stodginess. It was the first time that we'd all had a meeting together in the room.

I'd been counting on that. It would make this briefing memorable and important. And it was vital for them to be imbued with a sense of the grandeur of the operation. Human nature being what it is, this flourish would fix their loyalty, stimulate their willingness to work.

When the bell rang I motioned to Walpole to go down and let Strand in. Walpole was a short, tubby fellow with a bald head and a ginger moustache. There was an element of French farce about the situation when he tripped opening the door on his return, and then stood back with a sort of butlerish gesture to let the major by.

I can see Strand now, neat and erect there in the high opening, shaking water from his hair and slapping his hogskin gloves on his thighs. The pompous, silly mood of the occasion was shattered in a flash. This was the man who was going to change all our lives.

I rose to my feet. He was advancing across the room, stepping down the aisle through the rows of seats.

"Major Strand," I said, splaying my hand along the front stalls, "have a seat here, if you will."

After that it was easy. I snapped my fingers for Billington to draw the curtains behind my back. The huge board was revealed, and I pulled the cord for the linen-backed map of Southeast Asia to unroll like a blind. The arc of lights came on, silhouetting me against the theater of war.

I began to understand, as I spoke, what Chamberlain must have envisaged: the tiers of benches packed with his generals; the words of command or inspiration echoing back from the lofty cornices; the scrape of heels and the spark of matches in the darkness. For twenty minutes I manipulated his dream.

At the end I laid my pointer aside and ordered Walpole to put on the lights. Molly was leaning back with her eyes closed and her mouth open. She has no soul, that woman. Clark looked foxy but excited. Walpole was blinking by the doors; Billington, coughing into his handkerchief. I thought for a moment that Brundall might be going to clap. But he caught my eye and thought better of it.

Only Strand had the power to react in the appropriate way to the momentousness of the occasion. He sat perfectly still, Japanese to a fault. There was dead silence. Then he rose to his feet.

"I will do what you want," he said.

For a moment I felt a great relief, mixed with a huge joy. Then I took my feelings in hand and bent over my papers. To be fair to my staff, I could hear a murmur of approval as I gathered the papers together. It stayed with me as I led Strand into my office for a celebratory Scotch.

We were clinking glasses when Clark came in. He had the digests of the latest Cabinet committee on food rationing.

"They're talking about having a points system," he said, eyeing the bottle of Haig. "So many for whatever you want, from tinned salmon to fruitcake."

I was feeling bland. I offered him a glass, watching him pour an indecently large measure. He never had any sense of proportion. He couldn't even swallow the stuff without gulping. Strand's lip was curled.

"When the war's over," he said, rotating his drink, "I'm going to go into Simpson's and order a double helping of their steak-and-kidney pie. With roast and boiled potatoes and mushrooms. I got a lifelong taste for my English victuals at Wellington."

Clark sat with his whiskey awkwardly cradled in his lap.

"I thought you'd be more of a *sushi* man," he said. "Or didn't the Peers' School carry patriotism into its cuisine?"

He was trying to needle Strand. It seemed the wrong time to me, but I got the point. We might as well lay the pressure on him right from the start.

"We ate our rice," Strand was saying.

He was unruffled. He knew what Clark was doing. I liked his coolness, but there was something almost uncanny about it. I had a spurt of sympathy for my bumbling Clark with his questions.

"Another glass?" I suggested, topping Strand up.

I ignored the spasmodic twitch of the now empty glass on Clark's knee. The stuff was expensive, and hard to get. Let the lower orders stick to their beer and skittles, I always say.

Clark was discussing Japanese food with a show of expertise. I had to give him good marks for research. He'd never known this much about *yakitori* the week before last. He was reeling out his assessment of eels' livers like a fisherman from Kobe.

Strand was polite now, but bored. I could feel him circling Clark, ready for the kill. I let my adjutant off the hook.

"Let's turn to business," I said, fingering my letter opener. "First of all, the transfer arrangements. They should pose no problem."

I already knew about their accommodation difficulties in Camberley. I expected to have the paper work done within ten days, and there was a good chance Strand would be in training at our house in Elms Road by the end of June. In fact, I was a week out, but it made no difference.

I elaborated the details of the transfer procedure, and then summed up what would happen when it was completed.

"You look like a Japanese," I said, fixing Strand with my steely glare. "You sound like a Japanese."

I paused.

"For all normal circumstances, you can pass as a Japanese in the way you behave. At a business conference or a cocktail party you can probably get by with no risk at all. Our job, when you come over and settle down at Elms Road, will be to work out a thoroughgoing series of tests and traps that will flex your muscles in more dangerous situations. Major Strand," I concluded, "welcome to Department M. I look forward to our collaboration."

Clark was putting his glass on the edge of my table as Strand left the room. He turned to face me.

"Bloody amazing," he said. "He's almost too good to be true."

I leaned back in my chair and closed one eye. There were times when a touch of vulgar connivance was quite useful with Clark.

"He's convincing," I said judiciously. "But when you and Brundall have finished with him at Elms Road he'll be perfect enough to fool a *mako* girl on the Ginza."

My prediction turned out to be almost an understatement. What exactly Clark arranged to do to Strand over at Elms Road I never found out in full detail, but it certainly kept him busy. I got the reports on progress every day as I worked in my office on the arrangements for my trip to Singapore. They were more than satisfactory.

Meanwhile my own attention was focusing on the selection of a sleeper. As I've indicated, this was going to raise problems, but I thought I had a way of solving them.

We'd decided to give the operation a code name. That sort of thing was already all the rage. I think it was Churchill who brought it in. He was always a bit of a glamour boy when it came to the nomenclature.

At any rate, we were following the fashion, and we'd settled, with a fairly banal obviousness, on CHAMELEON. It looks better when you type it in capitals. We never did in those days. Strand himself was going to work under two separate aliases. On his trips to Singapore as a Japanese businessman with interests in rubber and tin he'd be known as Mr. Tanaka, and we had a passport made out accordingly. Within the operation, however, he would have a continuing identity under the general name of MAGNOLIA TREE.

One smiles, remembering. I have one in the garden now, down by the summerhouse, lifting its raw porcelain saucers into the sun. But it wasn't so much the flowers we had in mind when we chose the name. Clark was our horticultural expert in the Department, and it was Clark who wanted us all to have flower and tree names.

"You'd make a wonderful SYCAMORE, sir," I remember him saying. But I drew the line at MAGNOLIA TREE. One tree was enough. It was only later that Brundall reminded us all that magnolia wood was used for the hilts of Japanese swords.

In deference to Clark's interests and to preserve some hint of logic in the code names, we decided to categorize our base in Colombo, once we'd established it there, as LANDSCAPER. Clark himself had a fancy for something a bit more specific, like CAPABILITY BROWN or even HUMPHREY REPTON, but I managed to steer him clear. The clerks would never have got the spelling right, for one thing.

Finally, to keep matters simple at the spearhead, we agreed that Strand's control in Singapore, whoever he was to be, would be known as THE GARDENER. That completed the series. But not the difficulties, the worst of which lay in the roundabout way I had to contrive my connections. As I've been hinting, the most difficult element of all was that a colonel in British Army Intelligence, replete with official contacts in a British colony, should nevertheless have to make inquiries about the local Japanese spy network through the godfather of the most powerful local secret society, the Chinese Triad.

It was clear from very early on that it would have to be the Triad. Nowadays when you read about extortion and drug pushing, prostitution on an international scale, gang murders, all that sort of thing, you might well believe it was a hard decision to approach the Triad for help. It was. But they weren't quite so bad in those days, or so we deluded ourselves. And there was a war on. Remember that the Americans had to go to the Mafia to help them invade Sicily. It wasn't only Errol Flynn who won the war. It was Lucky Luciano.

I'd had numerous contacts with the Triad since my days in Tokyo. They were always a crucial source of information. In Singapore alone they had twelve thousand members, and you could have doubled that number if you took in the rest of Malaya.

Wherever you went in Singapore you were likely to be in the presence of a Triad member. He might be the Chinese waiter serving *stengahs* at the Coconut Grove, or whiskey ayers at the Raffles' bar. He might be the shoeshine boy with his brass box of brushes among the open-air diners in Bugie Street. He might be the operator at the central telephone exchange.

Whoever he was, he would be filing away the myriad tidbits of idle gossip or news he picked up. And these tidbits, when necessary, would all be filtered, classified, and eventually digested and passed on to the ultimate controller of this gigantic information network, the man regarded with awe and respect by all his subordinates, and indeed by every Chinese in Singapore, the man they called The One.

The Triad had been formed in the seventeenth century to fight the hated Manchu, the northern Chinese who had swept south and imposed their rule throughout the Empire. Their aim had been to restore the Ming dynasty, and their achievement, in result, after a whole string of revolutions, had been to bring the Kuomintang into power.

I had my doubts about Chiang, even in 1941. When you look at the way he caved in to Mao and the Communists in 1949 the doubts seem to have been well founded. He never had the guts or the integrity to hold the Chinese people in line.

They needed that, which was something the Triad recognized. In Singapore the manor was ruled with a rod of iron, but it was ruled with fairness, even with generosity. More than one small merchant was offered a favorable contract for rice or opium in hard times. It required a price, perhaps. But it was one usually computed in terms of loyalty. And it wasn't always ruthlessly exacted.

I'd never met the godfather of the Singapore branch of the

Triad. He was a famous figure, but he wasn't hard to meet. He was only hard to meet under his powerful but strictly unofficial hat. For the world's normal purposes he was Mr. Goh Han Peng, the affable and courteous proprietor of the House of Diamonds, the most long-standing and extensive dealers in precious stones in Malaya.

It was going to be easy enough to arrange an interview with Goh Han Peng to discuss diamonds. Over tea and bargaining I would have to manipulate the counters of disclosure. A lot would depend on the discretion with which I was able to overcome his initial and very much inbred caution.

The critical hinge might be just before my shift of alias. He would agree to an appointment in the first place on the assumption that I was a rich and potentially profitable client, a civilian. At some point I would have to reveal my true identity, and my mission.

Before that, of course, I might be dead. I had no illusions about the dangers. I was going to deal with a gangster. If he suspected me of being something other than I at first appeared he might have my throat slit first, and establish who I was afterward.

He wouldn't risk murdering a British officer, of course. But then he wouldn't risk dealing with a British officer through unofficial channels. He would first establish the reason for the interview through private inquiries among his local contacts. And I daren't jeopardize the whole operation by letting my approach to Goh Han Peng come to the ears of Fort Canning.

I needed a secret approach. And that meant risking my life. When I look back now I wonder if I'd do the same thing again. I suppose I would, if I were twenty years younger. It seemed the only way at the time. And it was nothing to the sort of risks that Strand would be taking.

I remember once seeing the body of an informer the Kempei Tai had released to the British authorities in Tokyo. He'd been a cook for a time in the staff canteen, and then someone had had the bright idea of planting him with the Japanese. They'd uncovered him in thirteen days. And then they'd made him cook and eat a blowfish.

Poor devil. He'd known what was coming to him. The books will all tell you the poison works fast. It doesn't. It's sure, dead sure; but it takes four hours to kill you. I wouldn't like to have ended my life on the floor of that stone dungeon in Kamakura the way that little cook must have done.

I had a silver pencil in 1941. My fingers were wet on the hexagon of the stem when I remembered. I'd just had Clark's daily bulletin from Elms Road. The magnolia tree was in bud, we'd soon have the first flowers, etc. The usual evasive ciphering.

Decoding the stuff revealed that apparently the curriculum at the Peers' School had included some judo. Strand was a green belt, and he'd picked up a few karate moves on the side as well. Clark was excited. He seemed to take a positive delight in the possibility of his pupil requiring the arts of defense as well as disguise.

It made me smile. I didn't want Strand to need his judo. I'd have been much happier if we could have planted him safely in his pot under the benign sun of our local Triad gardener. I even felt, in a mood of passing paranoia, that Clark might secretly be training Strand for a commando mission.

It would have been possible: there were all kinds of plots and counterplots in those days. I know now, of course, that he wasn't. It was just that he hated Strand's guts. Clark was a loyal officer, in his way. But he wouldn't have shed too many tears if his protégé had died in agony.

Poor Strand. He was having a rough time with his trainers over at Elms Road. He was learning, though. From a near-perfect imitation of a Japanese you could have relied on to fool a roomful of his compatriots at an embassy, or a *Noh* play, he was turning day by day into an exact replica who could step up to Hirohito at the Warriors' Shrine and be taken for the descendant of a *samurai*.

It was an astonishing transformation. All credit to Major Clark. I suppose the adrenaline was an advantage, really. It gave the edge of viciousness to the testing. It sharpened the blade in the fire. It gave me hope.

6

I flew out to Singapore in the last week of June. Nowadays you'd take a 747 from Heathrow and be there in under thirty hours, with stops at Frankfurt and Teheran, and perhaps Bombay and Bangkok. In 1941 it was different.

First of all I took the train down to Poole Harbor, in Dorset. There I boarded an Empire C Class Flying Boat of Imperial Airways, with a full complement of twenty-four passengers. They were deep, heavy-looking machines, those old flying boats, not so very unlike a 747 after all, if you imagine one rocking on waves.

I'd flown in flying boats several times before the war, and I never enjoyed the embarking business, with the cabin cruiser chugging across the water and the dinghy full of your luggage splashing along in the wake. Then up the short ladder and into that *art deco* hull bobbing like a cork in a basin of soapsuds.

I could never have been a success in the Navy. Even those rich Bloody Marys the steward always managed from his little pantry in the stern didn't override the nausea. And you knew, if you were flying to the Far East, that you'd be going through the whole roller-coaster ride again twice a day for much of the next fortnight.

This was still the fastest way to Singapore, and it took fourteen days. In 1939, as it happens, you could have saved a day or two. But in the bleak trough of 1941, with Rommel at the skirts of Cairo, the pilots had to avoid any risk of encountering Messerschmitt squadrons above the Western Desert.

This meant flying the so-called Horseshoe Route. If you open your *Times* atlas and take a look at the right-hand half of the globe in Mercator's projection, you'll see what this involved. It was basically a deep U down the left flank of the African coast to Lagos, via Lisbon, Bathurst and Freetown.

At the bottom of the U's first upright, there in Lagos, you were transferred to a land plane for a long hop across to Khartoum, in the Sudan. Seeing that vast four-winged bird come roaring down out of the sun would have been enough to give poor old Kitchener kittens, I remember thinking.

My father had charged with the cavalry there at Omdurman. It seemed strange to be soaring thousands of feet above his horse's hoof steps by courtesy of Mr. Handley Page and his twin-engined biplane. I looked down at the sand, the color of French mustard. It seemed a long way off.

Now it seems further, a lifetime and an ethos away. At least it was still *Imperial* Airways in 1941. None of your mealy-mouthed rubbish. I never had any time for the cant of calling it Commonwealth. It was them or us. We ruled, and we chucked it away, starting with India. I'll say this for Churchill: he had the guts to turn his face against hypocrisy, the old scoundrel.

I had plenty of time for this kind of reflection in my fourteen days in the air. A good chunk of the Empire went past under my heels. From Khartoum I flew up the Nile again, with a couple of stops before Rod-el-Faraq. I was back in the flying boat again, on the last leg of the U detour.

I would settle back in my padded seat after each landing with a kind of benevolent resignation now. There wasn't much to do except wait, read and think. The other passengers had almost all changed. Some had been civilians disembarking on business, a few had been soldiers in uniform, on undefined affairs concerned with the war.

None of us talked about our journeys. The specter of Hitler there in the next seat had been forcefully implanted by those Fougasse posters. At any rate, I wasn't anxious to be too convivial. For reasons of security I was traveling in civilian clothes myself, and I didn't want to have to waste energy on elaborating my cover story.

I watched the world pass by below. I slept. I got through *The Tale of Genji*, in the Waley translation. I still believe it's the best. You can keep your Seidensticker, for my money. I'm too old for a new version.

After the U detour there was the long series of hops across the Middle East and India. These too were done by flying boat. Some of the ports of call you might know, others are lost in history now. They make a splendid roll call of names, all places with water attached, of course, either still or moving, salt or fresh, for the flying boat to touch down on. Basra, Bahrain, Dubai. The old sheikdoms.

Jiwani, Karachi, Raj-Samund, Lake Gwalior. The old India. The siege of Lucknow and the massacre of Cawnpore. The wings flying on, the hull over water. The River Ganges at Allahabad, the River Hooghly at Calcutta. The starving millions down there in the streets.

Akyab, the island off the Arakan of Burma. Nearly there now. Rangoon, Bangkok, and Penang. It gave me an odd sensation. I was in Malaya, and only a narrow strip of land away, as I knew then, and as history proved later, from the place where Yamashita would land. Then back to my familiar corner at my window in the bows for the final hop to Singapore.

I shook myself. We were rocking at anchor, and the steward had his hand on my shoulder. I'd been asleep. We had landed in the rocks at Keppel Harbor. I was there.

The Raffles Hotel is a good deal changed, I expect. I haven't been back since 1947. I had a secretary once who made a stopover there on a flight to Australia in the early seventies, and she said there was still a touch of the old elegance. But I wonder. These things pass. I'll bet they have iced water and a coffee shop by now.

They didn't in 1941. You had your luggage carried in by a Malay porter in uniform, and you got your breakfast at breakfast time, and served at your table. The morning after I arrived, I was eating the best eggs and bacon I'd had since the war broke out. I'd slept on stiff sheets on a good, hard mattress, and I had the *Straits Times* folded beside my plate.

I always enjoyed the front page, with its advertisements for Robinsons store and Melrose's gin and the dinner-jacket outfitters. At this period they were crossed with air-raid precautions, including a warning about huddling against the sides of trenches, and one about avoiding bombs traveling diagonally. I turned to the inside pages with some amusement.

For once there wasn't a lot happening in the war. A few days before, Wavell had been appointed C-in-C in India, in a direct swap with Auchinleck. I was still smarting at the insanity of sending a desert general—and a failed one at that—to protect our interests in the jungle.

I was looking for some local commentary on Wavell's appointment when I came across an eyewitness account of the *Kelly* going down. It was five or six weeks since Mountbatten had been sunk by dive bombers in the Mediterranean, and apparently someone was talking about making a film of the whole business.

It had been pretty heroic, by present-day standards. The two destroyers, *Kashmir* and *Kelly*, sunk by waves of Ju 87s. The survivors machine-gunned in the water as they clung to the rubber life raft.

It had a disturbing similarity to what happened the other day in Ireland, I see that now. At the time it was just pride I felt, a stubborn pride that at least one gallant gentleman was left in our ruling class, one royal soldier-hero worthy to have served beside Richard in Bosworth Field.

But I didn't spend long with the news. I was too preoccupied with the man I'd flown out here to meet, the Chinese lion whose den I was going to enter in three-quarters of an hour's time. I didn't anticipate an easy morning.

I'd dressed in a cream duck suit, with a pair of rather flashy snakeskin shoes, and I was carrying my real means of identification in a small leather attaché case. I'd kept my pockets fairly empty, except for a silver cigarette case, but I'd made sure it was placed in an inside pocket, to cover my heart. It was a small precaution, but better than nothing.

I knew a man whose life was saved once by a pigskin cigar wallet. It took the edge off a .45 slug at forty yards. He was probably lucky, but then I would need luck, and it tends to follow the few who prepare.

I'd contemplated a weapon, too. But even a knife was bound to arouse suspicion. I could have slid one down my stocking like a Highlander's dagger, but the Chinese have their way of brushing calves. They'd know what I had, I was sure.

I contented myself with a nail file. It was a bit longer than usual, and it had an edge like a razor. Given time, and a man off guard, you could drive it home to the heart with a jab from a cigarette case. I'd seen one of Lovatt's boys do it with a dummy at a course in Rutland.

Of course, that was a dummy, and I'd be dealing with flesh-and-blood strong-arm men. But I didn't allow myself to dwell overlong on the flimsiness of my defenses. They were the best I could afford, and I had to live, or at worst die, with them.

Singapore's Chinatown has much the same features as Chinatown in New York, or even Limehouse. But it's bigger and it's much more bustling. It took me longer than I expected to walk the last few streets when I left my taxi.

I was sweating a little under the armpits, and my shoes had lost their morning shine, when I found the unobtrusive entrance of the House of Diamonds below the curving roofs and the upturned eaves of the Temple of Heavenly Happiness in Telok Ayer Street.

There was a counter, Western style. A number of tables edged with brass and covered with baize. Two or three Chinese and a single European were sitting or standing and examining stones.

I didn't believe in the customers. They had the look of practiced heavies from an American gangster film. The assistant who approached me with a smile and a bow might have been the brother of Charlie Chan.

"I have an appointment," I said, to forestall him.

I wanted my blow in first.

"Mr. Brown?" he suggested.

This was the alias we'd agreed on, the residue of Clark's dream. Brown I had allowed; the Capability had been dropped.

I followed the assistant and his bow through the lifted counter and along a short corridor, darker than the shop. I slid my hand into my pocket and fingered my nail file. I hoped that the gesture would strike any unseen watchers as natural.

The assistant was unlocking a door. Another bad sign, I thought. And he was standing aside. It added up to a dangerous combination.

But there wasn't much I could do. To the honest man, on a normal business errand, there was nothing overtly sinister. I had to maintain my cover. I advanced through the door, brushing the assistant with my shoulder as I passed.

It might have been imagination that I felt the hilt of a weapon under his close-fitting jacket as I heard him announce my name, or what sounded like it, in Cantonese.

When you work all day in an office, whatever you're doing, it makes all the difference to get out on a field trip. It shakes up the adrenaline. I used to find that even at the agency after the war, when I had a chance to take a client out to lunch. The sense of romance used to come into play. I was a great entrepreneur, doing deals.

In Intelligence work this operates even more dramatically. We're all spies at heart, as we slave at our desks. That was the slogan my old boss, Roger Newlove, always asked us to remember. He had Ian Fleming through his hands once, on a course, too. I've often thought those maxims of his made their contribution to the James Bond mythology.

It's not so mythological, either. Fleming knew his stuff. When you go out on the road you're psychologically predisposed to feel tough, and in danger. You positively *want* to feel that your skin's threatened, so that you can justify your training.

But you learn to allow for this. I was making allowances that morning as I went into Goh Han Peng's inner sanctum. Part of what I was feeling was the usual heightened sense of menace, the desire to make this job more important because more

61

frightening. But this wasn't the whole of it. There was a genuine residue of actual trouble brewing, and my antennae were twitching.

The room I'd come into was small but luxurious. It was furnished, surprisingly, with a tasteful blend of European fashion and Chinese tradition. There was a lot of black glass and chrome, but there were lions of Fu, too, and some exquisite lacquer cabinets.

The man who rose to greet me and beckon me to a broad, comfortable dragon-patterned sofa was a compact little demon with neat, peaked ears and a bald, shining head. He looked about fifty, and very fit. He was massaging his hands.

I could bore you with a long account of the preliminaries. The polite remarks about the weather, the sitting down and crossing my legs, the ordering of tea, and its arrival on a tray of filigreed red lacquer.

I pass this by. Business with diamonds, like all dealing involving large sums of money, tends to need the lubrication of time. I hadn't been expecting a rapid movement from generalities to the reason for my visit. So I kept my eyes open and chatted easily, or as easily as I could, as I sipped my aromatic infusion.

When it came, the transition was fast, and it leaped a stage. I hadn't been ready for anything quite so incisive, and I'm afraid my delicate cup rattled in its saucer.

"I know your business," Goh Han Peng was saying.

He had risen to his feet and was cracking his knuckles. He did a lot of things with his hands, I noticed. They were long and bony.

"Diamonds," he was continuing, in a kind of razor-edged purr. Then he paused, as if the precious word itself required a brief but holy silence. "Diamonds are often a cover," he suggested. "Men come to buy opium, or to arrange the disappearance of a friend. They require protection, or vengeance."

He had put his palms together, as if praying.

"Colonel," he said quietly, "I know who you are. A soldier is easy to recognize, in any clothes. And I have some pensioners at the Raffles. They owe me favors."

He was holding up his fingers now, preventing me from making any comment. I could feel the surge of his will, the imperious compulsion of a man used to being listened to without interruption. I gave him his head.

"Your work for the Japanese investigating committees of the British Army is known to me here," said Goh Han Peng.

His English, I was coming to see, was a curious patchwork of the orotund and the eccentric. It mingled an eighteenth-century magniloquence with a quirky invention.

"It has my respect," he was adding. "There are not many military men in Great Britain who are aware of the goals of the Japanese leaders. You have done your bit for peace."

He had seated himself again now, folding those amazing hypnotic hands in his lap. He stared at them as he spoke.

By now, of course, I was recovering my sense of balance. Goh Han Peng clearly had far more thorough sources of information than I had supposed. I could only rely on what appeared to be his good will. He was speaking again as I collected my thoughts.

"The island of Hainan," he was saying, pausing in what I began to see was a characteristic mannerism. "The island of Hainan is nearly six hundred miles around the perimeter. This is jungle country. This is more than the distance from the northern border of Malaya to Singapore."

Goh Han Peng had my attention. I let my right hand rest on the head of one of his lions as he spoke. It felt cold.

"I have heard only this morning about Unit 52."

He was glancing at me, but I shook my head. The name meant nothing to me then. So much for the completeness of British Intelligence.

"More tea?" said Goh Han Peng, pouring. "Unit 52 is a group of Japanese army officers," he continued. "It has three sections. One of them, commanded by Lieutenant Colonel Masanobu Tsuji, is planning the attack on Malaya and Singapore."

I felt a stab of joy, mingled with relief, and a kind of horror. This meant the confirmation of all my warnings to Whitehall. It also meant, in effect, a green light for Operation Chameleon. I had little doubt that Goh Han Peng's information was authoritative.

"Hainan," he was stressing. "The Japanese Fifth Division is training there in the jungle. They have a full-size natural assault course for their invasion of Malaya. They go around and around the island, and gradually they become perfect in every department of jungle warfare."

Goh Han Peng was holding a diamond up to a small table light at his elbow. He turned it once, and I saw the light flash and multiply from the facets. He laid it back in a velvet-lined case on his knee.

"Perfect," he emphasized. "Your British soldiers are fined five pounds when they damage a rubber tree. The Japanese are learning the fastest way to cut one down with a saw."

The box of diamonds had been snapped shut with a low, somber click. I stared at the top. It had a mountain and a bridge chased in fine metalwork.

"When your soldiers are doing exercises," said Goh Han Peng gently, "an officer stands on a bridge with a white armband and says that the bridge has been destroyed. He calculates the time it would take to repair, and when this time is up, the soldiers are allowed to cross. This is a game. The bridge has remained standing. It has not been destroyed. It has not been repaired. I have seen this happen."

So had I. His criticism struck home. The amount of time wasted on those jungle exercises was legendary. We paid the price, later. At this date no one knew how high it was going to be.

"On Hainan," said Goh Han Peng, laying his box of diamonds aside, "the Japanese Army has destroyed and repaired more than two hundred bridges. The bridges are blown up, then rebuilt. There are no games. Now tell me your business."

I told him. I put in the background and the foreground. The treatment of my reports in Whitehall. The reduction and exile of my Department. The arrival of Strand in my office. The germ of my plan.

I watched Goh Han Peng's face as I spoke, but it gave nothing away. He would sometimes open his box and fondle a stone; but there was no indication of his feelings. I concluded with the details of Strand's recruitment and training, and finally I came to our need for the help of the Triad in finding a sleeper in Singapore.

"This has to be unofficial," I said. "The British authorities have not the slightest interest in what I propose. They believe, still, that a war with the Japanese can be avoided. So I need your help."

One sees more with hindsight. I realize now that the precise nature of my request may have come as a surprise to Goh Han Peng. At the time I'd become so mesmerized by his awareness of my identity that I rather assumed he knew more than he did. In actual fact it occurred to me subsequently that he may have expected me to ask for something much more banal.

It could have been, for example, that he may have anticipated an appeal for pressure to be put on Sir Shenton Thomas to switch Chinese labor from the rubber plantations and tin mines to the building of defense works against a landward attack on Singapore. At that time there were only the guns pointing out to sea.

It would have been possible for Goh Han Peng to indicate the fears of his people, to hint at the likelihood even of strike action, unless something was done to make the city's defenses more practical. He would have had his opportunities at the Governor's weekly meetings with the Chinese Committee, on which the representatives were undoubtedly open to his influence.

This kind of pressure was never exercised. Looking back, it might have been effective. I can see now that it wouldn't have seemed out of character with my anxieties for me to have approached Goh Han Peng with a request for him to do what he could.

So his impassive response to my story about Strand, and the speed of his decision, may not have been quite so natural and automatic as they seemed after his information about Hainan. I remember watching him rise and take down a fan from a high shelf before he commented on my proposal.

At the time it seemed a casual gesture. With hindsight I can see that he may have been astonished enough to need a moment for thought. It was certainly only a short one, if he did. I recall him shooting the ivory spars open and shut, and then tapping the table with the end.

"Yes," he said. "I will help you."

I went back to the Raffles Hotel. The details had all to be worked out, but the main hurdle was over. I was to see Goh Han Peng again the following day, when he hoped to have some firmer proposals for discussion.

I ordered a Scotch and water from the kitchen and lay back on my bed watching the blades of the ceiling fan turning and turning above my head. I relaxed. For a few moments I felt safe again.

In a few days Strand would be flying out in my wake, on the first leg of his own journey to Rangoon, where he would assume his alias as Mr. Tanaka, a Japanese businessman traveling to and from Singapore in rubber and tin. I envied him. He was going to work at the spearhead. Every second of his time he would be in danger.

But I wondered, as I lay on my bed. I admired that kind of life; but could I sustain the pressure? My own job was going to be full of its dangers, too. They would surely be more subtle and tedious than Strand's. But none the less real, perhaps.

Even now, forty years on, one can see them so. Watching the sparrows gather for their bread at the little house in my rose garden, I can see that. I can see the dangers.

7

Digressions and anticipations are the bane of the storyteller. I never like them in books much myself, but I see now how hard they are to avoid. While Clark and Brundall and Strand and I were all in London together it was easy to keep a sort of chronological line. As soon as I flew to Singapore, there was a natural break in the development of our plans.

In a way it was a kind of explosion. We were all going in different directions suddenly, thrown apart, and moving at varying speeds. While I was traveling, and then negotiating with Goh Han Peng, Clark was completing his process of training Strand at Elms Road. The job was done well, as I've indicated, and our magnolia tree was potted and ready for planting in advance of my securing the cooperation of the gardener.

It's easy even now, as it was then, to lapse into the jargon. I still find myself doing it, almost without thinking, and I suppose Clark does too. Brundall, of course, was also busy, and this is what necessitates an anticipation. To be exact, in terms of time, what he did in order to obtain the radio transmitters we needed took place after the arrival of my cable from Singapore, some days later, saying that the arrangements with the Triad had been concluded.

But there are reasons for putting down this particular bit of the story out of sequence. For one thing, it's preying on my mind this morning, largely through having accidentally shaken out one of those curious pink letters in the handwriting of Warren Baltimore II. You'll realize what kind of impression they still make when I tell you I could swear there's an odor of Chanel there after nearly forty years.

Besides, I already had Brundall on my mind that first evening at the Raffles. I had an instinct that something was going to go obscurely wrong in the business of getting the radios. As it turned out, it did, though not at all as I had foreseen.

I don't imagine that anybody, least of all Brundall, could have foreseen Warren Baltimore. Nowadays I suppose that he'd have "come out," as I hear them say, and I'd have to be namby-pamby and call him gay. To be blunt, in the language of the 1940s he was a raving queer.

I only met him twice, but young Brundall's rather shy notes confirm my recollection. Baltimore was rich—new money, from oil, but plenty of it—and he was ambitious. He wore suits cut in Savile Row, but the handkerchiefs in his top pockets were lavender. He was using scent a generation before men were using scent.

I didn't like him, on a personal basis, but I'm bound to say that he had a certain power. You didn't get to be one of Roosevelt's invisible ambassadors without having a head on your shoulders. As for how Brundall got in touch with him, that never emerged.

There were clubs for homosexuals, even in those days, and I suppose that Brundall may have gone along for a lark one night.

Baltimore's offer of a place at a small supper party with some friends, and a talk afterward about the business of the radios Brundall had hinted at, must have seemed a tempting and indeed mildly luxurious proposition. Brundall implies as much in his notes.

Upstairs at Claridge's, of course, there were no friends, and supper was no more than a magnum of Moët et Chandon. There were dim lights, and a lot of cream silk cushions. Baltimore was in his shirt sleeves, and the shirt was open to the waist.

I imagine that Brundall can't have been entirely surprised.

He must have guessed what might be in Baltimore's mind. The proposition would have been covertly hinted at. It made me angry then, and it does now.

But it wasn't Brundall's fault. He needed those radios, and he took a risk. Without the Americans we had no way of getting our transmitters. And without transmitters we had no way of running Strand from Ceylon. It would have meant delays, information passed by hand and rendered useless before it arrived.

I suppose that we might have considered Rangoon again, if Brundall had come to me and explained his difficulty. But he didn't at first, and then I was away in Singapore, and he had to use his initiative. I can hardly blame him.

Frankly, I wouldn't have risked Rangoon anyway, so he'd have been wasting his time. No, it isn't anger at Brundall I feel again now, as I write. It's a cold, flat rage with that exploitative bugger, quite literally bugger, Warren Baltimore.

They say that the English public schools are a seedbed of inversion. Perhaps they are. There was often a bit of stroking and squeezing in my day. Crushes and pilling. Rather dirty horseplay. But it used to end with adolescence, whatever they say. Most of us grew up, and looked at women.

Baltimore didn't. He used his wealth and his connections to flatter his palate for boys. With Brundall he must have supposed he'd have no trouble. There was something for sale, on both sides. In return for a brace of American transmitters Brundall would lay his virtue down in front of the fire.

So Baltimore had his champagne ready and his jacket off. He probably motioned Brundall to one of those famous Claridge's sofas. He'd have taken his coat and stick, and passed him a drink, as an Indian maharajah might have done the night before to a girl from Lyle Street.

Outdoors, according to Brundall, there was the sound of sirens; but nobody came to warn them. Perhaps Baltimore had issued special instructions. Perhaps the hotel had a policy of waiting until the first bombs fell.

At any rate, there was a hand on Brundall's thigh, or somewhere near, and an arm around his shoulders.

"I'm sorry," Brundall reports that he said. "I came here to discuss business."

More probably there was swearing, even a scuffle perhaps. I can imagine a lewd roll on the carpet, heavy breathing, Baltimore on his feet in a white rage. Brundall nervous, determined, worried.

"Now see here," says Baltimore, very calm.

He pours himself more champagne, fifty-four, insulted, powerful. He knows how to handle this kind of situation.

"You need those radios," he is saying carefully, thoughtful. "I need your sweet young ass. We have the basis for a deal."

According to Brundall it took an hour of argument. I can see that it would. More reaching and liquor, too, no doubt. More angry words.

Gradually, as Brundall says he did, Baltimore would have cooled down. I said that he was ambitious, and he must have realized that a break in British security here would be bound to bring him kudos at the White House. I can well believe, as Brundall claims, that the idea of a *quid pro quo* in the shape of a detailed briefing about the operation would have originated with Baltimore.

So here he was, with his dove-gray jacket back on, and his tie knotted, squatting down on his heels in the best suite at Claridge's and draining my number three of the last drop of information about Operation Chameleon. To do him one solitary scrap of justice, he was impressed.

"Jesus," Brundall reports he said. "You Brits really moved your ass on this one."

For Brundall, it was a triumph, of a kind. He got his radios, and the operation depended on them. But he made a mistake—not surprisingly in the circumstances. He kept very quiet, for more than half a year, about the American connection.

I was able to infer it, eventually, though too late to be of much use. But for many months after my return from Singapore, preoccupied as I was with other details, I took on trust the report supplied by Brundall that the radios were a special order from Marconi.

It doesn't matter too much now, I suppose. The outcome might well have been the same through some other factor. There are a million ways of breaking secrecy, in Intelligence work.

Brundall's true report, I see, was written as late as October 1944, and Clark sealed it in with the rest of the papers. Reading it through again now, I note that the meeting at Claridge's must have taken place the night I touched down at Karachi on my flight back.

By then I had the business of the sleeper all arranged. I had Jimmy Fong in position, as well as Goh Han Peng, and I knew that Strand would be embarking for Rangoon before my flying boat was on the first upright of the Horseshoe Route home. I was a contented man.

But this is to anticipate. The morning after my first meeting with Goh Han Peng I returned to the House of Diamonds at the time we'd agreed.

Goh Han Peng came through his glass and lacquer to greet me with an expansive gesture of those eloquent hands. There was a young smiling Chinese in a low basket chair to his left, fingering a sandalwood paper knife. At least I hoped it was a paper knife. I hadn't entirely got over my sense of caution about Goh Han Peng and his establishment.

"Our friend here is my nephew, Jimmy Fong," Goh Han Peng was saying. "My nephew," he emphasized, with one of his pauses. "He is also a detective in the special branch of the Singapore police force."

This was good news. I had every reason to suppose that a connection inside the local police would be invaluable. I shook hands cordially with Jimmy Fong. He had limp, strange hands, very different from those of his uncle. You might have called them watchful hands. They contrasted uneasily with his perpetual smile.

"I believe that Jimmy has solved the problem you posed me," Goh Han Peng was continuing. "He has found you a sleeper."

I'd left a full-scale dossier on Strand with Goh Han Peng the previous day. There were dozens of photographs of him, from every angle, in black and white and in color, naked and clothed. There wasn't much they didn't reveal, from the mole on his forehead to the calluses on the soles of his feet.

It wasn't his feet, though, that seemed most remarkable in the photographs, at any rate the ones of him in the nude. The fact of the matter is that Strand had a damned big penis. Well endowed, I suppose you'd have to describe him as, if you wanted to keep it vague.

Molly had blushed when she saw the picture. Walpole, in a mood almost of alarm, had whistled. There was little doubt that Major Strand must have been able to give good value between the sheets.

As it happens, I'd seen this as a possible security risk. Men with a strong appetite for their pleasures tend to be easy targets for blackmail. However, there was no evidence from Strand's earlier military career that he'd given any cause for worry.

His private life had been exemplary, very quiet and uninvolved. There had once been a girl friend in Camberwell, but it doesn't seem to have gone beyond a bit of finger play in the back row of the Gaumont. It was obvious enough that Strand had been keeping himself in check.

Jimmy Fong was tapping the photographs with his paper knife. The tiny point ran up and down the glossy contours of Strand's body.

"You see," he was saying, "we need a cover. The facial similarities are essential. But much can be done with the training of expressions, too. The difficulty is very often the style of the man, the interests he has, the way he carries himself."

He was talking sense. I listened carefully as he ran smoothly through his analysis. The need for a sleeper whose whole physique would seem to echo, would lean in the same direction as, Strand's own. He was pausing.

"I think your Major Strand is a lover of women," he continued softly. "Your file has disguised this fact, or has failed to reveal its force. But it may be the key to our solution."

I nodded. I began to sense the direction his mind was moving in. A similarity in height or weight would hardly be enough. A man could seem to be taller or heavier than he was. An athlete would move with spring and grace, a clerk with lethargy.

"A lover," Goh Han Peng was saying, completing my thoughts. "A lover will go with women. He will be known and recognized for his prowess. He will give off an air of masculinity to those who observe him.

"There are nine or ten Japanese agents here who might easily make a physical match for your Major Strand," he was saying. "Of these at least four have been away from Japan for several years, and have the additional advantage of being single men. Only one, however, by a quirk of chance, is notorious for his interest in our Chinese brothels. His name is Captain Kato Ogawa."

I remember him laying a photograph on my knee. It was an odd moment. Here, all unknowing, was the agent whom Strand would replace, whose life, in just a few weeks, was going to lie in my hands. I felt a prickle of excitement, even of fear.

"Ogawa has a mistress, a Chinese girl," Jimmy Fong was saying. "Her name is Su Lin, and she works at the House of Happiness. She is beautiful, and she is very loyal. I pay her a small retainer for information. She will certainly cooperate."

I looked across at Goh Han Peng. He was cracking his knuckles again, a Dickensian gnome, fiendish and inexplicable, an Oriental Daniel Quilp.

"Look," I said, anxious suddenly to gain the initiative. "I begin to see what you're saying. When the Japanese invade—"

I paused. I had to take a chance.

"I take it we're all agreed," I said. "At the moment the British government is not at war with the Japanese. In theory, it may never be. In practice, I regard it as certain that hostilities will commence before the end of the year."

Jimmy Fong was shaking with weird laughter.

"Be reassured," he said. "There is no disagreement on that score. You see," he said, and for a second he seemed more human, "the Chinese people are already at war with Japan. We have lost many thousands of friends. Many thousands."

Goh Han Peng raised his hand. It halted Jimmy Fong. It was as if a colleague were directing traffic and had signaled him to stop.

"You fear disloyalty, Colonel," Goh Han Peng was saying. "You are a brave man, but even you are scarcely brave enough to put these fears into words."

I felt myself sweating, and wondered if I might have gone too far. The nail file was in my right-hand pocket, and I reached in to finger it out. It felt better, paring my nails.

"Forget your fears," Goh Han Peng continued. "There is a common cause. All information that passes through our hands will be open to your eyes. When the Japanese invade, my friends and I will be operating a resistance movement. You and your Major Strand will be part of that."

I eased myself in my chair. The main hurdles were over. It was as I had supposed. The Triad was too heavily committed to Chiang Kai-shek for any possibility of a local rapprochement with the invaders in the event of a Japanese victory.

There were risks in this, but at least I knew where I stood. I looked down again at the face of the man in my lap. I don't like violence, but there seemed no alternative. He would have to die.

"Be careful," I said. "I don't want anything to happen too soon. My colleague will be here shortly on the first of several visits from Rangoon as a Japanese businessman. He will have ample opportunity to make a close study of this man he is to replace."

Goh Han Peng was smoothing his bald head.

"Of course," he said.

We talked for a few moments longer. The plan was simple. Strand would assume the identity of the sleeper. He would go into hiding with Su Lin when the British plan to intern all Japanese residents of Singapore was put into effect. In the event, certain in our view, of a Japanese victory, he would emerge from the persuasive concealment of his mistress's arms.

It was a good plan. The Japanese would hardly find it surprising that the one agent to escape the British net was a man with the good fortune, or the good sense, to enjoy the services of a local Chinese prostitute. Su Lin would be a brilliant cover.

I found myself wondering, as I walked back to the Raffles, how far Strand would go with her. A lot would rest on this. She might succumb, in more ways than one, to his persuasiveness.

Looking back now, I see that Su Lin brought in our best hope of success, at any rate from the Singapore end. It didn't seem so later, of course. There were complications. But I could hardly have foreseen them.

I lunched at the Raffles on beef cutlets and some Bombay onions. Over a bottle of Tiger beer I thought about the sleeper. Death was there in the wings for him. Death, as if he had never been. Later the *kamikaze* program would make this sort of thing more acceptable, but this wasn't later.

It was early still, in 1941, and we weren't even at war yet. Ogawa was a Japanese officer, and he'd sworn an oath to his emperor. It was easy for him to die for what he believed in. It wasn't so easy for me. I had to order his death.

Sex and death, I remember thinking that day: the great absolutes. The operation was cutting down to the roots. What had started with envy was going to end with lust and rage. Three of the deadly sins already.

I thought about that as I finished my beer.

8

I never knew Captain Kato Ogawa. It seems strange, looking back. In a way he was the turning point of the whole operation, and without what he did, and what happened to him, I doubt if I'd be writing as I am. Things would have taken their course, but they'd have had a different dimension.

What I haven't yet mentioned is that Ogawa was a professional photographer. This became important as time went on, and it needs to be remembered.

Standing on the bridge this morning, I found it easy to remember. There was a young kingfisher diving from the alders, all wonderful blue and red against the water, and I came back up to the house to get my old box camera for some pictures.

But he'd gone. Taken his sharp beak and his wings into the trees, like the passing of grace into darkness. I held the little black rexine-covered box in my hands, and I thought of Ogawa there in Singapore, forty years ago, with the warships and the butterflies.

He must have been recruited by Yoshida sometime in the mid-thirties. I can imagine the situation. The dark little shop in Roppongi, near the underground station, the neat Intelligence major admiring the framed prints of mountains and weddings on the walls.

Ogawa, flattered, suave. Ogawa, ambitious.

"How would you like to assist the Emperor?" Yes, he'd have

been as blatant as that. It made its mark in those days. "Travel, perhaps. Would you like to travel?"

I can see Yoshida striding up and down, examining his fingernails. The spotless Gestapo man. Toothbrush moustache. Hitler look. "I need some help in Singapore. A few observations of roads, bridges, visiting ships maybe. Nothing illegal. Nothing more, really, than landscape studies. The sort of thing"—I can see the gloved hand gesturing at the walls—"you do all the time. And so well. So very well."

Ogawa preening himself. Ogawa excited.

"Your own shop, of course," Yoshida promises. "On capital from a long-term loan, without interest. Fares paid. You can visit your family once in a while."

Ogawa falling. Ogawa almost eager now.

Yoshida plays his trump card. A maroon album of "tasteful studies for gentlemen" slides in his squeaking palms. He taps the dark female buttocks with his pigskin index finger. Ogawa has perhaps drawn his attention to a particularly choice example.

"Women," he murmurs. "Whenever you need them, Kato. The finest Chinese whores in the world are available for the price of a cup of *sake* in Singapore."

I suppose you could say they exploited Ogawa. So did we. His Achilles' heel was a huge blister, burning for sex, burning for pictures, and Singapore gave him what he needed. In July 1941, when Jimmy Fong selected him to be Strand's sleeper, Kato Ogawa was well settled. He had a thriving photographic business, a willing British clientele, and a nimble Chinese mistress.

He was rich, satisfied and successful. At the age of thirty-eight he was fit and healthy. He fenced for exercise. He ate well but wisely. He dressed like a businessman, in the best English style. He even had a little moustache, like Clark Gable, like everybody else.

In every decade I suppose men of the same age tend to look alike. My generation squared their shoulders in the trenches, and you don't see too much to separate Macmillan from Attlee if you glance at the sepia prints, with their puttees on and their swagger sticks.

And Mick Jagger. He set a standard, too, with his long hair and his flabby mouth. I remember reading someone saying that Mick Jagger had made him handsome. By inventing, I suppose, the thin, unhealthy look.

At any rate, they were all alike in the sixties. The girls, too, for that matter. Silly kids. But you see my point. It's never hard, in Intelligence work, to find a double for somebody. Provided you pick from the same generation, and get the clothes right.

So Ogawa wasn't going to be hard to copy. He and Strand had the same physique, the same age, as it happened, to the month. The details would just be a matter of observation, and Strand would have plenty of time.

I thought about Strand at the Raffles, playing billiards with a man from Java who dealt in watches. I never discovered the export mechanism, in any sense, but they started from Yokohama. He showed me a suitcaseful, with their Mickey Mouse faces and Donald Duck hands.

Japan, like syphilis, has been the great imitator. The West has always known that, when it came to watches. It took a long time, though, to realize they could knock together a copy of a fighter aircraft as well as a clock movement.

Things had moved fast since I was in Tokyo. It was Strand who showed me drawings of a Japanese Hurricane he'd had from a colleague of his father's in the scrap-metal business. I'd never seen a Hurricane except in newspaper photographs, but I could appreciate how accurate that one was. Later they made them, as near as dammit, and wiser men than I learned their lesson.

Undressing for bed, I laid out the photographs of Ogawa I'd been given by Jimmy Fong. I glanced at my alarm clock. It was half past eleven. By now those supple muscles would be exercising themselves in the House of Happiness.

He'd be down to his underpants by the side of the bed. Or up to his elbows in hypo, perhaps. He might be a late worker. I visualized the image of a group of smiling British sailors, arms around each other's shoulders, the swelling hulk of their fresh destroyer clearly framed to the rear. I imagined Ogawa lifting the limp sheet out of the tray, holding it up to the red light.

I lay down on the bed, folding my arms under my head. I imagined Ogawa on the quayside, smiling and gesturing as he arranged his clients to bring out the best view of the bridge, the forward gun turrets. Poor devil, I thought, you're going to die.

Ogawa was a spy. Those photographs he was taking might send a thousand British sailors to their deaths. He was dangerous, and he had to go. When the Japanese invaded, and Strand assumed his identity, Ogawa would have to be killed.

It was hard, in a way, to see that as unfair. His colleagues in espionage in Singapore—and there were hundreds—would be interned. They would live out the war in British camps. Only Ogawa would die. But Ogawa's death was necessary. And Ogawa, like all the others when war broke out, would be liable to execution as a soldier out of uniform.

He would know that. We all knew that, on both sides. I turned on my hip and looked over at the drawn velvet curtains, the carafe of water on the dressing table, the rack for cases. It was a very British scene, here at the other side of the world.

I felt safe, protected by the long arm of the Empire on which the sun never set. And yet I was a murderer. We were not at war, not yet. And here was I condemning an innocent man to death for taking a few snapshots. It felt like that.

I rose, went over to the dressing table, and poured myself a glass of water. Drinking, I tried to assemble my feelings. Ogawa and his death were after all not the essentials at this stage. I had still to engineer the establishment of Strand in Singapore. I had cabled to London that the sleeper had been selected, and Strand would soon be on his flight, or series of flights, to Rangoon.

I focused my mind on Ogawa as I hoped that Strand would see him, as a subject for analysis and imitation. It was easy enough to imagine the public life, the erection of tripods on cobblestones, the manipulation of light meters, the soothing patter.

Working a camera, at least well enough for a convincing result by the frail standards of the 1940s, would hardly be a serious problem. Strand had a few days to have lessons in developing and printing with a professional like Billington, anyway. I made a mental note to send another cable on that subject tomorrow.

Since the Japanese would remember Ogawa as a photographer, an effective copy of his professional mannerisms would go a long way to making Strand accepted. He would have to try to acquire some of the more eccentric, more individual, tricks that Ogawa might use to put his sitters at ease.

It shouldn't be hard. He might even pick up some advice through British sailors who'd had their pictures taken. Following men to a bar, getting into conversation, bringing the talk around to needing a passport photograph. These games were the meat and drink of our business.

They still are, I'm sure. It was Ogawa's private life there was more to be guessed about. Su Lin was supposed to be Chinese, and a slave of the Triad. I had to rely on that, though I didn't want to.

Women are often a hazard, and foreign women are the worst of all. I remember an operation in the Dutch East Indies once that foundered on a native girl who fell in love with the enemy control. It's the kind of thing that happens, and you have to live with the possibility, but I never got used to it, then or later.

Su Lin, I said to myself. Su Lin, the little Chinese prostitute. I remember I lay back on the bed then and tried to visualize her relationship with Ogawa.

It was a pleasant enough task in those days, and I suppose it should be even now, at my age. I'm not too old to be charmed by a pair of pretty ankles in Oxford Street. It's not that. I could still manage whatever had to be done, if I was called on.

Writing now about Su Lin I realize there are things I shall have to say, if I tell the truth, and I have to, that can't be shown to Mary, after all. It's precious to read aloud to her what I've written, and to have her praise. It helps.

I didn't see, at first, how there might have to be an end to reading. Now that it's come, and I'll have to start with excuses,

I feel the change. Writing's a lonely business, after all.

I can't have anyone shown this chapter, until it's over. I mean, until either of us has gone, Mary or myself. It can't be all that long, I suppose, one way or another. I sometimes think, when she serves me dinner, and I hear the asthma catching her breath, we may not see another Christmas together.

Dear Mary. She'll be in the library now, sewing buttons on my shirts in the sun. Some things don't change. The stiffness may not come in my loins now when I see her stripping, but I still feel tears in my throat at the thought of her dying, or feeling pain.

God knows, I could do it still if she asked, if she wanted me to. There were good times. Nights with sweat running like condensation on windowpanes. You don't get a son and two daughters by pruning gooseberry bushes.

It could still happen. Affection rears like a snake to strike, and love can transform. It can open doors, too. It did for Su Lin, with her long cigarette holder and her Shanghai gown. She became a great lady in her way, after her mother died, and she played the brothels.

There's more to be said about her now. The report she made for Clark filled in a lot of the background. For most of us, in 1941, she was just a kind of blank sexual check, an empty sketchbook. The image we all drew in was a sort of Chinese Jane, or Betty Grable.

You remember Jane. The day she took off her knickers in the *Daily Mirror* the 4th Armored Division advanced eight miles in the Falaise Gap. There, or somewhere. There are several versions.

For us, I mean for Brundall and Clark and me, Su Lin was our Oriental equivalent. I don't suppose that we examined her possible motives or feelings for a moment in what she did with Strand or Ogawa. She was just a Chinese whore, a dream.

To be vulgar, I think we needed her body. It focused our sexuality, our repressed energies, in that gray trough of war. The pinups of Rita Hayworth did much the same. They gave us all some outlet for lust, and we needed that, whatever we say.

Su Lin was a real woman, though. She had broad shoulders,

I see now from the pictures, and scars on her thighs. She wasn't perfect, by any means, from a physical point of view, and she'd been through troubles. The six-inch heels and the slit skirt were simply the uniform of her profession.

Underneath her Shanghai gown a heart beat. And behind her makeup a brain ticked. She had feelings, and she had ideas. It's clear from her own report, or what passes for it in the desiccated English of the War Office translation, that she wanted to come to England. She even had some notion of going to university.

She played the piano a bit, rather well according to Strand, and she might have graduated to being a nightclub singer. But that wasn't her ambition. It was too low a goal. She wanted to stay where she was, at the bottom, until she got rich. Then leave, and soar.

As it turns out, she got very near. She had more than six thousand pounds, or the equivalent, in local currency and small stones. It wasn't lack of persistence that stopped her, or lack of skills, for that matter.

She was the best whore in the House of Happiness, according to the madam, or so Jimmy Fong reports. She could do things with her organs I don't really think it proper to write down. I saw her dance once, and she puffed a lighted cigar as she did so, but it wasn't the lips of her mouth she put it in.

She had the means to make herself very wealthy by pleasing men. There was never a doubt about that, according to Strand, and he was an expert. What stopped her was neither lack of will nor lack of power. It was a kind of excess of sweetness.

I like her better now, when I think of that. I stroke her hair in my mind, more gently. I walk with her like my daughter Alice, through a forest littered with bluebells. I read her Shakespeare, and explain the difficult words.

That's what she wanted, I suppose. And perhaps, too, it's what she got, more than I realized. Love calls to love, after all, and there are men, they say, who go to prostitutes to talk and hold hands as much as to screw and flog. I don't know. I was never one of those.

Anyway, it was long ago, the whole business. Ogawa's dead,

poor fellow, and Su Lin, too, for all I know. I wonder, though. I wonder if she ever did get to England, and go to university. I doubt it somehow, but I hope so, for her sake. She'd have learned all the wrong things, like the rest of them nowadays, but at least she'd have got what she wanted. Not many of us can say that we've had that, not any more.

9

Sometimes, by casual hindsight, I've recalled the operation as something we put together a couple of months before the Japanese invasion. But it wasn't that way at all, in reality. Time has a habit of telescoping, and memory plays tricks.

I realize, each day as I go through the file and check up the dates, what a very long business it all was. I tell the story, of course, to bring out what matters, or seems to me to matter, as I write in 1979. At the time, in 1941, there was a cloudiness, a kind of muzziness around the edges, that's hard to capture.

There was a war on: you have to remember that. Each episode in our planning took place against the background of hostilities against the Germans. Day by day, as I opened my *Telegraph*, I'd be reading about some new twist in the battles around Tobruk or some breakthrough in the Ukraine.

Most people were concerned about clothes rationing, or the bombing, or someone winning the George Cross. When Roosevelt froze Japanese assets in the USA and the British and Dutch governments followed suit, nobody paid much attention. That was in July. Even when General Tojo became Premier in Tokyo, in mid-October, the main news of the day was the torpedoing of Axis supply ships in the Mediterranean.

Much was talked about the exploits of the Commandos, with their newly appointed boss, Lord Louis Mountbatten.

Mountbatten had returned to London after the sinking of the H.M.S. *Kelly,* and in August had been consigned the command of an aircraft carrier, the *Illustrious.* But he'd been over in America, waiting for the ship to be fitted out, when he was recalled by Churchill in October and talked into becoming Adviser on Combined Operations.

It was an important appointment. Mountbatten seemed to enjoy the mixture of technology and old-fashioned high adventure. It suited his bent. The Commandos had already had one or two successes, with the Spitzbergen raid—evacuating a group of islands north of Norway—only one of the more spectacular.

Japan was far away, and there were problems and victories on the doorstep. I have to allow for that, I suppose.

I was trying this morning to pin down the day when I got back to London from Singapore. Curiously, there's no exact record in the file. It must have been well before the sinking of the *Ark Royal,* though, because I remember discussing Ronald Legge's dispatch with Molly Jenkins over my deadly coffee.

There's a piece about the sinking in Strand's diary, too, written during his stay at the Lotus Leaf Hotel, in mid-November. I suppose she was very much in all our minds, the *Ark Royal.* There's no precise evidence, but we know she did put in at Singapore, and it's possible, even probable, that Ogawa took photographs of the crew.

Strand was a lone wolf, always. This was what struck him. Only one sailor, apparently—Edward Mitchell—was lost out of the ship's total complement of sixteen hundred men. "*Ark Royal* sunk," Strand writes, in his neat *kanji.* "I wonder if the one casualty was photographed by Ogawa too?"

I've mentioned Strand's diary before. It's a crucial document, and at this stage I start relying on it quite heavily. We never talked about it at the time, oddly enough. He made the first entry at his hotel in Rangoon the day he arrived after his flight from England.

I was already back home, and our paths had crossed. The next time we met was to be many months ahead, and in circumstances neither of us had exactly foreseen. The last-minute

85

briefing was done by Clark. He might have regarded a diary, even one kept in Japanese, as a security risk. He might even have refused permission for one to be kept in England. I don't know. There's no record.

At any rate, it wasn't until he was on his own in Burma that Strand started the diary. It's here on my desk now. I can't help my hands trembling, even after forty years, when I finger the worn leaves. It means so much.

It's a plain black exercise book, unruled, with a handwritten date for each entry. Not every day has a record, and some are very short. The main events in Strand's establishment of himself are fairly fully treated, though, and this is what helps to make my story clear.

Diarists vary in how they approach their material, and some can be trusted more than others. There's often a weird mixture of fantasy and what the writer had for breakfast or dinner. It's been my job to wade through a good few specimens in my days of Intelligence work.

I'd rate Strand's diary rather low on imagination. He leaves his feelings out, for the most part, and he lacks skill in building up a picture. He tends to stick to the facts and to let the interpretation speak for itself. But this has its merits. He doesn't often lead me astray.

We know the books he read, and the times he went for his walks. We know the names of the restaurants he had meals in, the prices he paid for what he had to eat. It's all very much a correctly articulated skeleton, but it needs the flesh and blood.

I'm trying to use the diary fairly and at the same time to convey something of Strand's almost inhuman impersonality. He was a frightening man, if an admirable one. The diary shows his control but not his intensity.

Of course, both were important. In the early days, while he was establishing his identity as a Japanese businessman, it was necessary for Strand to appear relaxed. He was affable in the company of his peers, no doubt, and there are frequent references to meetings for lunch or drinks.

But he had to be careful. He made a point of dining alone, pleading the excuse of accounts to write up, and he kept early hours. He must have stretched his meditation techniques to keep his nerves in order when he went up those endless marble or rickety stairs to lie down for the night.

From what he says it was always the same. In Rangoon or in Singapore, on those early visits, he would kneel back on his heels in front of the *tokonoma*, letting his eyes go out of focus at the point where the branch of Heaven in a flower arrangement merged with the white of the wall.

It was the best way. He could easily have been watched, at any rate by the Chinese, and he needed to prove his alibi. It might have been nice to put his feet up on a leather Chesterfield with a Bulldog Drummond novel and a gin and tonic. I sometimes think that his Edgar Wallace side was about the only thing he retained from those years at Wellington.

It was always there. He had the healthy Englishman's love of roast beef and Yorkshire pudding, with a dose of rough justice handed out to give it spice. But he kept his clubman hero tastes well out of sight.

He was always the perfect Japanese. It must have cost him more than he shows. When I read some entries I think I can just sense the occasional underlying throb of a wire drawn a little too tight for calm. But it isn't easy.

He presents himself, with care, as what we all wanted him to seem. He sleeps on the floor, in a *ryokan*. He lunches off *yakitori*, with a bottle of Kirin beer. He buys the magazines about martial arts. It makes a fine cover.

Of course the nurturing of the magnolia tree, to revert to the jargon, was being efficiently carried out by the local gardener, and we have reports from Jimmy Fong to fill out the gaps in Strand's own account. These tell us the private life of the public man who appears in the diary.

It seems that, to begin with, matters went forward without any serious hitch. The intermediaries of the Triad, whether bootboys or chambermaids, would exchange the necessary messages in the form of pressed clothes with notes in the pockets, or bundles of laundry with rolled newspapers in the midst of shirts.

Strand was fully briefed about Ogawa by the end of his third day in Singapore. He had ample funds in the form of notes, gold and diamonds. He knew the emergency telephone procedures for getting in contact with Jimmy Fong. He was planted, in fact, and flourishing in his plot.

I can well imagine him on one of those walks he mentions to the Botanical Gardens in King George V Park, on the slopes of Fort Canning, closing his eyes in the scent of the frangipani flowers and dreaming of the girl with the six-inch heels whose photograph he had seen in the secret file.

He must have thought about her, by then. He must have worried about the security risks. He was a cautious man. But he must have felt some tingle of anticipation too, as he contemplated his long weeks of concealment after the Japanese invasion.

He was a great lover. It redeemed him, and made him human. It gave him a subtle extra dimension. It could also, of course, have been his one weakness—was, according to Brundall and Clark, who had reasons of their own to be careful. But I wonder.

What happened to Strand was affected by love, but not in the way we thought, and not at the time it might have been. He moved in a charmed circle with Su Lin, at least for some weeks. She was in his mind and in his heart. Perhaps even then, in late November, before he knew her, he plucked a frangipani blossom from the tree in the park and thought about her, the unknown girl whom his mind already knew.

He may have remembered other girls, in Hawaii, when he traveled there for his father. In the tropical night, with the sun setting into the Pacific, perhaps a Chinese girl had opened the Pandora's box of sex to the boy Strand on the warm evening sand, with the tiny popping eyes of crabs watching them as they moved in each other's arms.

It may be a romantic thought, but it enriches the trivial minutiae of the operation, and it may have happened. There must have been something more than the bare facts of the diary, and the secret plans in Jimmy Fong's files. There always is, and always will be.

Intelligence work, at its best, depends on knowing that. It also depends on the boredom, and, more than that, on the nastiness. There was plenty of that, of course, and Strand was equipped to handle it.

We learned this gradually, but the point was made early on by Clark, and it formed an important part of his assessment of Strand. He was sure it would help, and he was right.

The arrangements for killing someone are always complicated, and they can be messy. I've already indicated that I don't like violence, and I was unhappy about the necessity of disposing of Ogawa, particularly in time of what was still, technically, peace. It seemed like a betrayal.

Unfortunately there was no alternative. So I'd had to consider how it was going to be done. The obvious method might have seemed to be by issuing what I believe the Americans now call a "contract," and making this arrangement through the Triad.

However, I was by no means keen on this. We'd already had to go further than I wanted in asking a favor by getting Jimmy Fong to make the selection of the sleeper in the first place. Beyond that he was going to have a continuing position as Strand's local control. If I took him on as a spare-time hatchet man as well, I felt that I'd be in the pocket of the Triad for life.

At any rate, I had doubts about their willingness to do the job. Manipulation of a British agent might well seem a good deal less involving and dangerous than straightforward murder. Certainly at this stage, before the Japanese invasion.

So I went along, albeit a little reluctantly, with the suggestion made by Clark that Strand should handle the business himself. We'd gone out for a stroll and were watching boys throwing stones in the plague pond on the Common when he broached the idea.

"He can use a commando knife," said Clark. "I've seen him at work. And he's got the grip in his bare hands, if need be."

The surviving mallards were squawking indignantly.

"I wonder," I said. "Has he got the will?"

Clark looked at me.

"You know he has," he said.

We walked on in silence for a time, while I thought things out in my mind.

"Of course, we could hardly order him," Clark was continuing. "I know that it's not exactly part of the requirements of his attachment. Not according to the book, anyway. But he's bound to love the idea. He'll volunteer like a shot."

There was no problem. Strand had agreed without question, and the general plans had been made before Ogawa was even chosen, while I was still in England.

As it turned out the idea was a very practical one. In his role as a Japanese businessman it was easy and natural for Strand to make visits to Ogawa's shop to buy film, and we know from his diary that he had little difficulty in striking up an acquaintance.

You might imagine that the two of them would have got into the habit of joking about their similarity in appearance. I doubt if Ogawa noticed. People don't. And, besides, Strand was wearing clear spectacles as a cover, and he grew his moustache later, when he was in hiding with Su Lin. They can't have seemed that much alike.

I've said that Strand had a vicious streak. He must have had, you might suppose, to survive three weeks of accepting discounts, and enjoying conversations about the weather, with an innocent fellow countryman he was going to kill.

It's the cold-blooded, slow calculation of Strand I wonder at, and perhaps even admire, in a perverse, fascinated way. He could bottle up his emotions, good and bad, and then let them out in a smooth, even burst with precision.

That happened with Su Lin just as it did with Ogawa, perhaps. There's one passage in Strand's diary that gives a clue. He's describing an occasion when he went into the shop on the excuse of buying a new camera.

There were several on the counter, let's assume. He doesn't give us the details, but I can imagine the scene. There must have been one or two other people there, to judge from the tone of the conversation, according to Strand's notes. They may have been standing near at hand, sailors with their fresh glossy snaps, a girl or two holding negatives to the light.

"I like this German one," I hear Strand saying.

He works the shutter, testing the mechanism.

A Leica, apparently. Ogawa was full of praise for the workmanship, annoyed obviously, with a glance at those British sailors maybe, that the war had made such fine Teutonic instruments hard to obtain.

They discussed shutter speeds, exposures, prices. Strand had been well briefed by our pimply Billington. Those days at the Bournemouth chemist's had turned out to be a blessing.

They passed from photography to the war. The Germans were always good, like the Swiss, with fine equipment, Ogawa thought. Their binoculars were the best in the world. Their tanks, too, to judge from the news.

Von Leeb was clearly doing well that day outside Leningrad. Strand nodded, agreeing, noncommittal.

"We too one day perhaps," Ogawa murmured, watching the door close on the British. "Toys are a small beginning. The factories in Osaka are capable of producing watches, lenses. Machine guns, too, of course."

He smiled, at ease with a fellow Japanese.

"We have centuries of experience," he went on. "I have a cousin, Mr. Tanaka. His family have been makers of sword guards since the Ashikaga shogunate. You would need a magnifying glass to see the little black cups of the *nanako* on the *shakudo* grounds. Each one as exact as if laid on by machine. But laid by a hand punch, by a man sitting cross-legged on the ground. This kind of skill, this kind of precision, will make us the trade masters of the world."

He was eloquent, in his element, so Strand records. He watched the hand gestures, the way Ogawa had of tilting his head sometimes, as if pausing to glance at a picture he was painting. He made a mental note, and indeed one in his diary, to copy that.

The story of Ogawa's cousin had been a long one. Like many such narratives it brought out the inner garrulousness to which even the most reticent of men are sometimes prone. Strand was aware of this. He led Ogawa on. He was learning by tone as well as by fact. He was already sculpting his own internal Ogawa behind the quiet, attentive facade of Mr. Tanaka, the visiting businessman.

When the Japanese invaded, the curtain would be stripped aside and the carefully hidden model would come to life—a breathing, walking memorial to the real Ogawa, by then translated to another and more illusive sphere. The zombie Ogawa, the one survivor of the great battleship of Japanese Intelligence in Singapore, would rise and plot again.

The story was reaching its climax. Leicas and clients were forgotten. The cousin was having his troubles, you know how it is. Strand knew. He pursed his lips. The importers in all the British colonies were refusing to accept his wares. Even here, in Singapore, where the dealer, a Japanese himself, a peasant if ever there was one, had gone so far as to dishonor his commitments.

Ogawa sucked in his breath. He knew this dealer well. He'd spent some years at school with him in Nagoya. He was always a racketeer, a traitor.

He stopped suddenly, in mid-tirade. The shop was empty.

"Come upstairs," he said. "I'll show you one or two of my cousin's guards. I have a fair collection, and a good bottle of *sake* to set them off with."

It was as quick as that. I can believe Strand's jubilation. It comes through the bare prose like a bud opening. A receptive silence, and a well-judged interest in cameras, had brought him a precious visit to Ogawa's home ground. He was trusted.

He glanced around Ogawa's neat seven-mat room with a calm pleasure. The rack of swords. The *hibachi* with the pot of *sake* on to heat. The sliding doors beside the single ink painting.

A frowning *samurai*, school of Kuniyoshi. And then the other, smaller room, with the low lacquer table and the cupboard for bedding. The place where Ogawa would sleep.

Already Strand was making plans. He knew exactly what he would have to do. As he relaxed on the *tatami* and spoke with polite approval of the cousin's *tsuba*, he was formulating the words he would have to use to Jimmy Fong on the telephone.

He would need some help, and a large measure of luck. But

the chances were on his side, or at least some of them were. I imagine him there in Ogawa's flat, absorbed, on his knees. The account his diary gives of that moment is one of the most revealing he wrote.

One final detail I shall always remember. It seems that the last guard Ogawa passed him, an iron one from the eighteenth century, had an exquisite silver inlay of a crane. "A crane," Strand writes. "The symbol of longevity. You can guess that it gave me something to think about when I left Ogawa that night and walked home to my hotel."

At the age of sixty-nine, it gives your colonel something to think about, too, Major Strand. A sense of irony. A sense of obligation. So few of us have lived in the shadow of the crane. You deserve our respect. We deserve, perhaps, your envy.

10

Whenever events begin to move more quickly things tend to come with a rush. At the agency in the 1950s we'd work for months on a new campaign and then, one day, in a flash, the product would be launched and the men would be out on the road selling.

It was much the same with Operation Chameleon. I still feel vaguely irritated when I have to call it that. The only chameleon I ever saw was in a zoo, and it spent its time very conspicuously flicking tiny insects out of the air with a long tongue. You could see it quite clearly on its branch; it didn't merge into its background at all.

I'd like to think that I had better luck. The operation wasn't entirely a failure. There were moments of greatness, touches of real excitement, some satisfactions.

I've stressed that we all knew war was inevitable from at least the spring of 1941. Unfortunately there was never any cast-iron evidence to back us up. For those who chose to be blind—and there were plenty of them—every incident, every pointer, was construed as leading to a different conclusion.

My clerk, Walpole, had moments of real doubt, I know. One day in November he came into my office to ask for a transfer. He sat there in front of the maps of Southeast Asia, smoothing the remaining strands of hair over his bald head with his fingers.

"Sir," he said awkwardly, "it's really the Huns we're after, you see. According to my way of thinking."

I saw his point. The battles of Sidi Rezegh, in the desert, were at their crucial stage. We'd just lost thirty-seven bombers in a raid on Mannheim in bad weather. It was rough going, that week.

Walpole was elaborating.

"My brother's in the Merchant Navy," he said. "We've just heard his ship was torpedoed off Norway."

I was starting to frame some words of sympathy, but he forged through my attempts.

"It's not that," he insisted, shaking his hand. "We're all taking our chances, I know that. It's just I'm not sure I'm doing my bit here. I mean, we're not at war with the Japs, are we? Not yet, anyway. I feel I'm not pulling my weight. I'm on the sidelines."

I can see his creased, heavy face now, squeezing the tears back in his little eyes.

"I owe it to my brother," he said. "I'm sorry, sir."

I didn't try to talk him out of it. I gave him a stiff Haig and filled out the transfer papers. I knew the Director would never agree to a replacement. The establishment was about to be reduced to five.

It was the invasion that saved me, the very day the transfer was about to go through. The Reuter's report was on my desk a few hours after it originated in Indochina. The *Malayan News* had it up in banner headlines before it reached the streets in England.

A fleet of twenty-seven Japanese transports had been sighted off Cambodia Point. They were steaming west across the Gulf of Siam toward the east coast of Malaya.

I tore up Walpole's transfer papers and shredded them one by one into my wastepaper basket. We were going to need him here after all. Within twenty-four hours there would be a state of war with Japan. I'd been proved right.

Everything I'd spent my time on for the last four months was finally going to be justified. I'd correctly foreseen exactly what was going to happen.

I ran the wall map down and rocked in front of it on my toes. I had that *Old Moore's Almanac* sort of feeling. I told you so, I found myself saying inside my head. I was already drafting an imaginary vicious memo to the Director.

Perhaps it isn't surprising that I was excited. I'd waited a long time for this. I never doubted for a second what the outcome would be. This was simply the first stage in the inevitable sequence of events that I'd been predicting. The second and subsequent stages would logically follow.

They did, too. We know that now. But it wasn't so clear to everyone at the time. Sir Robert Brooke-Popham, then Commander in Chief of the Far East, appears to have been furious when he read the headlines. He rang up the editor of the *Malayan News* to say he thought it most improper to print such alarmist views.

Fortunately this wasn't Goh Han Peng's opinion. I know now that the news of the Japanese fleet sailing from Hainan was in the hands of the Triad long before it got to Reuter's, and it was passed on to Strand immediately.

The contingency plan for the assassination of Ogawa and the hiding of Strand with Su Lin was quickly reduced to its final details. It was only a question of timing. The basic necessities for the job were in readiness more than a week before the Japanese landings.

In all, Strand had been able to make three visits to Ogawa's apartment above the shop, and he'd got to know the lay of the land well. He knew the width of the stairs and the way to open the door at the top. He knew exactly how many strides it was from the door to the *shoji*, and then from the screens to where the bedding was laid.

He'd even had a chance to make a wax impression of the key to the shop and to get a copy cut. It was one of many details that Jimmy Fong reports as having particularly impressed him. It obviously helped in getting the Triad's cooperation. They liked to work with professionals.

The actual killing was going to be Strand's business, as already planned. It would have been possible—and Strand discussed it on the telephone with Jimmy Fong, he says—for the body to be left where it was going to be laid, in Ogawa's flat. An unsolved murder, though, was undoubtedly going to create a great deal of trouble, even in the turmoil of a Japanese invasion, and Jimmy Fong was clearly unenthusiastic about that.

On balance, there seemed to be a good case, he maintained, for allowing Ogawa simply to "disappear." In other words, to get rid of his body and make it seem as though he'd had warning of police intentions and gone into hiding to escape internment.

This wasn't exactly the safest choice from Strand's point of view. He was going to take enough risks as it was. Multiplying them by involving himself in a complex procedure to dispose of a corpse can't have seemed an attractive idea.

It would have been ironic in the extreme to be hanged by a British court for what they might claim was a civil offense. And I don't suppose he had any illusions, despite Clark's promises, that we'd step forward from the shadows to bail him out. What happened later was ironic enough as it was, but it had the dimension of something else as well, of a kind of tragedy. This was a different matter. Nevertheless, the cooperation of the Triad was essential. Strand didn't have much room for maneuver.

So the joint decision was finally made to allow Ogawa to "leave town," as I believe the Mafia used to say. Jimmy Fong agreed to supply Strand with transport, assistance and means of concealment for the corpse.

It was ten o'clock on the evening of Sunday, 7 December, when—and forgive my jargon—the magnolia tree received an instruction in a parcel of laundered shirts. Strand was to telephone a certain number in precisely half an hour. He'd spoken twice before to the gardener on the telephone, but never, as now, at the same number.

The voice at the other end of the line was clipped. It seemed to Strand, in the dingy box across the hall of the Lotus Leaf Hotel, that Jimmy Fong was under pressure.

"The Japanese have landed near Kota Bharu," the voice said. "The orders to begin the internment are bound to be given as soon as the news reaches the Governor."

"How long?" said Strand.

He could feel the armpits of his shirt wet with sweat.

"I'll have the car and the man outside Ogawa's shop in exactly two hours. You'll need to be fast. The whole thing has to flow. Good luck, Magnolia Tree."

Strand placed the long brass bell of the mouthpiece back in its cradle and walked to the desk.

"Urgent business," he murmured.

Within three-quarters of an hour he had checked out and was walking through the streets of Chinatown with his neat leather suitcase and his coat over his arm. He had no fear of being attacked. Inside his jacket pocket he was carrying a Napoleon razor. It was honed ready to draw blood at a touch.

The events of the next few hours are, in some respects, the kernel of my story. I've already said it was Strand's story more than mine, and I wish he were here to tell it. The wind's up tonight, and it's howling around these eighteenth-century bricks as I write.

It would be nice if Strand were beside the fire here with me, to check the details and get the color right. We could drink some brandy together in a pair of those good balloons, and reminisce like a couple of old heroes from The Runagates Club.

I wonder, though. It's not a Buchan romance, however much I may make it sound like one. They were real people, Jimmy Fong and Ogawa. Strand and I would agree on that. He'd want me to make them true to what they were.

True to their selves, true to their dreams. There was drama and mystery that night, as well as the dull business of police work. I can't avoid some hint of those. There was a full moon, for instance, and the long shadows beneath the screw pines.

Toward the northeast, on the high ground, the huge bulk of Government House, overlooking the city, was ablaze with lights. At the intersections of streets Strand could see them, and the lights of Fort Canning, fifteen hundred yards away.

What he couldn't see, four hundred miles farther north, in the light of the same moon, were the thirty thousand Japanese assault troops, dressed in battle order on the decks of their

98

transports, already only seventy miles from their landing points.

He couldn't see them; but he knew they were there. It must have stiffened his resolution. He at least was ready for action.

The walk to the corner of South Bridge Road took nearly half an hour. A single car was cruising in the moonlight, the Chinese driver leaning with his elbow along the open window. He glanced at the neat figure of Mr. Tanaka, the Japanese businessman who so obviously needed a taxi.

As the car drew up, the back door was already opening. Strand had his case in and was levering himself up over the running board as the driver began to accelerate.

"One-thirty," the driver said, in bad Japanese. "Internments to begin without warning. You have to hurry."

"Fifteen minutes," Strand replied. "It can't be less."

His watch said five to twelve. He closed his eyes in the darkness of the car. Just over an hour and a half to get up to Ogawa's apartment, finish the job, carry the body down to the car, drive out to the swamp and back to the House of Happiness. It wasn't going to be easy.

But it had to be done. The whole city would be swarming with policemen as soon as the signal to make the swoop was given. Every moving vehicle would be stopped. Anyone Japanese or looking Japanese would be seized.

The car slowed at the corner, and Strand stepped through the other door, on the street side, and walked back up the line of shops. There was no light in Ogawa's window. He must have paused, and tensed himself.

Just before you kill someone time always seems to slow. There's a long moment to visualize the whole surrounding scene. I've done it twice, that way, with knowledge that it was coming, and it was exactly the same both times.

You have the weapon's weight in your hand, the loaded springs in your forearms. There's wine, or food, maybe, stale in your mouth. A twilight intensity of the sense of vision. Perhaps you know what I mean: the sort of edgy clearness you get before a storm.

Of course, there's none of this in the diary. Only the bones of the work. The walk across the road, the silent, slow turn of the Yale. Shedding shoes, tiptoeing up the stairs in stockinged feet. The faint odor of spiced meat in the darkness.

And then the Glasgow business, as Brundall once referred to it. It can't have taken more than a few seconds, at the crucial point. The swing, the gasp, and the hiss. And then the quick, fumbling getting into the mailbag brought up from the car. The head first, then the legs.

Through the window Strand saw the car draw in to the curb and the Chinese driver looking up. He left the engine running, and Strand saw him enter the door. He took the stairs very light and fast, and helped Strand tuck the bare feet inside. There was blood on the sheet, the report he gave to Jimmy Fong says. Not much of it, but there wouldn't be with a slit throat. So they rolled the sheet, too, and stuffed it away.

Imagine the two of them humping that ugly sack on the dark stairs. Cramming the grim bulk of it into the rear seat of the car. The Chinese vanishing down the street, and Strand with a drive ahead through the suburbs of Singapore to the swampland.

I wouldn't like to have had to lug a corpse out on my own there, by the side of the stinking mud, and watch it sinking down in the sucking ooze. With a slow, bubbling noise, and taking its time.

Strand was a cool one. He doesn't mention the swamp, or the horror. The awkward business of gripping cloth in your fingers and lifting. The other, cold awkwardness of having to change into a new suit of clothes in the front of the car. Rolling up the striped English suit, the shirt, maybe the stained shoes, in another bundle. Or simply tossing them all out on the sludge. Watching them, maddeningly, fail to go down. Searching around for a long stick. And having to prod, and wait.

It must all have taken a long time. On the drive back into Singapore he must have glanced more than once at the racing hands on his wrists. From the bare facts of his own account it was one–twenty-five when he ditched the car, as instructed, near the Raffles.

He must have had to run to reach the House of Happiness before the floodlights came on and the sirens moaned. Overhead the crews of seventeen Japanese bombers circled the city. The lights continued to blaze at Government House, where the Governor paced the lawns.

The bombs fell, killing sixty-one and injuring a hundred and thirty-three, in Chinatown. The war had begun. In the moonlight the enemy made a perfect target, according to the pilot of an ancient Brewster Buffalo, gunned-up and ready to fly. But no orders came to take off. The antiaircraft gunners were untrained, and the RAF feared they would shoot down their own planes.

It was a bizarre night, one to confirm all my hopes and fears. When the roundup of Japanese was completed it was found that only a handful were missing. Among these the photographer Ogawa's absence failed to surprise.

"He's a shrewd bugger," Jimmy Fong confided to his subordinate. "He probably got a tip-off. We'll find him, though, one way or another."

It seemed likely. The others in due course turned up, alive or dead, and the list of absentees grew shorter. It was generally assumed that Ogawa would surface, from the bog or the brothels.

But when the British Army began to retreat, the interest in Ogawa and his fate soon shriveled away. There were more pressing matters to attend to.

But not that night. That night the new Ogawa assumed his identity, and entered his kingdom. The magnolia tree put out its first flowers in the darkness, under the moon and the circling bombers.

11

It was a quarter to four on the morning of Monday, 8 December. A Chinese woman, naked to the waist, was kneeling over the supine body of a man on an old brass Western bed in a back room at the House of Happiness. The slats of a venetian blind rattled a little in the wind from an open window.

The woman was wearing some kind of silk garment, loosened from her broad shoulders, and allowed to fall to her hips. The bottom half had been rucked up, to gather in heavy folds around her powerful thighs, where the blue scars gleamed under tensed muscles.

The man lay very still. The invisible point where his body was joined to the woman's rustled in the darkness as she forced her belly up and down on him in regular motions. There was no other sound in the room except the gasp of her breath.

Outside, in a hundred other rooms in Chinatown, Japanese men very like the man on the bed were being wakened, forced to dress, and transported from their homes to ships waiting in the Telok Ayer Basin. Four hundred miles away, more Japanese men, fully armed and clothed, were wading through choppy waves on the beaches at Singora and Pattani.

The war that had been so slow in coming was at last in swift progress. The man knew this, and he lay, perhaps, and thought about it. The woman, whose thoughts were only on the man's body, advanced herself toward her climax.

She was an expert in how to reach what she wanted, and how to do it quickly. There were times in her profession when you gave the man what he needed, and detached yourself. There were other times, less frequent but more amusing, when you got the chance to be wholly fulfilled. This was one of those, and the woman was taking it.

The sheets had been thrown aside onto the floor, the man's clothes piled neatly on a cushion. The scent of incense, faint from something burning in a corner, provided a subtle background.

The woman released her breath in a long sigh. She was near. Very carefully, she leaned forward and put her mouth on the man's shoulder. Her nipples brushed the dark hair on his chest. She rested.

Then, with a roll of her hips to one side, she allowed one leg to slide down and along the inside of the man's thighs, which had parted slightly to make this possible. The woman shuddered expectantly. With a slight roll of her hips to the other side, she allowed her remaining leg to come down, sheathing her whole body inside the man's.

It was how she liked it best. The man's hands came around and fondled her buttocks roughly under the Shanghai gown, then fell away, neglectful, as if bored. The woman trembled. She felt the final surge rising.

Heaving herself on the man's belly, she began to moan and plead into his neck. She felt the fluttering come, the huge growth of the sleeping chrysalis into the wild moth in her groin. The frantic beating of its wings, the sudden release. And then the flight, for a brief forever, into the night.

It was a quarter to four. Su Lin knew this because she had trained herself always to look at the time on her diamond wristwatch at the point of climax. Time was money. However relaxed or exhausted, she kept her eye on it.

They made love for just under two hours that first night. It wasn't a record, either for Strand or for Su Lin, but it made an excellent start. She felt his power, she said, the moment he came in through the door.

She was on the cane sofa, curled up under the rose light from a jade lamp, and he stripped her to her American briefs with one slash of his eyes. She didn't love him then. He hadn't even spoken. But she felt the onset of a sudden, trickling lust.

He'd drawn her hair back with one hand and kissed her eyes. Then he'd levered her down to the floor, peeled that Boston silk to the backs of her knees, and put his mouth from behind to the wet lips between her buttocks.

She remembered later, and wanted to be accurate. She got it all down on the Dictaphone for Jimmy Fong. Her voice was low and sweet on the tape, like treacle flowing out of the tin.

They were on the bed, after her climax, talking. It was nearly dawn when she realized that she loved him. It had happened before, more than once, but it never lasted, and it never started so quickly.

It wasn't how big he was. She makes a point of that. It wasn't his pace either, or his coldness. Though both helped.

It was how he talked, after they finished. He had such total honesty, she said. She felt that she'd known him all her life, as if they were made for each other, and had just been waiting to meet.

She wasn't a fool either. She had her head screwed on the right way, and more than an eye for the main chance. You had to have, in the House of Happiness. She wanted to come to England, as I've said, and she knew very soon that Strand could never be the way.

But she didn't mind. He made her feel he was giving her all he had, and without trying, or charm. He was more himself, she said, than anyone she'd ever known. And he opened the doors, and let her in.

It's hard to believe, knowing Strand as I did. I saw only the ice and the drive, never the openness that she did. It takes a woman, I suppose. There was one fragment of their conversation that night that might explain what it was. It was when they made love again, during the raid.

The bombs had started to fall at a quarter past four. Su Lin had looked up, her whole body alert, when the first explosion came. It was over somewhere by the docks, to judge from the sound. The second rattled the window in its frame, and Su Lin swung her scarred legs to the floor.

"Come back to bed," said Strand, very gently, it seems.

He lifted her legs, rolling her over beside him again.

"It's the Japanese," he said. "The war has begun. We shall have to live with bombs and shells for a long time now, my little squirrel."

"It's been a long time already," said Su Lin. "I had family in Manchuria. They raped my cousins, in Nanking."

"Soldiers are all the same," said Strand. "They rape, and they kill. And the Japanese are the worst. That's why I'm here."

She felt the lax machine turn into the hard sword. It thrust at her. It plowed through the riven soil of her groin. It sowed the seed—albeit, one might add, in the bare ground of her Dutch cap—of a mood of revenge, a crop of warriors, an army of the will.

So they turned in each other's arms, cruel, plotting, and calm. They made love with fevered skill. They ate each other's powers. They knew, in their different ways, that what each was doing was temporary, and political, that it had to end.

They knew, but they didn't care. A kind of love had taken root in the stews, and it would flourish. For ten weeks they could live out of time.

It gives some decency to my bitter tale to remember this. In the windy summer of 1979 I salute you, Su Lin. And you too, Strand, in your brief madness. Such daft work as we two did requires these interludes. I cherish yours, those hot days in the House of Happiness.

It was a curious time. In London, for us in the Department, there was a lull in tension. It was natural, but it was hard to bear. I took some leave and went down early to spend Christmas with my mother in Brighton.

The Japanese advance in Malaya was proving faster than even I had expected. The official news, of course, disguised the true facts, but the inevitable tenor of the war was clear enough even to Molly Jenkins when she heard on the wireless that the *Prince of Wales* and the *Repulse* had been sunk by Japanese torpedo planes.

It seemed incredible to most people at the time. Here was a brand-new 35,000-ton battleship, escorted by a large battle cruiser, the pride of the greatest naval power in the world—as the British all believed themselves to be—sent to the bottom of the sea by a mere sixty little Asian flying machines three miles above them in the sky. It was as if a whale had been harpooned by a flock of gulls.

"Well," said Molly, as she brought me in my leave papers to sign. "It's what you've always said, sir. They're not such fools after all, the Japanese."

I was unscrewing my new Waterman. I was about to have two weeks away from it all, relaxing with Mother's collection of hunting prints behind the stuccoed facades of Brunswick Crescent. I signed my name with a flourish.

"It means the fall of Singapore, Molly," I said. "And rather soon, I'm afraid."

I was right. The airfield at Kota Bharu was captured after minimal resistance—minimal in my opinion, at any rate—in the first week of the campaign. After that there was virtually no air cover. The troops, poor devils, had no experience of what it was like to be constantly bombarded from the sky. There were cases when a single 250-pound bomb could cause panic in towns with a frightened Asiatic population and no proper air-raid precautions.

The army of Malaya began to fall back, overloaded with all the paraphernalia of European warfare. The Japanese carried what they needed for the jungle; our men had steel helmets and gas masks. It's a wonder they were able to retreat as fast as they did with all that rubbish on their shoulders.

Here was this great British army then, drawn from the Highlands of Scotland and the wilds of the Australian bush, almost to a man untrained in jungle warfare, fighting for their lives against a highly skilled and totally alien force and without support for their efforts, either from the sea or the air.

This was, of course, the deciding factor. It explains, though it doesn't excuse, what finally happened in the Ford Motor Factory at Singapore on the morning of 15 February, 1942—the surrender of by far the largest British army ever to lay down its arms to an enemy it outnumbered almost three to one.

It still makes me flush with shame. Hong Kong was bad enough. It was on Boxing Day, over plates of plum pudding with dried milk custard, listening to the old Pye in its walnut case by the bay window toward the sea, that Mother and I heard the news that Hong Kong had fallen.

Sir Mark Young had surrendered with eight thousand men after a siege of seven days by two entire Japanese divisions. They made it sound like a victory. I switched the set off and cradled Mother's head in my arms.

She came of a military family, as had my father. We weren't used to hearing of British defeats, not in the East. In the Afghan wars, Asians had fought bravely. So they had in India, many times. But they always lost, in the end. They were savages, after all. We were the British, the bearers of a sacred mission to civilize the world. Surely our last great poet, Rudyard Kipling, had told us so?

Things were changing. I poured Mother a glass of sweet sherry and tried to talk. She knew how I felt about the Japanese, but it was hard for her to understand. I sympathized. I'd felt the same.

It was a bitter thing to see what you'd been brought up to admire and respect thrown down and shown to be a sham. It was a cruel truth to have to accept your ideals as threatened, abandoned by those who were supposed to defend them.

I drank my Haig and tried to tell her that Percival would make a stand in Malaya. I knew he wouldn't. He had an MC and a DSO, and he'd commanded a battalion, with some distinction, in the Great War. He'd once been a brave man, I'm sure. But he'd lost his nerve.

He'd thought the Japanese were little yellow fuzzy-wuzzies, and he couldn't adjust. He let them come on and on, down the whole length of that elegant peninsula he was being paid to defend. And then he handed over his command, his honor and his men, after one day, just one day, without water, when his reservoirs were taken. He didn't even mount a counterattack.

I despised him already, that Christmas, for failing to make a stand at the beaches. I despised him more in February. I despise him still, even more, when I take up that photograph and see the flag slanting, and Yamashita dictating his terms. That was the end of Singapore, a squalid plea and a bitter compromise.

I'd known it would come, but hardly quite so soon. And it was hard to accept. One part of me, of course, had still to rejoice at being right, and at having the means to snatch one burning ember from the dying fire of defeat.

I thought a lot about Strand, although there was nothing at this stage that I could do to help him. I could only hope he was out of sight and safe, as we had planned. There was news from Jimmy Fong, by coded cable, that the arrangements for disposing of Ogawa and seeing Strand into hiding had worked out all right. There would be no more news, almost certainly, until after the fall of Singapore.

That would be the moment of supreme danger. Unfortunately it would also be the moment when I could do nothing to support Strand. He would be on his own. His neck on the line.

I walked along the beach and thought about Strand. I watched the waves come in and curl back on the pebbles. I wrapped a scarf around my face and sat reading Basho in the flying spray under a groyne. It was a good Christmas, lonely and satisfying.

I felt better for the rest when I got back to the bunker early in January. I wasn't alone in having traveled. Eden had been in Moscow for discussions with Stalin and Molotov. Churchill had got his pact signed in Washington, for twenty-six nations to fight the war to a finish.

Wavell, I read, of all people General Sir Archibald Wavell, after his failures in the desert had been promoted from his Indian command to be given supreme control of all allied forces in the southwest Pacific.

"It can't be true," I said to Brundall, as we washed our hands at the ancient porcelain basins.

"We need a proper leader," said Brundall, drying his face. "A shogun the Japanese will respect."

I turned off the dull brass tap. I would have to get Walpole to see that it was polished. Our standards were dropping.

"You're right," I agreed. "When Wavell's finished mucking everything up perhaps we will."

Brundall was cogitating by the table of clothes brushes.

"It won't need to be just a general," he said. "Morale will require a touch of mystique, too. Something royal, maybe."

I laughed, I remember.

"I can't quite see the king in person going out," I said. "We might try making a little Joan of Arc out of Princess Margaret Rose, I suppose."

I was joking then, but I did see what he meant. I'd guessed already the name he was going to mention, but I think it was the first time any of us had spoken it out loud. It was early days, after all.

"Mountbatten," said Brundall quietly, by the door. "He's the only man. He has the charisma of royalty. It'll put a bit of life in our chaps if they try him out. And the fear of death in the Japs. They'll respect his blood."

It was a prescient notion, but then Brundall was a bright young sprig, in his way, as I've suggested.

"He's young, too," I said. "He may get his chance."

Later he did, as we all know, but it was still in the far realm of guesswork that morning in January when they gave us Wavell. In two weeks the Japanese were a hundred miles from Singapore. They'd made a series of landings behind our lines, on the west coast, and our army was withdrawing fast.

On 28 January the Japanese were sixty miles from Singapore. On the thirty-first the battle of Malaya was over. The causeway to the island of Singapore was blown up, and the huge, dispirited forces of Percival's army began to dig in for their last stand.

It was brief. On 8 January the Japanese landed in the north of the island. Apart from a handful of obsolete Wildebeests the only aircraft in the skies were their bombers. The oil tanks at Kranj were exploding within hours. The reservoirs to the north of Singapore town were captured in days.

Propaganda was skillfully used. A single Japanese light aircraft dropped a series of eighteen-inch bamboo tubes over the center of Singapore. When opened each was found to contain a message to the British High Command, written both in Japanese and English. It praised the fighting spirit of the British army. It subtly threatened a direct attack on the city itself. It outlined the procedures for a surrender.

A large Japanese flag was raised, by prearrangement, on the roof of Singapore's tallest building, the Cathay. It was the signal that General Percival was coming into the enemy lines to negotiate terms.

It was 8:30 P.M., according to Percival's own account in his book *The War in Malaya*, when hostilities finally ceased. It may be so. According to Jimmy Fong the Chinese resistance had already begun its war of sabotage. According to my own records Major Strand was already preparing to emerge from hiding. Hostilities, alas, had not ceased. Not by a long chalk.

12

It had been a long war, I suppose, for the eighty-five thousand defeated troops who laid down their arms in the streets of Singapore and waited for what was going to happen to them. It always seems a long war to those who lose.

One and all, Highlanders and Indians and Australians, they'd fought their way over four hundred alien miles of tropical jungle to those burning stones at the end of the line. They were exhausted and frightened and some of them, to their credit, vaguely angry.

For most of them, as they thought back, the war divided into weeks. The first hopeful weeks at the bridgeheads, believing each tactical withdrawal was what their officers claimed, a chance to regroup before a counterattack. Then the longer, disillusioned weeks of the gradual retreat through the length of Malaya, weeks broken by an occasional desperate stand, a brief flutter of disorganized heroism. And finally the last despairing week of withdrawal to the island, knowing the bridges were being burned, and the only outcome was going to be death or surrender.

For the British troops the war was fought in weeks, but for Strand, in his hideaway with Su Lin, it was fought in days. It was a strange, lyrical time. Each night, before he set the alarm clock, he made a note in his diary of the events of the day, together with a synopsis of the censored news as he'd picked it up from Singapore Radio.

He didn't believe what he heard, but he wrote it down. It makes grim, silly reading in 1979. They can surely hardly have expected their listeners to believe the exaggerations as Strand records them. Perhaps morale was sustained, but I doubt it.

Strand's own morale had a more direct source of support. The night after his arrival he'd moved to Su Lin's tiny apartment in Waveney Place, and he spent his time there reading and meditating while Su Lin went out to shop or work.

It was an old house she lived in, and the square had been named by someone from Norfolk long ago, she told Strand. It was a magic word for her, Norfolk. It seemed to sum up all she believed that England could offer her.

"Fields," she said once, when he asked her what that was. "Cows, boats, horses. Men farming. Thatch houses, are they? Dogs."

From somewhere, Strand never found out how, she'd got a reproduction of an early nineteenth-century hunting print, with a group of men in tight trousers shooting pheasants. All the other things she mentioned were shown in the background.

"Thatch houses," he said, leading her on. "What are those?"

She was standing with only a towel around her waist. She'd been washing, as she always did, in a small tin bath on the floor. Her neat upturned breasts were glittering with soap.

"Made of twigs," she said seriously. "Surely you know what roofs are made of in England. Look."

She went to a drawer and took out a battered magazine, an old copy of *Country Life*. Fingering through, she knelt beside him on the edge of the bed and pointed to an illustrated article on the decline of the craft of thatching.

Strand reached up and put his arm around her wet shoulders. He was amused, he writes, and amazed too. She could read some English, but not quite enough to get the main point. She didn't realize that thatching was dying out.

"England has changed a lot," he told her. "Parts of it, the big cities at any rate, are not so very different from Singapore."

112

Su Lin had risen and started to dry herself. She did it with care, Strand says, and a kind of love. She knew that her body, scarred and eccentric as it was, was the one means she had of buying the time in England she craved.

"England is beautiful," she said simply. "I have seen many photographs of it. There are flowers everywhere."

"It's true," Strand had agreed, and then, anxious to be clear. "But the war changes places. It will change Singapore."

Su Lin had turned away. She was modest, in the way they say good whores can often be. She was drying between her legs, and it mattered that Strand, her constant companion, should accept her modesty. Even as a kind of coyness. Even, if only that, as a stimulus to his lust.

She replied, speaking with her head down, her voice muffled by the long hair falling across her mouth.

"The war won't change England," she said. "Your song says so. There will always be an England."

"Yes," Strand agreed. "There will always be an England."

I wonder if he believed it, then. Certainly, he saw his own mission as under a terrible threat. In his arms he held her, and knew the threat, feeling her Chinese warmth against his own half-Chinese skin.

"Make some tea," he suggested.

He watched her capable hands as she lit the gas ring, arranged porcelain on a lacquer tray, shook tea from a tin, poured water. She was the kind of woman, he writes, that in other circumstances he might have wanted to marry.

That was going a long way, for Strand. He did go a long way, in his diary, those winter days. While Su Lin was out at the vegetable market or serving time in her room at the House of Happiness, he had ample leisure to write, and he used it well. For seventy days what he did and what he thought is documented with detail, and in depth.

I admire it even now, going through those ink-stained pages. It isn't easy to write your experiences down and be true to how it was. For men of action and intrigue, as Strand and I were, it takes an effort and it needs faith.

Strand had his faith, and it kept him going. It may have

been no more than a mixture of hatred and self-pride, a kind of amalgam of desperate negatives and indulgences. I've sometimes thought that, in my sour moments, but it served its purpose, whatever it was.

It can't have been easy when Su Lin was away. He was cooped up for seventy days in a room only twelve by nine, with a single window he had to remember to stay clear of. It was cluttered, too. He had no space to exercise, except on the floor beside the bed. He had no space either for a *tokonoma* to practice his Japaneseness, or for a nostalgic corner to remind him of England.

There was only that solitary, surreal image of the hunters in Norfolk, and the worn-out red and gold oversumptuousness of a typical Chinese interior. A mass of fraying cushions and flaking gilt dragons. Bad, overdecorated lacquer and cheap ornaments.

"There used to be a saying," Strand wrote. "Hell is where the policemen are German, the cooking English and the interior decorators Chinese." He often remembered that in Su Lin's apartment.

He would lie back in his underpants on the bed, letting his hands lace and press on the back of his neck until he felt the slight floating disorientation he could always induce, he says, at the dentist's. Then he would let his eyes blur and dissolve against some arbitrary point on the broken surface of the wall.

That way he could forget where he was. That way he could forget who he was, and what he was doing. That way he could remember who he really was, and where he was going.

Then Su Lin would return, coming through the door and shaking the bead curtain with a slight wave of whatever scent she was wearing that day. Arms full of packages, if she'd been shopping. Tumbling rice and celery as she rolled down into his arms.

She would kiss him, and talk, if it was the daytime. Or if she'd come back from her night's work at the House of Happiness she'd throw her black shawl aside, hitch up her skirt and kneel at once into the tin bath she always kept filled in the cor-

114

ner, presenting her supple back to him as she cleaned what needed attention.

He would watch her then, and wait, feeling the eagerness as a growing pressure under the sheet. Hating himself a little for feeling this extra desire for her at the thought of those other men. Puzzled a little, too, at the weakness of need he felt, the simple anxiety to be holding her, and knowing she was back, and his, and no one else's.

"I love you, Michael," she said, always. And he knew it was true. She could lease her body to whoever paid for it, exactly as before, with a kind of professional abandon. She could do it well, and without exciting any suspicion that something had changed, he was sure of that. And yet something had changed. She was his.

"Let's go to England after the war," she would say, as they lay smoking opium and watching the ceiling through a blue haze.

"Let's go to Norfolk," he'd agree, and hug her.

But he knew they never would.

Su Lin would never go to Norfolk, and Warren Baltimore, five thousand miles away across the oceans, would never go to Arizona. That was his ambition, he told Brundall, to buy a plot of land and build a Frank Lloyd Wright mansion there in the desert. His heart attack put a stop to that, in 1946.

It seems an abrupt transition, perhaps. It isn't, really. The Japanese raid on Pearl Harbor took place only a few hours before the invasion of Malaya, and in one deadly swoop bound the Americans to us with hoops of steel. They lost five battleships and had three more damaged in the space of half an hour. Two hundred airplanes, more or less, were destroyed, and they had more than three thousand casualties. It was a bitter defeat.

It was also, from the Japanese point of view, a mixed blessing. They'd struck a telling blow, but they hadn't achieved the crippling effect they must have hoped for. No American aircraft carriers were sunk, for the simple reason that they were all out on an exercise when the raid took place. And, as it turned out, aircraft carriers were going to be the crucial sea weapon of the war.

This wasn't all. The Americans were shocked, and wounded, but they were also galvanized into a brutal desire for vengeance. They felt that they'd been cheated, and they reacted like spoiled but energetic children. They cried for justice, and they worked to get it.

Of course, the surprise was in many ways their own fault. They knew perfectly well that the Japanese were desperate for oil. They knew, too, or they ought to have known if they'd read their history books, that the Japanese were traditionally un-Western in their attitude to declarations of war. They hadn't declared war either on China in 1894 or on Russia in 1904. Why should they make an exception for the Americans?

In fact they did, or so one may argue. Their declaration was delivered to the American Embassy in Tokyo some hours before the attack, but it wasn't translated in time. I have a suspicion that they guessed it wouldn't be.

It may have lain unread in someone's files for a month or two. It must have acquired a little dust. It was Pearl Harbor, and Wild Bill Donovan's drive to fork the OSS into life, that really brought American Intelligence into existence. Up until 1941, as Mussolini once remarked, it was so well disguised that nobody had ever found any signs of it.

Roosevelt changed all that. He made the money flow, and he brought in a first-class lawyer who also happened to be a hero of the Great War. In no time at all there were classified files on everything under the sun, from Peruvian guano to short-horned cattle in Turkestan. And there were men like Jake Lawson to administer them.

Colonel Lawson was typical. He came from Houston, and he wore a white ten-gallon hat at all times, indoors and out. He had the kind of slow drawl that suggests a python in a dried-up watercourse. Before the war he'd been in oil, and he was still in oil the last time I heard of him in 1974. He was founding an art gallery in Dallas, no doubt to make a tax saving.

I hated Lawson's guts, but he wasn't a fool. I see him there with his feet in his fire-sewn cowboy boots, trying to look like a cattle baron, and reading the Baltimore report. I see him pressing a bell for some vast young aide, all ears and blue eyes.

"Walter Brown," he says, very quiet. "I just hope and pray you aren't the one who kept this from me all these months."

Maybe the aide swallows, watching the hickories through the plate glass. Maybe he just sits very still, keeping a low profile, as we learned to say later.

"Now, Walter," says Lawson. "I like you very much, boy. I really do. But I need to know who held this information back. Real fast. So start talking."

The aide has ideas. He keeps those big ears open. He recommends a name or two for the chop. The axes fall, the heads roll. Days pass, and the colonel rocks in his armchair, chewing the same gum, drawing the same caricature of himself.

"You all listen to this," he says to his staff. "This war with the Japs ain't gonna be won over the weekend. We're gonna need what extra handholds we can get."

He taps the Baltimore file.

"I don't have much time for the Brits," he says. "But they got the Japs by the balls on this one. And we're going to take a squeeze of our own. So how do we get it?"

He leans over the desk, snapping with his fingers.

"Ideas, boys."

I don't know who it was. Not one of the Texas lobby, for sure. There must have been some suppressed, seconded young West Pointer with a New England ingenuity.

"Sir," I hear him say. "This smells to me like private enterprise. A low-echelon venture without high-level support. Supposing we have the man in the wheelchair speak to the fat boy."

They had that kind of arrogance. For Jake Lawson and his cowboys, Roosevelt and Churchill were only counters to be maneuvered on a board. They liked to see themselves as the real power, the belted eminences behind the paper thrones.

"A touch of praise in high places," the clever one continues. "I do believe it may do the job."

It did, and it probably made our young friend a captain.

They moved up fast at the OSS in those first heady days. From our own point of view, as I've said before, it was inevitable, no doubt. At some stage or another, the war being as it was, we'd have had to take the Yanks into our confidence.

It led to the worst of our difficulties, and the most intense of my frustrations. But at best the liaison could only have been postponed. I have to forgive Brundall. And Warren Baltimore, God rot him, has long had his deserts.

In the short run there were certainly some advantages. In particular, the American connection both accelerated and dramatized my own return to favor with the Director of Far Eastern Intelligence, and thus provided the money, the staff and the time to establish our base effectively in Ceylon.

It would have happened anyway, but without the panache. I liked that, I must confess. The time in Clapham had been well spent, but the unfairness had been very hard to bear. I was more than glad to see some recompense made.

It came one icy morning in February 1942. The Japanese had won their victories on Guam and on Wake Island, and MacArthur had withdrawn to make his final stand in Bataan. It was a bad time for the Americans, and they needed something to cheer them up.

So for that matter did we. We were in full retreat in Burma, and the best they'd done was to replace one desert general with another. The troops had been given an Alexander for a Wavell. It was as if the High Command believed the whole world was a wilderness of sand. The idea of jungle was beyond their ken.

In these circumstances our magnolia tree was indeed the one fruit of an oasis in the desert. It was a lonely blossom, and I was its begetter. I deserved the telephone call I got one morning from that remote fortress, as it now seemed, in Whitehall.

"Thank you," I said, and replaced the receiver. "I'll be there at two o'clock."

I'd been summoned for an urgent conference with the Director of Far Eastern Intelligence.

13

To be honest, I was worried. I had no idea of what had been going on behind the scenes in America, and there was no reason to suppose the Director had any good news for me. I was still playing my cards close to my chest, and it seemed improbable that the Director had heard any whisper of our real activities. But we couldn't be sure.

Admittedly, the landings in Malaya had fulfilled all my prophecies, but those who predict ill news are rarely regarded well for their foresight. I hadn't been recalled from Clapham, and indeed had had little contact at all with the Director's office since our exile.

There were routine exchanges of memoranda, of course, and one or two departmental meetings. But we hadn't spoken in person, and I'd watched his fake-squared back from a vengeful distance. I didn't like his occasional braying laugh when I saw him chatting to more favored colleagues, and I'd kept well away.

So I took my time on my walk to Whitehall, and I thought out my position. It was a fairly clear one. Supposing the Director was going to announce further economies, which I judged possible, I was ready to make a stand against them. I didn't, in fact, think the moment was quite ripe to bring up the subject of Operation Chameleon. It would be better to draw it out into the open when I had some positive Intelligence to offer,

119

and that could only be when Strand was finally entrenched in the Kempei Tai.

On the other hand, supposing the Director had gleaned some hint of what was going on, it might well be necessary to have a kind of showdown. I was prepared for that, and had some views on how I might make my defense.

I reviewed the situation as I strode across Battersea Bridge. I made a neat military figure in those days, with my boots gleaming and the brass locks of my attaché case catching the sun. I took a salute or two as I walked, and it helped my confidence. I was still a colonel in the British Army, whatever happened.

Short of a court-martial, that is. I thought about that as I glanced over the Moorish parapet at a barge of wood plying down toward the Port of London. It was hardly likely. What had I done, after all? I'd used official time and money in the pursuit of an unofficial operation.

Yes, but it was surely one in the best interests of my country. "I'll be the judge of that, Colonel," I could hear the Director saying. "You're not to play God, you know."

Looking back, I'm amazed, in some ways, at my paranoia. I automatically assumed that my summons was a prelude to trouble. And yet there was no possibility that the Director could have found out what was going on. And that was what mattered most of all.

As it turned out, of course, the interview ran completely contrary to my expectations. I crossed Parliament Square as a light drizzle started to fall. It gave a slight Wagnerian air to the old Foreign Office building. I went up the marble stairs with a Death of Siegfried feeling. This was going to be the end.

The Director's secretary was smiling. That didn't alter my mood. They always did. She showed me in, without waiting, through the enormous double doors, a little khaki-clad foot-woman with bobbed hair and a high voice.

I took in the room with a jaundiced sense of familiarity. The coal fire was blazing, and the Director was there again with his back to it, warming his buttocks. The desk, as usual, was bare except for a solitary puce file.

But there was one difference. The magnificent leather-topped drum table in the window was loaded with the remains of a very peacetime-looking meal. There seemed to be caviar. There was a massacred but still substantial turkey. Plates of roast potatoes. Remains of an apple pie.

"Sir," I said.

An insane desire was going through my head to add something. Alternatives occurred. "Late Christmas, I see" was one. "P.M.'s just left, has he?" was another. But I stuck with my monosyllable.

It wouldn't have mattered. I still didn't know it, but this was my day. I could have done no wrong. The Director was already coming forward, away from the fire, an amazing concession. His hand was out, and he was drawing me toward the wreck of his feast.

"This calls for champagne," he said.

I hadn't noticed the pier table against the wall. It was groaning under the stuff. Most of the bottles, admittedly, were empty, but the Director was reaching in for a full one. Fairly full, anyway, although the cork had been drawn some time ago.

"Sorry I couldn't have you in for luncheon," the Director was continuing as he poured a couple of glasses.

I took one, bemused still. It was fizzing, anyway. A fair Krug, to my palate, even if it wasn't entirely fresh. I took another sip and started to listen.

"Busy times, you know," the Director suggested. "Spend all my days at conferences of one kind or another. Can't even find an hour to eat a meal by myself."

He waved his free hand at the food.

"This was just a little working picnic for some of Beaverbrook's people. Conversation about the supply of Blenheims for Java, you know. Tedious business, but we have to keep the Dutch happy."

He seemed to realize suddenly that we were still both on our feet, as if at a cocktail party, enjoying the view of the gardens. It clearly wouldn't do. It was too civilian. He gestured at an armchair beside his desk.

"Alastair," he said, as he sat down facing me.

I'd been half expecting this. Nobody ever uses my Christian name, or did then, but I'd always believed the Director was capable of it. He was running true to form.

"Your initiative," he was saying now, spreading his hands on the desk, and I could feel the Churchillian surge starting—we all did it in those days, of course, even down to the ers—"has, er, given us," he was continuing, with a long pause, "one of the great Intelligence coups of the war so far."

I leaned back in my chair. So it was out, after all. I listened with half an ear to the rest of the prepared speech. It had all the expected sonorities, and figures. Behind it—and this was what interested me—there must lie some complex process of leakage and assessment.

I tried to work out what it was as I basked in the Director's change of heart. A question or two here and there, while he rested for inspiration, elicited some background information. The Prime Minister himself had expressed his congratulations. There must, of course, be full cooperation from now on with our American allies. Needless to say, facilities for a proper servicing of our agent would be made instantly available.

I began to get the picture. Somehow the OSS had got wind of the operation and were using high-level praise of our initiative as a means of getting in on the act. It was clever.

It was also, I realized, as I sat there, something that had an immediate cash value. I couldn't resist turning the screws a little.

"May I have another glass of this excellent Krug, sir," I said.

It got him out of his chair and across to the table. I guessed there wasn't another unopened bottle, but he wasn't ready to say no to me. I watched him frown as he wrapped a napkin around the neck of the new bottle and pulled the cork.

"That's why they never used to insure waiters for blindness," he said as the cork flew with a sharp pluck and hit the paneling.

Point to you, I thought, as he handed me a full glass. He wasn't going to be thrown from his stride so easily. I sipped with enjoyment. Then I put the boot in harder.

"Sir," I said, "we shall need extensive American funding. Your original requisition for the operation was only sufficient, as you'll remember, to launch the initial planting."

That got him. He swallowed hard, and I saw his color rising. He knew damned well he'd requisitioned nothing, and never would have done. But I had him in a cleft stick. Either he agreed, even tacitly, with what I was implying, and took the responsibility for Chameleon in retrospect, or he denied his involvement and lost the credit he'd already been given by the P.M.

I knew that he'd dearly like to have had his cake and eaten it. He would have loved to keep the praise and manage to reprimand me into the bargain. But I wasn't having any. I felt the tide running, and I wanted blood.

"So may I take it, sir," I continued, and paused, "that American money will be forthcoming in adequate quantities to establish our base of operations in Ceylon, as you and I originally planned?"

There was what you might call a pregnant silence for a while. I drained my glass and set it down on the floor. Then I spoke, very quietly and without looking up.

"I'd like to express my congratulations to you and your staff here in this building, sir," I said. "Without your full cooperation, as well as your original concept, the Department would have been unable to achieve what has so far been done. Knowing your modesty in these matters, sir, I can hardly anticipate your making an official minute of this. But I feel it proper to see that something is privately filed and circulated on my own authority."

I looked up then and caught his eye. He was angry, but he knew he was beaten. Perhaps, to be fair to the bastard, he felt that I deserved my revenge. He breathed in, and nodded.

"Thank you, Colonel," he said. "That won't be necessary."

It wasn't the end of the interview but it was the end of the messing about. After ten more minutes discussing details I knew that everything was going to be all right. I walked out through the double doors with whatever I wanted. Staff. Money. Offices. Time. I had everything.

So had Strand, I suppose, in his own way, in those rich days with Su Lin. They couldn't last, of course, and he knew that. They both did, and it added a spice to their strange love.

The end was delicate. All through early February they'd known from the radio, hour by hour, something of how bad the situation was. Not even the most outrageous British propaganda, Strand says, could disguise the true facts. But it was when the water stopped flowing from the taps that he knew the end had come.

It was on the night of 14 February, when Su Lin called from the little stone sink outside on the landing they shared with four other apartments.

"No water, Michael," she said.

He went through the door, alert for a footstep on the stair, his hands loose at his sides. The other rooms, he knew, were occupied by girls out at work in the brothels, but they often came home with men, and he'd learned to listen with care. Noises, and voices, in Su Lin's room would excite no comment. A face was different. It might be remembered.

Su Lin had her hand on the brass faucet. It was open, full. Strand ran his finger around the mouth of the pipe. His mind moved fast. He knew what it was.

"Leave it a moment," he said, resting his arm on Su Lin's shoulder. "It may come back."

The water did come back, but not that day, and not under British rule. There was another flag, with a rising sun across it, over Government House, when the water flowed again. And that was five days later.

Beside the bed Strand was kneeling at the radio. He found the station and tuned the static out. There was continuous music now, fairly martial, and breaks for news bulletins. He waited for one.

When it came it was no surprise. There was heavy fighting on the outskirts of the city. Nine Japanese fighters had been shot down. Our units were holding firm. There was no mention of the reservoirs.

Strand sat with his hands clasped in his lap. He knew that

the news of the Japanese cutting the city's water supply would remain unmentioned. It wouldn't be long, though, before everyone realized what had happened. It would mean surrender.

No British general was going to hold out while people died of thirst. There might have been a final counterattack, and the numbers of troops available would surely have given it a chance. I know that now, and I thought so then. But Strand was disillusioned. He had no more faith in the British High Command.

Singapore was perched on the brink of a Japanese victory. The moment had come to be aware of this. In a few hours, Strand felt certain, his mission was going to begin. The days of passion were over.

"Su Lin," he said, smiling. "Am I like Ogawa?"

In the distance there was the sound of shellfire.

He waited for her to reply, thinking of the swamp outside the city and the neat, friendly man who had passed him sword guards to admire. He waited, but Su Lin was slow to speak. She was kneeling back on her heels, looking up at him. She didn't smile at his smile.

"In bed, no," she said. "You know that. In appearance, in ways, yes. Very like."

He knew she was lying. To her he was a completely unique person, as unlike Ogawa as the sun is unlike the moon. He gave some light to Ogawa in retrospect, that was all.

Surprisingly, perhaps, there had been little talk between them about Strand's mission. According to Strand's diary, this was partly the natural reticence of agents in the field. They fixed their attention on the job at hand, at the time concerned. For Su Lin the job was to keep a man in hiding, not to speculate about his past or future.

But it was more than that. In whatever else they discussed, they were one. There were no barriers. They talked as partners, sharing the earth. In this one area they both recognized the eventual withering of the idyll, the worm eating the heart out of their world.

It had to be so. They knew that. It was hard, and it hurt. Even an old man, as I am, can sense a little of how it was.

"I have to be more than like him," Strand said, leaning forward and stroking Su Lin's hair. "I have to be what he was, and what he would still have been. I have to be Japanese. I have to be victorious, exultant, superior."

Su Lin laughed. It was unexpected, and it broke the mood. She rolled away and sat up, still laughing.

"You find that easy," she said. "In bed, anyway."

Strand rose and lifted her into the air, swinging her skirt open, a Western tweed with lisle stockings underneath. Lechery makes his diary best on that kind of detail. He branched her legs, he says, forking her body above his hips. An airplane came over, very low, and there was the sound of machine guns.

"Little squirrel," he said.

He sat down, holding her in his lap, and the words flowed. It became easy, feeling the warmth of her flesh, to discuss their separation. It became a notion in the abstract realm of ideas. It lost its weight, its painfulness.

They listened to the news together, and Strand explained what he planned to do. He would dress himself in his neat Ogawa clothes and take his film and his cameras. He would set out through the streets in a search for a Japanese patrol. He would give himself up and be taken for questioning.

"Very soon, I think," he added. "When the Japanese and not the British are giving the news, the time will have come to go out."

Su Lin was cooking now. She gave him a spoonful of soup to taste, and he swallowed egg and chicken. She watched his mouth moving, serious, detached. It was as if she was trying to remember whatever he did, store it away, pin it down as it was.

Strand ate their last meal, he writes, with a sense of being in a film. They seemed to be almost more themselves than usual, as if they were both acting their proper roles, without distractions, without additions. They were finalizing everything they'd been.

Awkwardly, Strand spoke once.

"It isn't forever," he said.

Over by the docks there was the crump of bombs falling. They sounded remote, unreal.

126

He realized then, Strand writes, that Su Lin believed he would die at the hands of the Kempei Tai. She had no faith in his mission succeeding. For her, he was a brave soldier going to his death without illusions and without hope. She was already building his memory.

It gave him a touch of fear, perhaps. Even Strand, with all his arrogance, can hardly have been immune to doubts that night. He mentions none, of course, but that was his way.

"I'll see you quite soon," he said. "Whenever I need to use the radio."

It was breaking security, but what could he do? He knew, and she knew he knew, that the future plan was to use the House of Happiness as their place of liaison. Su Lin was going to be the continuing link with Ceylon, run, as she would be, by Jimmy Fong.

But this wasn't her business now, nor Strand's. There might have had to be changes, for a dozen reasons. Another girl might have come to do the job. It was the House of Happiness, the golden alibi of the brothel, the lure for Japanese and British alike, that was the vital element. Not the individual whore.

That made no difference, or very little. But he wanted to reassure her, Strand writes, and perhaps he wanted to take some reassurance as well. It gives him a touch of humanity, that need for a lifeline. I admire it in him.

"Of course, Michael," Su Lin said. "Of course I'll see you soon." And she served his meal.

Before he left in the morning they lay naked on the low mattress watching the light filtered in through the slats of the blind. Su Lin was flat on his belly, her breasts heaving a little as she breathed.

"Michael," she said, making it a question.

He didn't answer, cautious, already half alone.

"Let's go to Swaffham first," she went on, her voice muffled against his neck. "Where the thatch houses are. With English muffins for tea. Then"—and her voice was breaking—"then we'll get married."

Then she was crying, and then she was on her back, and Strand was up and washing. Then he was packing his film and cameras, and then he was dressing. And then he was kissing her cheek, and then he was gone.

Outside there was silence. No shelling, no gunfire. Singapore was in the hands of the Japanese.

14

This morning I drove Mary to Ludlow to do some shopping. There's a baker here who still does crumpets the way my mother made them, and we were buying half a dozen for tea. I was crossing the street to my car when I saw the Japanese, a flood of tourists back like spring birds.

There was a charabanc, parked over a double yellow line. They were out with their cameras, thirty or so, snapping a bed of uneasy daffodils in front of the Town Hall. One saw me watching and came over to ask a question.

It was the usual thing, his English was unintelligible. I tried my Japanese, the first time in years, and he nearly dropped his Minolta onto my toes. He wanted to know if the flowers were crocuses, and I told him no.

He was very neat, with a green English Burberry and a trilby hat. You can never tell their age, not easily, but I guessed he must have been old enough to have served in the war; old enough to have been a double for Strand.

I stood in the square, safe in England, and it all seemed to grow up again in my mind. The war was over, many years, and the conquerors were here in Ludlow, like the Germans in Paris, taking pictures and admiring flowers. They'd won. Oh, yes, they'd won, just as surely as if their guns had come rolling up Whitehall to Trafalgar Square.

I wonder, though. Reversals of fortune are hard to bear. A

man of prudence is always ready, they say, for whatever changes in circumstances the years may bring. I never was, myself. The shocks came out of clear skies, whenever they came, and they used to hurt. They still do, even with age.

At the beginning of March 1942 we were all ready to leave for Ceylon. I'd been offered fresh accommodation in the Foreign Office building, to service the Far Eastern base at home, but I'd decided to keep a presence in Clapham. I'd acquired a sort of affection for our old concrete mansion, and it had the advantage of being more independent of the rest of the Department.

To begin with, Brundall was to remain in England, with Walpole to support him. Within weeks, however, there were going to be seven additional clerks and secretaries, even a porter again. All this would act as broad support for the narrow spearhead represented by Clark and myself, with Molly Jenkins and Billington, on the outskirts of Kandy.

The war, as usual, was going badly. Apart from Timoshenko's gains around Kharkov and the torpedoing of the *Prinz Eugen*, there hadn't been much to give grounds for hope. By 9 March the Japanese had landed in New Guinea and the Dutch had surrendered in Java. Rangoon was being evacuated.

Against this background our own exhilaration had a weird, unfair quality. What right had Department M to be so successful in waging war when the rest of the allied forces were in the doldrums? I remember how Clark put it in one of those labored memoranda of his.

"It was certainly a spirit of irony that was to control our destinies for the near future. Whatever went well for us was really the source of our downfall. We labored in ignorance, and our labors destroyed us while they prospered."

It was seeing that little Japanese this morning in his trilby hat that made me realize I'd have to explain how this came to be.

I remember discussing the whole affair with Clark one day in 1947. We'd met for a drink in The Salisbury, the sort of compulsive reminiscing kind of drink so many old soldiers used to have in those dry demob years.

We were in the back room, framed by the red plush and mirrors. Couples were holding hands, actors posing. I lit my pipe. We talked of this and that for a time, and then it came.

"He had us by the short hairs," Clark said, suddenly bitter, clenching his glass at the end of a story, all tit-and-bum stuff: I don't remember the details.

His mind had moved. Like so many conscript veterans, he'd been drawn back into his war.

"Right from the start," he was saying, flushed with gin, "we were sitting ducks for the whole business."

It wasn't the first time we'd discussed the operation, but it was the first time I'd sensed the full depth of Clark's bitterness. He felt betrayed, exploited. More than Brundall, more, almost, than I did, he felt a kind of fool, deeply deceived, deeply guilty. I got him another drink while I thought what to say.

I'd been around this particular track every day since the war ended. There were a hundred ways of explaining what happened, a dozen excuses. I carried the glasses back and sat down.

"You're blaming yourself too much," I said.

Clark gulped his gin.

"I wonder," he said. "I had him for almost eight weeks in Elms Road, remember. I sweated blood to make him what he was, a perfect Japanese. Jesus."

I said nothing.

"Colonel," said Clark, only half joking, "he was half Chinese, half British, remember. The blood was ours. I had a chance," he insisted, squeezing my knee. "I might have turned him. I really think I might."

Across the room I watched a wide boy, a spiv, as we called them then, doing a deal. He was using his hands like an Italian, spreading imaginary nylons. I was sure that Clark was wrong. The bitter truth was there on the table between us, and nothing could move it away. All along Major Michael Strand had been an agent of the Kempei Tai, placed in England to infiltrate the British Army's Intelligence Department.

I stood up, lifting my raincoat from the seat. I felt very sure

131

of what I was saying, and I wanted Clark to believe it. I spoke with emphasis.

"You had no chance," I said.

I went back to the office, I remember, and tried to write some copy for a new detergent. It was hard to concentrate. The war leaked in through my closed door and ran like blood across the floor.

I remember Brundall, once, as we waited for a bus in Cavendish Road—it must have been right at the end of February 1942—saying, "It's quite fantastic, sir. I can't imagine it. Walking out. Knowing that you're a fake. In the midst of the enemy."

He paused.

"I doubt if I could have done it," he said simply.

That was just before I flew out to Kandy. It was long before there was any suspicion. There was mist in Clapham, sounds of heels on the pavement. It seemed a long way from the dangerous markets and brothels of Singapore.

Brundall lowered his voice as the bus drew up.

"I admire his guts," he said. "It seems so cozy here by comparison."

In the autumn of 1945 I met Yoshida. He was a prisoner of war in Yokohama, and I had a chance to interrogate him. We sat there in a little plain room, with a crew-cut young American typing notes, and he told me what had happened.

He was still doing the SS act, fanatical, elegant, and he cut his throat with a penknife a few days later. But he gave me enough to reconstruct that first meeting he had with Strand in Singapore when he flew down from Tokyo.

It must have been early in March 1942, before the Japanese cut the Burma Road. They met in a long, open, sunny room, overlooking the harbor in the distance. It had once been the British Governor's study.

I can see Yoshida there at the heavy mahogany table, a case closed in front of him. I can see Strand as he must have been, coming through the double doors.

They face each other in uniform, two Japanese Intelligence

officers. The British major, now a captain in the Kempei Tai. The full colonel from Tokyo, who recruited him.

Outside the window there is the sound of a hedge cutter. Yoshida rises and turns on a radio. Music mixes with the sounds from the garden, a Western orchestra.

"Richard Strauss," Yoshida murmurs, heels clicking, Prussian to a fault.

He comes forward, stares closely, perhaps with a slight smile.

"The resemblance is truly remarkable," he says. "Not in the features; but in the expression."

Then the mask relaxes, and he bows, grateful.

"Michael," he says, "it's so good to see you."

They were at school together: it went as far back as that. I gathered from Yoshida that they'd even gone on holiday together, walking in Hokkaido. Talking about the state of the world over their campfires, as though in the Dolomites. Like any other pair of young intellectuals the world over in the early 1930s.

They were men of the right, even then. Yoshida admired the diplomacy of Bismarck, the iron of Mussolini. Strand still felt some pride in the British Empire, the fields on which the sun never set. It was the new Japan, though, that held his keenest admiration. He came to believe that the laws of *bushido* were the most honorable code ever devised for a man or a nation to live by. He swore to work for a country in which these laws had free play.

It was four years later that Yoshida recruited Strand into the Kempei Tai. There might be a war. They needed a man in England. The old lion was dying, corrupt. It had no teeth, no power. It was up to Strand. He might be the one man to resolve the crisis, to save his country.

Strand agreed. The mechanics were complicated, but not impossible. Strand's mother and father were on the verge of a divorce. Their separation allowed the fiction of her murder to gain some easy color. She returned to China and disappeared. Strand and his father came to England.

I went through the dossier many times. There was never a

point where we could have put our finger on a falsity, a clue. What was there was true. What wasn't there could never be checked. From the time Strand landed at Croydon he was firmly in place.

After four years it must have been satisfying, and moving, to meet Yoshida again. Even Strand, with all his weird coldness, could hardly have been unaffected.

But it isn't that which his diary mentions, and dwells on. It's what he felt about the sword. I took it out this morning, before I started to write. It needed cleaning, and I took some Duraglit to the *soritsuno*, the returning-horn. The *menuki*, the black studs with their golden paulownia flowers, are a little loose. But the blade—the double wave soaring from the dulled brass of the *habaki*: it brought the tears to my eyes.

I know what he felt when Yoshida opened that case there on the table, and gave him the brocade bag, with the hilt protruding. It was an honor beyond a medal, to receive a *tanto* from Hirohito himself. It was something the imperial fingers, the divine flesh, had touched and held.

He fell to his knees, bowing over the rounded *kashira*. "Thank you," he said.

The mood lightened after that, and they talked of other things. Yoshida, playful with his German brusqueness. Strand allowing himself a touch of that English contemptuousness.

"You've been taking photographs, I hear," said Yoshida. "Saito tells me he has an officer with a real eye for a picture."

"Ogawa had," said Strand, fumbling for his wallet. "These are some of mine from the last few weeks. They don't match his."

He showed the pictures, accepting comment, approval. Four or five are still here in the file. They draw a brutal image of the occupation, dog-eared as they are after all these years. One of a huge brute, like a sumo wrestler, swinging a long *katana*, surrounded by a terrified crowd of Chinese. Another of twelve severed heads, laid out in a neat row, like turnips.

"Looters," Strand has written on the back, in Japanese.

"Nobody knows you here," Yoshida said, as he handed the prints back. "They all believe you're Ogawa, the one spy who had the luck and the skill to escape internment. That's why it was easy to see you. I've heard a hundred embroidered stories of how you managed to evade the British police. You're a hero. You've killed at least a dozen men with your bare hands to survive."

Yoshida laughed his dry, barking laugh.

"They'll think the sword is for that," he said. "You've got the perfect alibi."

Then he was serious.

"Michael," he said, "I want to keep you in place. The last few weeks have established your cover beyond breaking. Your acceptance here as Ogawa is bound to convince the British, as it does me, of your power to pass as a Japanese. You're in the socket. One turn of the handle and they believe they can manipulate you."

Yoshida snapped his fingers.

"And we can manipulate their manipulation," he said softly.

The tone poem on the radio had risen to a crescendo of romantic splendor. The hedge cutter was obliterated. Then there was a crash of cymbals, and the music was over.

"Let's walk in the garden," Yoshida said.

He led the way through the French windows and they struck out side by side across the lawn. Well away from the house, they paused by a clump of lilacs, admiring a blossom.

"Tell me about the whore," Yoshida said.

He was worried, he told me in 1945. He hated using women in Intelligence work, as I did. As we all do. But he hated them more than the rest of us. He was as queer as a clockwork orange, I'd say, but he kept it very quiet.

He may have been in love with Strand. It's possible. But he never showed any signs, nothing physical, anyway. He kept his doubts of Su Lin at the military level, strictly as a security risk.

He was right to be worried, even as a lover would be. I've often wondered what Strand told him that day about Su Lin. I see him there, as if from the windows of the house, holding a cone of bloom in his fingers, his lips moving. But the words he speaks are inaudible, blown away by the wind.

Whatever he said, whatever squalid or lewd or romantic picture he drew of his time with her, whatever private doubts or fears or hopes he may have had of her loyalty or her insight, whatever he may have wanted to conceal or adorn or play down, the words were ones that brought reassurance.

Yoshida walked through the beds of roses, whipping at some with his cane. He took Strand by the arm and showed him the views.

"You see, she could have an accident," he suggested.

"It won't be necessary," said Strand.

Yoshida was looking out to sea. Two battle cruisers, flying the Japanese flag, were steaming into harbor.

"The war is going well," he said. "We shall capture Burma, and the Philippines. Even India, maybe."

He turned and led the way back toward the house.

"Our star is in the ascendant," he said slowly. "But a time of reversals may come. The British being as they are, Michael, like the tortoise, will bide their time. They may learn to choose a better general."

They were passing a bed of tulips, brilliant, ordered.

"Someone to strike fear in our breasts," he added. "A royal leader like the kings of old."

He paused, slashing down a long swath of tulips with his cane.

"Then we shall need your help," he said. "More than now."

They were walking up over the shaved lawns to the balustrade. A sprinkler was moving water evenly. It was still all very British.

"There are two ways we could use you," Yoshida said. "In the short run you could grease the wheels a little. Speed our advance here and there. Filter some false information."

He lifted his free hand, breathing on it.

"And be blown in four months, a husk of what you were."

Strand was waiting. He had a great power of stillness, like an Indian. He could wait forever, it sometimes seemed.

"I'm a pessimist, even now," Yoshida said. "I feel the storm on the flowers. I sense the turn of the tide, even in the hour of victory. I want to keep you for that, Michael. It means risks,

136

and a waste of time. The men in Tokyo may not approve. But I mean to have my way."

In the hiss of the sprinkler his words took on a sibilance, a kind of prophetic message.

"For as long as necessary," he said, "I want you to feed the British with sound information, of limited usefulness. I want them to trust you up to the hilt. And that means giving them help."

He sat down cross-legged on the grass, playing with his cane.

"One week from today," he said, "I want you to call on Su Lin again at the House of Happiness. Two weeks from today, on your second visit, I want you to pass our order of battle to her."

Strand was beside him, very quiet.

"It may be a year, two years," Yoshida said. "Your moment will come, Michael. You'll have your chance to be our Horatius, holding the bridge. Our Achilles, even."

"I'll wait," said Strand. Then, with an attempt at jocularity, "I'll try to improve my photography."

Yoshida was on his feet, looking down.

"Goodbye, Michael," he said.

Then he was walking fast toward his car in the drive. That stiff, rather goose-stepping walk he had. It was Strand who gave me that, from his diary. The rest was mostly Yoshida, dry-voiced there in the camp at Yokohama, a few days before he killed himself, remembering. He had a good memory, and a fine style.

I suppose that Strand was thinking the same, as he sat there with his sword on the lawn. He was condemned to an indefinite routine as a minor Intelligence officer in Singapore, taking photographs of his colleagues at parties, passing second-rate, accurate information through Jimmy Fong.

And waiting like a weapon in the scabbard for his day of blood. It was to be a boring, easy time. He had one consolation. Once a week he could leave his normal Japanese life behind and slip naked into the passionate, loving arms of Su Lin. Once a week, and once a week only.

That would be the hard part.

15

Betrayal takes many forms. I remember a cat we had once in Devon when I was a child, a little fluffy Persian thing. It used to come onto my lap when we were eating, and I'd stroke its neck and feed it scraps of bacon rind.

One day when I made my kitten noise it wouldn't come. It swept around the table, tail in the air, and rubbed its flank on my older sister's ankle until she lifted it up and held it against her cheek. I ran to my own room and lay on the bed and cried.

It was hours before I came down. I felt as if the whole stock of love concentrated in the kitten's care had been abused. I was only four years old, but I'd learned one of life's first lessons. You give them what you want, and they take what they need.

I didn't understand. I thought the kitten enjoyed being up on my lap more than anything else in the world. I'd only to make my kitten noise and it would always come. I didn't realize that I was only one among competing attractions.

I felt betrayed. It was the first time, and perhaps the worst. It took me days and much hatred of that vicious kitten before I recovered. In the end I took my revenge with a brutal kick against it in the dairy, and then I felt better. A little. But I still had the wound, and the scar.

There were other betrayals. The native girl in Lahore who took me up to her bedroom and laughed when I showed her the kind of machine I had with my Sam Browne loose. She did what I wanted, flexing her gross belly under the cheap sheets, but she didn't show much interest, or response. I never forgot that laugh of hers. It had all the scorn of the well endowed for the underprivileged. It taught me the limits of ambition, and the hierarchies of desire. I felt betrayed by God, by my own body, by the mean dowry I'd been given.

I was a young officer, only eighteen. When I was twenty-five I was engaged to be married. I met the girl on leave, in the hills. We rode together, ate ice cream, went to tea dances. It was all rather late Kipling, early nineteen thirtyish.

There were kisses below the cherry laurels, fumblings with awkward buttons against the arms of Chesterfields. I got no farther than the rims of her tight bras, thumbs under sweating armpits at the smooth edges. But I felt her pelvis arched up under my tunic, and I knew she wanted me.

I never tried the rest. There was always that funny laugh in the back of my mind. I held my fire. One day when I called with an armful of gladioli there was a new face on the terrace. A pair of squared shoulders and a cheeky grin.

We were introduced. We played billiards. I rather liked the man—he had a boyish charm, a cocky humor. In four months the girl was engaged to him. In seven months they were married, her belly already swelling with his groping child.

I could go on listing betrayals. The women lost, the jobs never given. The endless day-by-day betrayals. The losses of face, the casual insults, the unnoticed forgetfulness. We all have our list, I suppose.

With Michael Strand, our own list at Department M came up to date. It wasn't just the sense of betrayal. We'd put our dreams in him. For Corporal Walpole, who'd opened the door of the lecture room that first morning to a kind of hero, it was just as bad as it was for Clark, who'd trained him to his own specifications for nearly eight weeks.

For Molly, he was the deep secret we had to keep quiet about, a kind of Tyrone Power of the spy world. For Brundall he was what he was working for, the white spearhead of the

British counterattack in the East. Even for Billington, poor Bolshy little Billington, with his pills and his acne, he was the elegant underpinning for a torrent of gripes and grouses.

In London, from the date we recruited him, Strand was the major reason for our existence. He was like a myth, or a flag, even a kind of god. Whenever I needed something difficult, or time-wasting, or simply boring, done, I had only to appeal to the damage it would do to the magnolia tree to overcome all slacking off.

Strand was the physical embodiment of our ideals, whatever these were. For Brundall, they were moralistic, abstract. For Molly, they were glamorous, with a touch of Hollywood and *Woman's Own*. For Walpole, they were decent, and English.

Even though Strand was underground, a hidden thorn in the waist of the Enemy, he was still our weapon, and our support, the one means we had to justify our labor, our time, and, most of all, our silence.

At home or on the streets, talking to relatives or friends, in uniform or out, our lips were icily sealed. Even among ourselves, the jargon tended to be maintained. It was the magnolia tree we spoke about, how well it was blossoming, how exposed its situation was, how many threats there were to its roots or its blooms.

When we moved to Colombo, the background omnipresence of Strand in our thoughts and our talk became a foreground obsession in all our work. We lived for Strand, and one of us, Billington, almost died for him.

There was a fault in the transmitter, and the engineer was away with flu. It was Billington who went up the mast and tinkered with the aerial, rocking in the girders of our miniature Eiffel Tower, nearly sixty feet above the villa in a butting wind.

I saw his face when he came down, white with fear and gross with satisfaction. It was always like that. However nasty or intricate or alarming the task I had to impose, its outcome would reveal, as after a successful seduction, the lineaments of gratified desire.

We were lucky, I suppose. In many departments, over many theaters of war, they were fighting only for the king, for Britannia, for Winston Churchill, maybe. We had someone more real, more enticing. We had our *femme fatale*, and her name was Michael Strand.

As long as it lasted, it worked with power, and subtlety. It was as if we were married, like everyone else, to a good cause, which had its public expression in the newspapers and on the wireless. But, unlike others, we also had our private cause, our wicked reason, for what we did. It was as if we had a mistress.

She was loyal, we thought. We paid her the tribute of our total attention. We waited until she called, which was not often. Whenever she did, we listened with bated breath to whatever she said. We hung on her words. We believed her, and used her advice.

In return, we asked very little. She never came, and we never saw her, not for years on end. When she did come, it was briefly, and toward the end of our long affair. Soon after that, we discovered what she really was, and how she had let us down.

Strand was our woman. Strand was our lord and master. No wonder the sense of betrayal would last a lifetime. No wonder that for some of us, like Major Clark, it would never end.

The move to Colombo was the crux. It was after that we were in the grip of our plot, our own trap. The bait had been laid with care, and we'd eaten it ourselves.

Clark had been the first to fly out to Ceylon, and he'd done the preliminary work of renting accommodation and arranging for the construction of the transmitter and the installation of the equipment. It was a fussy job, and he did it well.

If you've ever had to try to get a spare part for your car at the Leyland depot in Southall, you'll know what it's like doing business with the Indians. I had years of it, in the thirties. It was no accident that I sent our Clark on ahead to do the tedious bit.

I can imagine that rough Yorkshire tongue of his may have had its uses. It can sometimes pay to spell out the requirements with a certain brashness. At any rate, we had a sizable stone bungalow on the edge of the Ridgeway golf links and a ninety-foot metal wireless tower, capable of picking up a signal from as far away as Singapore, by the time Molly and I arrived in mid-March.

It was sweltering then. I knew what to expect, and I had a suitcase of the right sort of clothes from Alkit. I was met at the harbor by a Clark still in London-weight uniform and suffering from Egyptian tummy.

Kaolin, I suggested, and let him off the hook.

He went off to try to buy some Chlorodyne and I waited to hear the details of what he'd hired until he was better. We put up at the Galle Face for a night, watching the palms move in the wind from the sea. The villa could hold for tomorrow.

I forewent the dubious pleasure of introducing Molly to the delights of a good curry and left her to settle down with her knitting in the annex. It was cool on the terrace, and the drinks were British India at its best. Served on a silver tray and laid on a cane table by a boy in a clean turban.

We taught them that, like so many other things. I sipped my Haig, in a cut-glass tumbler, and thought about India. It was a wonderful country, even then. But it wouldn't last, whoever won the war. Ceylon was the first salty tear. It wouldn't be the last.

The following morning I went out to the bungalow. It was a comfortable two-story acquisition, rented from a teak exporter who'd gone up to Kerulia for the summer. There were oleanders and bougainvillea blooming when we came up the drive in our dwindling Sunbeam Talbot.

The morning sun beat down on the long, pillared sweep of the verandah, with its array of worn basket chairs and bamboo occasional tables. It was a shadowy, inviting spot. Above it, the line of arched windows on the second story had louvred shutters drawn. It would be cool inside, too.

I spent many a happy hour over the next few weeks, reading Basho and drinking stingers. I played croquet with Billington and Molly on the shaved lawn, enjoying the nostalgic click of the mallets on the wooden balls. I walked under the mangoes at night, listening to the endless rustles in the undergrowth.

Most of the work simply consisted of waiting. Our days were

filled with reports, idle gossip, and meetings. Now that the Department was in favor again, I could afford to spread myself on the propaganda side. I seized the opportunity.

Money and praise flowed in with equal regularity. Every post brought more appreciative memoranda, more curious inquiries. I read, filed and ignored them. What I wanted I asked for, and usually got. It might be a new houseboy, or a filing cabinet, or a bracket clock for my study.

What I didn't want, I managed to avoid. There was no visit from the Director. No assistance from M15. No surveillance device in the hall.

The one thing I couldn't avoid was an American presence. They put the money in, in large dollops, and they had to have their finger on the button. Or so the Director instructed.

I saw his point. From what I'd heard of Jake Lawson, he was hardly the man to be satisfied with his news through a British filter. He wanted information from the horse's mouth. His own horse.

So one quiet afternoon when I was eating crumpets in a rocking chair on the terrace I found myself looking up at a rangy young American in a stetson.

"John Q. Vonnegut, sir," he said. "The third."

I never did find out what the Q stood for. I assumed for a while that the whole rigmarole was a pseudonym, but there turned out to be an aged parent who wrote weekly letters from Palm Beach. Neither, as it turned out, was related to the science-fiction writer, but we didn't know about him either in those days.

I got Vonnegut and his leather cases into a bedroom, and he soon settled down to the daily routine. I knew he was on his guard, and probably ready to catch us out at the drop of a blueberry muffin, but he wasn't an onerous watchdog.

He'd come from money, somewhere in the Midwest, and he liked his wines and his hunting. By the time the transmitter was finished, and we were getting the first signals from Jimmy Fong, I'd taken quite a fancy to him.

We used to play billiards after dinner in the room at the back of the house under the tigers' heads, and he gave me a good game. Chalking cues, or sipping coffee on the buttoned leather bench, we'd discuss cattle, or the best way to skin carcasses.

That was for the first few days. When the transmitter was ready, we had to switch our time. Every night, from then on, was given up to our main task, the regular attempt to make contact with Strand.

The arrangement had been that we'd send out our call signal every night at exactly nine o'clock, Far Eastern Time. We'd wait for an answer, and then repeat the call at regular intervals over the next hour. It was a cumbersome procedure, but nobody could think of anything better.

It meant that most of the calls, inevitably, would go unanswered, and this was bound to be demoralizing. But it also meant that Strand had a daily hour in which he could be certain of getting in touch with us. In the event of an emergency, or any news of urgent topicality, this would surely be invaluable.

So from early April 1942 I spent every evening after dinner cramped in the attic at the top of the house with Vonnegut, Billington, and Molly. I've never known quite why all wireless communication seems to require inelegant and uncomfortable conditions. It was the same in the BBC always, when you went in to broadcast. They could never manage anything better than a decrepit studio and a pair of creaking chairs. Even Churchill, they used to say, had to make do with a hard back and a glass of whiskey.

It was best to be high up, the engineers had said. As it happens, the house was on high ground anyway, and, besides, it was the tapering ninety-foot mast in the shrubbery that collected the signals. But never mind. It was better to put the receiver in the attic.

We had folding camp chairs, the sort of thing Victorian generals crouched on in the Afghan wars. The beams came down low, and nobody bothered to do much dusting up there. There was a good deal of suppressed sneezing.

Billington sat at the trestle table, dedicated, with his headphones, at the platter of pots and dials. Molly would be over to his right, sharpening a pencil into an empty paint tin. Vonnegut was bent with his fist on his chin, like a constipation advert.

It was a ludicrous contrast to the style of our downstairs accommodation. We'd all rise from a twelve-foot Hepplewhite table on a pair of tripods, with a chandelier above it imported from Nancy, and silver serving dishes that wouldn't have been a disgrace to George III. Then up the uncarpeted attic stairs, and through the trapdoor, to this.

We'd been calling and listening for fifteen nights when the first response came. I can well remember the moment. Vonnegut had been smoking one of his Camels, and I was thinking we ought to be taking more care about the possibility of a fire.

It seemed so unlikely we'd have a contact. One's mind was sure to wander. It hit me like a blow in the stomach when the usual crackle of static disintegrated into Morse.

Vonnegut was stubbing out his cigarette on the floor, Molly had her pencil hard down on the note pad, Billington was shaking with excitement.

The message came through Billington's fingers onto the page. The letter groups as encoded by Jimmy Fong at the other end soon yielded up their information, weird in places in their English, but incisive in what they disclosed.

It took Molly only a few minutes to decode the first sentence. The magnolia tree was safe and thriving. He sent the following details about the Japanese order of battle.

Vonnegut whistled through his teeth as he read the translation over Molly's shoulder.

"My God," he said slowly. "This looks like real meat."

An hour later we were downstairs in the library. I sat at the head of the colonial Jacobean table, a single sheet of flimsy paper in my hand. I passed the paper across to Vonnegut.

When he'd finished reading, he laid it aside, almost with a touch of reverence. He pretended to wipe his brow.

"Wow," he said softly.

I nodded.

"The Twenty-fifth Army," I said. "We have details here of all three divisions, the brigades and regiments, and the support groups."

Vonnegut reached his hand across the table.

"Congratulations, Colonel," he said. "You've justified the whole operation already. There's enough here to slow down the advance in Burma by months."

There was. It's amazing, looking back. There was nothing false in that first message, nothing invented, nothing distorted. It was the pure milk of hard fact. It's hard to believe that the Japanese would have taken such a risk. They must have been dizzy, intoxicated, with their victory.

I got Molly in straightaway. We had secret memoranda on their way to the High Command in Delhi within two hours. I had Billington telephone for a dispatch rider, and he came to the door with his goggles in his hand when the hall clock was chiming one.

The message could have been in London by the following evening. It might have reached Churchill himself as he forked down his sausages before his Cabinet meeting. He could have given orders that would have reached HQ on the ground beyond Rangoon within two days. Our whole lines of battle could have been shifted to take advantage of what we knew.

So far as I know, it never happened. Within the week, the Japanese had captured Lashio, the starting point of the Burma Road. In a few more days they'd captured Mandalay. Whatever the destination of Strand's information, it made no difference. British inefficiency continued unabated.

I can scarcely credit it, even now. This was only the first of a number of messages from Strand over many months, and all were as accurate, as punctual, and as potentially devastating to Japanese interests as the first one. None was made adequate use of.

They were believed, of course. The star of Department M was truly in the ascendant at last. We could do no wrong. Our agent was in place, and in action. The Americans had confirmed it. We had achieved one of the great Intelligence coups of the war.

146

But it was useless. The time was not yet ripe. The man had still to be chosen. The desert generals continued their jungle bungling, and the British armies withdrew and withdrew. Whatever we offered, and it was always gold, its import was ignored, or misapplied, and its influence was minimal.

One day I was making out my report on the month's gleanings, and their potential application, when Vonnegut asked me a question. We were in the office, which had once been the drawing room, with a metal fan spinning in the plaster ceiling to keep us cool.

"Who is this guy Mountbatten?" he said, looking up from a file. "There's a report here on what he did with the St. Nazaire raid. They say he's a candidate for the C-in-C job."

I remembered Brundall, with his prescient suggestion more than a year earlier, as we washed our hands together in Clapham. I told Vonnegut what he wanted to know.

"He's the king's blood relation," I ended. "He has a charisma the Japanese might understand. He could be the right choice."

Vonnegut looked out the window.

"MacArthur needs a right-hand man," he said. "He's an arrogant bastard. I wonder how he and your Lord Louis would hit it off."

Within four months we were going to know.

16

There was a long lull after those first heady weeks of messages. The monsoon came, and we sat watching the rain lash down in long strips amidst the dazzling green of the hibiscus. I played bezique with Vonnegut, and sometimes patience with myself.

It was a time for patience. I read through a battered history of the Great War, all twelve red friable volumes of it, breathing in the musty odor of the unturned pages like a spell against the damp. I improved my billiards, even tried to introduce the recalcitrant Clark to the game's pleasures.

He was a poor player. I wonder sometimes how we failed to get on each other's nerves more than we did. It must have been the euphoria of success. I could even swallow an occasional dig of Clark's cue in the perfect baize of the table without exploding.

I was at ease, more than often before, or since. I would sit for hours under the green shade of the lamp at my writing table, filing butterflies in a glass case, or studying pressed flowers. I was living the life of a gentleman in the colonies, knowing that all was well with the world.

It wasn't, of course. But my own contribution to its welfare was the best it could be, and I was basking for a time in contentment. Things moved with a slow dreaminess through the rain. It seemed to work like a screen, holding back the dark realities of the war.

I remember calculating once that I'd been in Colombo for well over a year. It was late August 1943, and the months had slipped away without leaving their mark. Molly, I saw across the room, was typing a report. In the hall I could hear Clark on the telephone. He was ordering fruit.

That day I wrote a letter to my mother, in Hove. She'd been suffering badly from her arthritis, and she'd moved to a smaller flat farther along the coast. I found the letter again this morning, thick with dust among all the others I'd written her from Ceylon, tied with a purple ribbon. I don't know why I kept them after she died. They made sense to her; they were all she had while I was abroad. But the style makes me wince. The avoided subjects, the circumlocutions, they're all so predictable.

I loathe my pompous young self as I read them over. But at least he gives the abstracted feel of the time. I might have forgotten that sense of distance, and calm, without the letter.

"Dear Mother," it begins. I see it's dated August 20, five days before Mountbatten was appointed Supremo.

"We've been here now for almost eighteen months," I say. "Today it's still raining, the kind of torrential stuff we used to get in the Lake District. Remember? Only worse. It cuts through everything, and goes on and on. But I'm well, and getting work done. I only wish we had something more dramatic to show for our efforts, the way the Russians do, and the chaps in Sicily. They all say there'll be new appointments soon, and that may make a change. We'll have to see."

I didn't know, of course, about Mountbatten. But it wouldn't have taken a genius at that date to see we were due for a shake-up. Since the victory at El Alamein in November 1942, we'd had nothing but Monty's antics right along Africa, and across the Mediterranean. It was refreshing news, if you had a taste for showmanship. In Russia, after the Germans had ground to a halt at Stalingrad, Zhukov had begun to roll their tanks back over the great plains toward Kharkov.

It was a turn of the tide, all right. What nobody tended to remember was how fast the direction of a mechanized war could change over even terrain, either in a desert or a series of cornfields. One day you went one way; the next, the other. There'd been plenty of to-ing and fro-ing the length of Libya in earlier years.

In the jungle, it was different. Since the Japanese had reached the Chindwin, in May 1942, not very much had happened. In England, the scruffy munitions workers and the fat old profiteers never realized why. They thought the troops, on both sides, were squatting back on their arses and drinking gin fizzes.

It wasn't like that. When the monsoon broke in Burma, it went on for months. It brought malaria. One hundred and twenty British soldiers were dying of disease in Burma for every one killed in battle. I don't suppose it was all that better for the Japanese.

They had another problem, too. Despite the fact that the British had been in Burma for more than a hundred years, the only roads over the border into India were three mule tracks. They weren't going to make the advance of a modern army very easy.

So the Japanese had our prisoners of war building roads, and were calculating the likelihood, a not inconsiderable one, in my opinion, of the population of Bengal rising in their favor in the event of a frontier crossing. The British, desperate for supplies, and now regarding the Japanese troops as invincible, which they weren't, were picking leeches off their legs and waiting for someone with a new idea.

The only someone who'd come forward was another showman, this time the T. E. Lawrence type. I have a grudging admiration for Orde Wingate. He was lucky to get the ear of Churchill, and he failed to see the limits of his behind-the-lines raids. But at least he led his men from the front, and he got results.

Between February and May 1943, the Chindits were the only people who seemed to be doing anything to keep the war in Burma going. It was a dull time, as I've said, and we were all waiting.

It was on the wireless that I first heard of Mountbatten's appointment. We'd had tiffin late on the twenty-fifth of August, and the usual heavy afternoon shower had set in, the rain falling in straight vertical lines beyond the verandah as I finished off my papaya.

We'd had chicken with sultanas and rice, and the sweet flesh of the fruit was a gentle aftermath. I was feeling sleepy, and I'd switched on the battery set more to wake me up than from any expectation of hearing important news.

There was a break in transmission of some music program—Vera Lynn, no doubt, with one of her usual crooning numbers—and the announcer was suddenly telling me that we'd at last got the leader we needed.

I rang the bell for the *khimutgar*.

"Champagne," I said. "Ask Corporal Walpole to get out a bottle of our best Moët et Chandon."

We were all excited. Brundall, I believe, was the most.

"By God, sir," he said. "We'll show them now."

Vonnegut was stirring his black coffee.

"You sure do admire this guy," he said.

Brundall was enthusiastic. He'd been informing himself about Mountbatten's background for some time.

"He's a wizard at public relations," he said. "Look at what he's done with the Chief of Staff's Committee. He has the whole lot of them eating out of his hand—generals, air vice marshals, the whole bag of tricks."

Clark swallowed his last chunk of papaya. He wiped his mouth.

"You're all snobs in America," he said flatly to Vonnegut. "Mountbatten's exactly what you need. He's the great-grandson of Queen Victoria, and his manners are impeccable."

Vonnegut smiled into his cup.

"He's not just that," I put in. "Mountbatten's achievements have at least been offensive ones. It makes a change. Remember Bruneval, when his Commandos captured those German radar installations. And, of course, the St. Nazaire raid."

We'd all been impressed by that. In a war where the whole effort had seemed to be concentrated on defense, it was refreshing to hear of a destroyer packed with explosives and wheeled in like a Trojan horse to blow up a whole shipload of

Nazi officers. Mountbatten's people had certainly come up with some daredevil stuff.

Churchill approved, of course. For him, Lord Louis could do no wrong. He even managed to ignore the shambles of the Dieppe raid, where three thousand men out of five thousand landed never came back. A defeat became a kind of victory. It was adapted to show the lesson of needing to support an armed landing with sufficient reserves to keep them ashore.

"St. Nazaire was another triumph for the policy of having friends in high places," said Clark slowly. "And using the gift of the gab to make a silk purse out of a sow's ear."

"Perhaps," agreed Brundall. "But we do need that kind of gift. Look," he went on, leaning forward eagerly over the table. "There are basically three problems to be solved out here if the war's to be turned to our advantage."

"Controlling malaria for a start," I said.

The champagne had arrived, and I watched as the table boy wrapped a napkin around the bottle's neck and drew the cork. I reached forward my glass and took the first foaming, exuberant effusion. I rose to my feet.

"Gentlemen," I said, "to Lord Louis Mountbatten, our new C-in-C."

We drank and settled ourselves again as Brundall continued.

"Controlling malaria's important," he said. "And Mountbatten is the man to do it. He's the one leader we're likely to get with enough interest in scientific progress to spread new medical techniques."

It was another of Brundall's prescient remarks. By 1945 Mountbatten had cut our casualties from malaria down to only ten for every soldier killed in battle. That may sound bad enough, but this was the jungle. This was only six years after slum children in Glasgow were dying of rickets for lack of milk. There was no National Health Service, and no free penicillin, in those days. It was rough when I was young, and we all took illness, and what it did, for granted.

"Your second basic problem just has to be the monsoon," said Vonnegut suddenly. He was growing tired of Brundall's malaria statistics.

"Right," said Brundall, quick off the mark. "And the third, if I may anticipate your interruption, is the problem of transport."

They debated the issues, and the coffee shrank in the little blue Japanese cups, and the rain slackened into the brightness of early evening. It was a classic debate, and one repeated, no doubt, throughout the length and breadth of India that afternoon.

At last our new leader had arrived. What was he going to do to turn the tide of war? We were soon to see.

It wasn't solving transport problems, though, that mattered most about Mountbatten. It wasn't his battle against malaria, or his fighting through the monsoon. It was the third of what he once called his "three M's." It was what he did for morale.

In 1943, the British army in Burma was a broken force. It had no faith in its power to win. It felt, with some justification, that the powers that be had forgotten it was there. Mountbatten changed all that. He put the Burmese army back on the map.

Once he was there, the situation looked brighter. After all, the king had sent one of his own relations, his own royal blood, to restore the faith of his men. It was in the Agincourt tradition. If someone who was a possible heir to the throne had come out to lead the army in the jungle, their cause must surely be a great and noble one.

It was their duty to live up to it. Men straightened their backs and cleaned their rifles. A new spirit was in the air. A fresh wind was blowing. The Japanese might have had their victories, but they weren't supermen.

It wasn't only on the Irrawaddy and the Chindwin that this feeling began to gain ground. It seeped across the border into Malaya; it ran down the peninsula. It even penetrated to Singapore, and to Tokyo, where it nurtured its own special paranoia.

All Intelligence agents have their paranoia, and the senses are their early-warning system. I've known men who could see Reds under the bed, in plenty, but I've also known men who could sniff imaginary gas leaks in all-electric kitchens. Men who would go to safe houses and taste poison in their soup. Men who could feel stilettos bulging in the pockets of their mother's aprons.

It's always like that. The organs become too acute, and they create the bogey they're alert to prevent. With some, the nose will grow its own aroma of burned almonds. With others, it'll be the tongue, or the palms of the hands, itching for the texture of buried steel.

With Yoshida, it seems to have been the ears. He had small, neat ears, I remember, and they always seem to have been tuned in for trouble. In Tokyo, or even Singapore, it can hardly have been assassins he was listening out for. It was eavesdroppers he feared.

So whenever Strand met him, on the rare occasions he flew down for a personal briefing, there had to be elaborate, and sometimes ludicrous, precautions against being overheard. One conversation they had was in the front row of the stalls at a performance of the *Götterdämmerung*. Another took place while Yoshida was overtly supervising the testing of a new submachine gun.

It was staccato, Strand notes in his diary, with one of his infrequent lapses into humor. The time the two met for their Mountbatten discussion was in June 1944, just after the retreat from Kohima, and the precautions were athletic. They played a game of table tennis.

Yoshida was very fit. He spent more than an hour a day on *kendo* practice, and his arm muscles were supple and powerful. But he hadn't, evidently, been keeping up his game. Strand notes that he wasn't extended in the early sets, and he had to work hard to avoid overcoming his superior officer by too large a margin.

I don't suppose that Yoshida liked to be beaten, even when he was using the game as a cover for another purpose. He had the single-mindedness of the Prussians he so much admired.

I can picture the two of them there, stripped to the waist in the gymnasium. They'd have kept their baggy trousers on, and perhaps their boots. But they'd want to make some gesture toward the seriousness of their contest, even with something as trivial as table tennis.

Removal of jackets and shirts would have marked the ritual. Perhaps they even tied white bands around their foreheads, like navvies and *kamikaze* pilots.

There were plenty of other sports they could have tried, more martial pursuits with flashing blades and gripping hands. The gymnasium had been built in the basement of Fort Canning for the British officers, and it was well appointed with hobbyhorses, and parallel bars too.

It was noise paranoia that led to table tennis. But it was also a kind of caste paranoia. Yoshida didn't want to attract attention by being seen engaging in a noble exercise with a local junior officer. It would have seemed suspicious, and been bad for morale.

On the other hand, it would appear a magnanimous gesture to indulge in a more demeaning pastime, and one, to improve the figure of his gesture, which had assumed some current popularity with the younger men.

Strand himself had been playing every day. He had a good eye and quick wrists, and his clients for photographs were often the more vain and dandified of his colleagues who enjoyed showing off their torsos. He would sometimes snap them after games, wet with sweat and standing with arms folded and a rubber bat across their chests.

He kept a couple of prints crushed in the back of the diary. One has a signature on the back, in Japanese. "Saito, your friend." And then some numbers, twenty-one–five. It must be the score.

Yoshida kept that aloud, as they played.

"Nine–five," he said, serving fast with his backhand.

It was another technical fault. He always kept his other hand on the ball, and imparted spin with his fingers. But Strand had never bothered to explain the rule.

By now the style of play had established itself. Yoshida wanted an easy exchange of shots while he rapidly conveyed one passage of what he needed to say. At the end of this, he would exert himself to concentrate and attempt to win the point. It made for an odd sort of game, I imagine.

Fortunately, this last meeting was one that mattered a lot to Strand, and he clearly spent a lot of time in getting his account of it down on paper in the way he felt right. I can feel that game as if I were playing myself.

So we have the perpetual click of the tiny balls. The slither of booted heels on the wooden floor. The echoing blur of Yoshida's voice.

"At Kohima," he said, "they put up the best fight they've done so far. It wasn't all in the news, Michael."

"Fourteen all," said Strand. "Your serve."

He'd guessed the siege of Kohima had marked some change in the British fighting spirit. For thirteen days an outnumbered force of twenty-five hundred men had held out until they were relieved. There had probably been the usual bungling, hospitals overrun, and senior officers vanishing into the jungle in their pajamas, but for once, and perhaps for the first time in this war, the line had held.

It was Lucknow all over again. The imperial lion had started to grit its teeth, and it must have been their new Supremo, Mountbatten, who'd done the training.

"Fourteen–fifteen," said Yoshida, serving again.

He'd lost the point, no doubt by a wasted smash. He was a player for the offensive, Strand had found. It made it even harder to let him win, or at least lose with dignity. He had to waste his own smashes, and he didn't like that.

"It was air cover that made the difference," Yoshida was saying. "He's getting ninety-six percent of his supplies in by air, and he's talked the Americans into flying all day for seven days a week. It's a kind of charisma he has. The royal style. The royal blood."

He had lost again, the same way. Strand took his time walking back to the table with the ball. He thought about Mountbatten. It might be true, he thought. It might be more than true. It might be the way they were going to win the war.

With the traditional English sangfroid, and a few graceful

156

speeches made by an elegant fop whose grandfather had been sacked from the Navy. It made Strand savage. He waited for Yoshida's third serve crouched slightly to one side.

When the ball came looping slowly over the net he waited, watching for the swerve as it spun from its contact with his side of the table. He didn't, as he'd done before, pat it gently back. He let his right hand slide across his body, then flick up and out, like a penknife blade jackknifing shut.

It was a classic backhand drive. Yoshida never saw the ball before it was past his guard and traveling fast away to the wall. "I'm sorry," Strand said. "I didn't see you weren't ready."

He felt the savage impulse die away as he ran politely to retrieve the ball for Yoshida. He waited, relaxed, for the fourth serve in the set. It came, bouncing, genuinely casual this time, a rather cunning variant on the hard spin series.

You're trying, Strand thought, as he eased it back, but he said aloud, against the clicks of the ball: "I was thinking about Mountbatten. It made me angry."

"You're playing well," Yoshida said, flicking the ball high.

He watched it bounce high for Strand, and hang, the perfect target for a hard forehand smash. He watched Strand knock it gently back, smiling as he did so. He smiled himself, returning Strand's return.

"You're playing with me, Michael," he said, laughing. "But I rather like it. I'm getting back in practice."

Then, with a sudden lunge, he put all his strength into a forehand jab, ramming the ball hard away to Strand's left. It was a wonderful stroke, and Strand flung himself full length, paying it the tribute of a desperate attempt to get it back. He was too late, and the ball ripped past his ear as he fell.

"Fifteen–seventeen," said Yoshida, grinning.

He was proud of himself.

"You were lucky," said Strand, rising to his knees.

"I know," said Yoshida, still grinning.

His last serve was a medium one, and they kept the ball going through a series of returns.

"In a few weeks," said Yoshida, as he moved his bat,

"there'll be an offensive. Stilwell is on his way toward Myit-kyina. If they capture the airfields there they can link up with the Chinese. They have to be stopped."

He took a sharp swipe, like a man cutting at nettles with a sickle, and the ball jerked from the edge of his bat into the net.

"Fifteen–eighteen," he murmured, as Strand served.

He caught the ball in his hand and threw it back. It was far too fast for him. Exactly the same thing happened with the next.

"Fifteen–twenty, Michael," he said softly.

He crouched, waiting, and Strand served more slowly. He had a sense that this was the crucial moment. He knew already what Yoshida was going to say, but he felt a prickle of something strange, even so. It was hardly anticipation, or fear. It was more like a kind of sadness.

Yoshida spoke as he knocked the ball back over the net.

"There's only one way to do it," he said. "They need a psychic shock."

He waited for Strand's return. It was an easy, rising ball, and he lashed at it with a firm, vicious forehand stab.

"Mountbatten must die," he said as he hit the ball. "And you must kill him, Michael."

The ball missed the edge of the table by a tiny margin. They both watched as it skimmed away across the floor.

"Game," said Yoshida gently. "I think that makes it three all."

"Let's play another," said Strand.

They passed each other as they changed ends, and he smelled the healthy, dry odor of Yoshida's body. He wondered, he writes in his diary, what it would have been like to have to kill Yoshida, on the orders of the British, then and there.

He felt a firm sense of death, and the terrible means toward death, and he knew, suddenly, he says, that he would undertake what he was ordered to do by Yoshida, and that his mission would not be easy. He knew, too, he says, and he knew it without anxiety or horror or any uneasiness, that he would never return from it.

Whatever the outcome of the mission, his own life, he felt sure, would be part of the price of success.

The room was suddenly full of spirits. As he played on, and listened to Yoshida's plan, they began to desert him, one by one, slowly and inexorably, as bees detach themselves from their cells and desert a burning hive.

He must have seen that in Somerset, as a boy at school. It brought tears into the corners of my eyes as I read the lovely, reticent *kanji* this morning, walking among my roses and hearing the wood pigeons.

There are spirits left, Strand. A few here. Not many. But more than there might have been, but for that war, and its honors, and treacheries. I remember those. I shall always remember.

17

Two and a half years is a long time in any love affair. For some lovers it may simply span the introductory period between meeting and consummation, the prologue to years of bliss. For others it may exhaust their dreams, and their hopes.

To Su Lin, the return of Strand after his first departure was like a rising from the dead. She never expected to see him again when he left, and his first reappearance, after the Japanese occupation, was like a kind of bizarre resurrection.

Her lover had been miraculously reborn, but not, as he had been before, as a vulnerable secret, a precious trust to be kept hidden and enjoyed only in private. He was back as a public spectacle, a Japanese officer to be feted and treated with respect.

The House of Happiness was a place of pragmatism. Those who ruled its destiny, and pocketed its profits, were all Chinese. They would have preferred to make their squalid money out of British foibles, and they did their bit, for the most part, to assist the resistance.

But there were limits. When Goh Han Peng appeared, with his cracking knuckles, and his bald dome glistening with desire, the coffers were opened freely, and the talk was all of victory. The Triad was too powerful to oppose, and the Triad was committed to Chiang Kai-shek.

It was different when General Yamashita, or one of his men, came knocking at the door. In particular, any officer in the Kempei Tai was assured of an obsequious reception. Too many heads had rolled, literally, for any less welcome style to be appropriate.

So Strand was able to click his heels, and clean his hands with warm towels, and everyone thought how lucky Su Lin was to have retained a lover who had risen and prospered. They remembered the athletic and generous Ogawa *san* from his previous instantiation as a civilian photographer.

It was intriguing to learn of his double life, and of his time spent underground with Su Lin in her apartment, and to find that he was now as frequent in his visits, and as liberal with his payments, as he'd been before.

He took more photographs, too. Strand was evidently not one to waste his opportunities, provided they could be seized with safety. The disappearance of two or three rather prominent citizens working for the resistance was never connected with the fulsome Mr. Ogawa, and his eagerness to get all the bystanders into his pictures.

Human nature is very trusting. No one realized that it was work not leisure for Strand when he came to the House of Happiness with his camera, just as it was work when he fulfilled his office duties at Fort Canning. His cover as Ogawa was well maintained, and it yielded advantages.

I marvel at the narrow line Strand was able to walk. He might have risked some dangerous and rewarding coup. It must have been tempting, for example, to consider unveiling Jimmy Fong.

There was plenty of resistance work, apart from the running of our wireless link, that was being cleverly channeled through local police procedures, and it would have saved much trouble to the Kempei Tai if Jimmy Fong had been arrested.

But Strand was a cautious man. He knew that the prime consideration must be the absolute preservation of his own credit with British Intelligence. Nothing, not even the neutralization of someone as destructive as Jimmy Fong, could be allowed to interfere with that.

161

Su Lin, of course, believed in him totally. His very flamboyance in his public portrait of Ogawa convinced her. She came to see him as a great actor, as well as a great lover. It underlined her faith, and it deepened her joy.

It wasn't until the very end that she came to accept how Strand was able to deceive even her by his acting. It was hard to believe. After all, she, too, was going through a public deception in pretending that he was Ogawa. But in bed, with Strand, her Strand, she was honest to her bones.

Two and a half years was a long time, but for Su Lin it came to seem like a kind of apprenticeship. As the weeks went by, and the shape of the war changed, her suppressed fears had a chance to thaw into hopes. She began to see her voyage to Norfolk in new terms.

It was no longer an escape route from reality. It was what she was going to do with Strand when the war was over, and the British had won. It was where they would live together, and marry perhaps, and have their children.

It took time for this dream to gather force. It fought its way with Orde Wingate, cutting the railway from Mandalay to Myitkyina. It made a stand with Richards at Kohima. It began to creep forward in greater power with Stilwell.

Strand's visits were only once a week, or sometimes less, and they rarely lasted more than an hour or two. There was never time, or reason, to go home to the little room they had shared for nearly ten weeks like man and wife.

Their meetings took place in the casual, sumptuous decor of the House of Happiness. Accomplished with a vulgar grossness in the seedy grandeur of the public salons, amid black garters and pipes of opium. Or snatched, with a more affectionate but no less threatened transitoriness, in whatever bedroom was allocated that day for their privacies.

It was very sad, perhaps, in its way. But that was Su Lin's world. She could rise above the coarseness; she was used to doing this. But she could also step below her dreams, into the morasses of lust.

She was a practical girl. Whatever went on in her physical

environment, she could adapt it for her own purposes. It was the furnishings of her spirit that mattered.

With Strand it might well have been the same. There were things they had in common. We know that. Exactly how or why it happened I shall never plumb, but for those ten weeks in 1941–42 Strand was in tune with Su Lin.

It changed his soul. He may even have been in love, in his fashion, for a time. I believe he was, and it altered his stride, and he nearly faltered.

As it was, he hesitated, and then he went forward again. He went up the road to Fort Canning, and he never looked back. From the day he returned in his Japanese uniform, he was dressed as he felt he should be. He was Japanese to the pith.

He was tender in bed, as he'd been before. He spoke, when he had the chance, like a British agent. He watched the myth of Norfolk as it budded and flowered in its bowl. But his heart was outside now, in its own world.

Su Lin was there to be used. She was good to use, and he took his pleasure with skill. Washing, or eating, with her, lying naked against her undraped skin, or simply talking, Strand was to all appearances the same.

But he was bored. It may be the way with all love affairs. I think it was Balzac who said in love there is always one who is hurt and one who is bored.

For Strand the weekly visits were growing to be a chore. He was starting to chafe at the long isolation of doing a dreary desk job with men he despised. He wanted the secrecy of action again, the shift into enemy territory that the trained agent always craves.

From the beginning he knew it would come. Yoshida had promised, or hinted, a special role. It was only a question of time. But the waiting was hard to bear. I suppose that a man with more imagination could have seen himself as already in the field every time he visited the House of Happiness.

But for Strand it was all too comfortable. He needed the extra salt of danger. He wanted to feel his life on the line, and he didn't see that it was in Singapore.

It's all there in his diary. The frustration. The sense of waste. The bitterness. Every time he records a visit to Su Lin there's a vicious joke in those last days about her manners or her appearance.

He was venting his rage. At first he did it all on paper, and that was no problem. Once or twice, recalling some features in Su Lin's report, it may have leaked through to her face. But whatever came out, she was always able to put it down as a passing quirk, a little irritation that would soon fade.

It was only that last day that he let the mask slip. I suppose you could say there were excuses. He was exultant at what he'd been told by Yoshida. It brought all his emotions to a curious head.

They were quarreling before either of them knew it. In the basement of the House of Happiness there was a laundry room, and on certain afternoons, in a dry season, it was leased out to a client for his own amusement.

Su Lin and Strand had been down there before, and they'd found the huge baskets and the wet linen an enticing inducement to their appetite. There were sinks, and faucets with hoses, and a high Edwardian mangle with a screw on a ratchet and smooth wooden rollers.

They had water on, and she'd let him jet the nozzle up through the cheeks of her anus. You can visualize the scene. The horseplay and the lewdness.

Usually, it would have ended in gentleness, on the crisp linen in a hamper. But not today. They were quarreling, as I've said. They'd been bickering, and it escalated. And then the whole thing was on fire.

Su Lin could never remember how it began. But she had the last sequences by heart.

"All right," she remembers Strand saying, and he was standing buttoning his trousers beside the wringer. "I know you want me to stay. But I have to go. I've explained why. I have to go."

"You rotten bugger," she says she said.

She'd learned the words, and she knew the ones that would move the handles in him. It was the first time she'd used the power to annoy, and not to amuse, him. It was the first time, and it was the wrong time.

Something went across his face, she said, like the shadow of a swallow on a wall. Then she doesn't remember any more except a cracking noise, like nuts breaking. And looking down at her two fingers hanging loose.

You get the pain later always. And she did. But that's another story. He must have reached down and swung her up from the basket by her arm, and then laid her hand on the bottom roller and turned the iron handle before he knew what he was doing.

That's what he said, when the madness was over. When he realized he'd gone crazy for a second, when he knew he had to get the stocking back over his face before she recognized she was talking to a killer.

But it was too late. He got her a doctor, and they had the fingers bandaged, and money changed hands, and the usual explanations. It wasn't the first time they'd had accidents in the laundry room, and they were quick to accept their client's explanation. Particularly when they saw the look in his eye.

He gave a good performance. Anguished, in a kind of controlled way. Apologizing. But it didn't work. Su Lin had had a kind of revelation.

Her lover, the one man she'd pinned all her hopes on for two and a half years, her beautiful, expert Michael, who was half Chinese and would take her to England, her lovely, unreachable Major Strand, was tired of her. It was over.

So Su Lin did exactly what a wise girl, in the circumstances, was bound to have done. She'd been beaten up by men before. There were scars from knife slashes on her thighs, and a stab wound in her back from a ship's engineer.

It had never paid to complain. The customer was always right. You smiled, and you nodded, and you pretended that it didn't hurt. And later on, if you were lucky, you got a special present, and even a bonus for good behavior from the powers that be.

So she kissed Strand for the last time, closing her eyes, and her mind. She let him go with the special caress he liked on the side of his neck. He may even have believed he'd got away with it.

Strand left the House of Happiness, and two days later, on Su Lin's instructions, Jimmy Fong sent a message to Colombo. It was exactly as Strand had encoded it.

It was Clark who got the news. We'd begun to take it in turns to do the regular nine o'clock stint, and most of the time there was no reason for the man on duty to bother the rest of us. Night after night he'd sit up there in the dust and the cobwebs, and nothing would happen to drag his eyes from his book.

This particular Friday was different. In general, Strand had been making contact about once a fortnight, or less, and the normal drill for these occasions was clear-cut. The duty officer would see that the message was decoded and present me with a translation before he went to bed.

In the interval between coming off the air at ten and finding Molly with her cipher key, he'd alert me in the library or the billiard room, and I'd be standing by for the details. The system worked quite well, and it meant we could spread the labor and the boredom and still keep on our toes.

I'd several times had to call out a dispatch rider after midnight, and the messages he carried were frequently urgent. The fact that very little effective use was ever made of them, even after Mountbatten came to be appointed, fails to undermine the value of Strand's information, and the extreme nature of the risks the Japanese were taking.

This particular Friday, as I've said, was different. It was the night we discovered the reason for those Japanese risks. It was the night, too, that the Kempei Tai tried, and succeeded, with their final, most hair-raising bluff.

No wonder, I sometimes think, that Clark was so bitter in his self-recrimination. After all, when it came to the point, it was Clark, the cautious, no-nonsense Yorkshire Clark, with his Peter Cheyney novel on his knees and a bottle of Guinness at his elbow, who heard the signal from Jimmy Fong and took down the exact words of the original message.

It couldn't have made any difference. There was no direct

contact with Strand, no chance to pick up any false nuance in
his tone or manner. There was just the warm, slightly humor-
ous Chinese lilt of Jimmy Fong, and that never changed, whatever he had to say.

No one, not even Clark, could have seen through the message at the point of transmission. But we were a superstitious
team. Like all those involved in secret work, we believed in
omens, in strange marks and signals.

For Clark, it was always a bad sign, and a cause for a kind of
sinister disquiet, that it was he who'd been on duty and
brought the news downstairs the night that we heard of the
Japanese plan. He never forgave himself, and I don't suppose
that Brundall or Vonnegut did either.

We were drinking port in the billiard room, the three of us.
The size of the villa had lent itself to a simple after-dinner
convention, so that the lower ranks—I mean Walpole and Billington, with occasional visits from Molly—were relegated to
an upstairs parlor.

They used to sit there for hours over endless games of pon-
toon, winning and losing their mild fortunes, while Molly pla-
cidly knitted. It wasn't so very different, I suppose, from what
was going on all over the world that year in a dozen armies and
stations.

It was still, thank God, a world where the classes knew their
places. The officers changed for dinner; I insisted on that. The
other ranks could do as they pleased, in the servants' hall.

So there was Vonnegut, with his jacket off, and his crew cut
like a shoe brush under the lights, a mini-Eisenhower chalking
his cue. Brundall had gone to the sideboard to refresh our
glasses from the decanter of Sandeman's, and I was aligning
the table rest for my third cannon.

There was a moment of complete silence, and I could hear
the insects outside in the bougainvillea through the mosquito
screens. Then Clark was in the room, clumsy as a moth.

"Sir," he said, anxious, and fluttering, as it seemed, at the
back of my legs. "There's a message."

I was feeling testy. He'd broken the drift of my thoughts for
the shot, and that's always fatal at billiards.

167

"Can't it wait?" I said. "I'm in the middle of a game."

"It's the longest I ever remember," said Clark quietly.

There was something in the air suddenly. A kind of tension. I sensed an intuition of what was coming in the very awkwardness of Clark's manner.

"Get Molly in here," I said. "We'll evaluate the message line by line as she decodes."

Brundall was handing me a glass, his quick eyes scanning my face. Vonnegut had laid his cue aside. We didn't often interrupt our game so brusquely.

Then Molly was in the room, and Brundall was dragging a table over for her to write at. We clustered over her shoulder, and the fateful, unbelievable words began to come out into sober English.

It took an hour for Molly to complete the decoding, and it was another five, deep into the coffee-sodden small hours, before the implications were entirely clear.

By then we were in the library, surrounded by piles of old *Tatlers* and volumes of the *Handbook of British Ceylon* going back to the turn of the century. It was the right environment for a decision about a matter affecting the future of the Empire.

You felt its power there, in the elephant's foot umbrella stand, in the sepia photographs of servants in turbans. Even Vonnegut, with his West Point detachment and his false democracy, was aware of what it meant.

"I'll recapitulate the main points," Brundall was saying, the brisk young subaltern.

I could almost hear the bugles blowing behind his words.

"Strand has reported that the Japanese have a plan to assassinate the Supremo. Point one."

"Hardly surprising," said Vonnegut.

He'd said it before. The Americans, of course, are used to assassination. I didn't realize this, fully, until the 1960s and the death of Kennedy. It struck me then that that was the sort of thing that had happened in America, ever since Lincoln was killed.

For Clark and Brundall, in 1944, even in the middle of the

war, this kind of thing was harder to get used to. It was scarcely cricket.

My own view was that what the Japanese had in mind had become inevitable. All wars are won and lost by myths, and, in this war, the myth had changed. The myth of the invincible Japanese Army had, very gradually but emphatically, been deflated.

It had been replaced by the myth of Mountbatten, the invulnerable shogun, who could work miracles by a wave of his hand. The only way to win the war was to explode this myth. By removing its point of origin, by revealing the mortality of the royal superman, the Japanese could restore the faith of their troops in their own power.

So I agreed privately with Vonnegut. It was hardly surprising that a plan should have been devised to assassinate the Supremo. Only its imagination, and audacity, might seem surprising.

"They mean to use Strand himself," said Brundall, "as their assassination weapon. He will be planted, as Ogawa was before, behind the British lines."

"That was before the war, of course," Clark interposed. "The idea of landing Strand by submarine on the coast of Ceylon seems a very different affair. Even supposing his papers are in order, as a Chinese photographer, I can hardly believe they expect him to stay alive for long."

"They won't," said Vonnegut crisply. "It's a suicide mission."

Strand had suggested as much in his report. The scheme was hazardous, he implied, even in the eyes of the Japanese High Command, and they were banking only on a fifty-fifty chance of success. But the dividends, even at these odds, were worth the attempt.

"You know," said Clark thoughtfully, "in the crowds at the festival, there won't be much chance of anyone picking out an assassin. Once they get Strand ashore, the job won't be so very difficult. The one thing it requires is a man who doesn't need to be got out alive."

"A suicide volunteer," said Brundall.

"You know what they're like," I said. "That's not a problem. I agree with what Strand says. They won't find anything unusual in his being willing to sacrifice his life in the mission."

This was before Admiral Onishi had launched the *kamikaze* program, but we'd had a score of incidents that made clear the Japanese approach to the business of last stands, and fighting to the death.

"So Strand will be landed from a Japanese submarine," said Vonnegut slowly. "He'll make his way down the coast and then inland to Kandy. He'll mingle with the crowds at the festival of the Temple of the Tooth. When Mountbatten appears at the shrine, as planned, Strand will devise a chance to get close enough to shoot him under cover of taking his photograph."

"Not really," I said gently. "That's just the plan."

They were losing their grip on reality.

"It's feasible," said Brundall. "Hideously feasible."

There was a short silence. Vonnegut creaked in his cane chair. He was worried. I could see he was thinking about MacArthur. He was wondering where this kind of risk would end.

"Look," said Clark. "There are two problems. It's clear that Strand has perfected his cover as Ogawa. It's become a seamless garment. The Japanese believe they have an expert agent whose commitment goes back to the 1930s. He's proved his ingenuity by keeping out of internment at the fall of Singapore, and he's managed to continue his work with the Kempei Tai while supplying us with a steady flow of first-class information."

"That's obvious enough," said Brundall. "What are your problems?"

Tempers were getting frayed at the edges. I could feel my own tiredness leaking down from my brain. I'd said very little myself in the discussion, but I was thinking hard. I knew that we had to finish soon.

"Forgive me, Clark," I said, slicing in. "The problems are these. One, how will Strand unveil the local Japanese agent in Kandy? Unfortunately, we don't know, and neither does he. He'll have to wait to be contacted, and make his plans on the ground. That's *our* problem, remember. Not one for the Japanese."

I paused, then went on, speaking more slowly for emphasis.

"This is the central point," I said. "The Japanese have an agent in Kandy, someone at or near Mountbatten's HQ at SEAC.

"Now, as this agent has given no indication whatsoever of his presence, and presumably isn't likely to, we have virtually no chance of winkling him out without appearing to align ourselves with the Japanese plan and waiting for him to make himself known to Strand. It's a huge risk, as Strand himself says, but there seems no alternative."

There was a long silence.

"At this stage in the war," I continued, "it's obviously intolerable that there should be a Japanese agent under cover somewhere at SEAC HQ. He has to be found and eliminated. And soon. Bringing back Strand and appearing to cooperate with him in the assassination attempt seems the only way."

I poured myself a last cup of coffee. It tasted cold, and burned. The time had come to push things to a decision.

"The Japanese," I said, "have only one problem. It's the naval one. They can't hope to be sure of getting their submarine through our blockade. They must be anticipating their maximum risk while Strand is still at sea. They're clearly prepared to risk losing a submarine. This must be a vital operation for them."

"So what do we do?" asked Vonnegut.

I drained my cup and looked at my watch. It was six-thirty and none of us had slept. I did my Churchill act.

"I have no doubt of what to do," I said roundly. "We shall facilitate, as Major Strand requests, the arrival and departure of the Japanese submarine, and his own safe landing on the shore of Ceylon. There must be no question, I repeat, no question, of his mission failing before he has uncovered the Japanese agent in Kandy."

I paused. I had them now, even Vonnegut, wrinkle-browed over his biscuits.

"That means," I continued, "the, er, cooperation of the

171

British and American navies. With your help, gentlemen, I shall see that we get this. This may be a turning point in the war. We have a chance to save the life of the one man, perhaps, who can turn the tide against our enemies. We have to take it, at whatever cost."

This kind of rhetoric goes down well at six-thirty in the morning. We broke up in a spirit of euphoria. The details, of course, were going to require a lot of work. It wasn't going to be easy to arrange for the navy to hold its fire against a Japanese submarine off the shores of Ceylon. Too many people were likely to see it as the spearhead of an invasion by sea.

However, it had to be tried. I went upstairs to bed in a strange mood. I was thinking, most of all, about Strand himself. It was three years since I'd seen him, and yet he'd been the central pivot of all our lives, day after day, night after night.

It would be good to see him again. I undressed and climbed between the sheets, wondering. Perhaps I would never see him again. Perhaps, after all, this was going to be the end of the line.

I fell asleep as the sun rose and burned through the slats of my blind, waiting for the nine o'clock alarm I'd set, and feeling the huge web of bluff and counterbluff surge and grow in my dreams.

I woke tired at the buzzing of the alarm. The climax of all my work was at hand. I had to be ready for it. I rose and called for Molly. Razor in hand, I began to dictate.

18

You can imagine the next few weeks. It was a hectic time. Despite the Churchillian tone I'd taken in my final briefing, the decision about what to do was obviously not going to be mine. It would be taken at a much higher level.

In the event, it took place at the highest. I'd already foreseen this, right from the start. I went through the motions of reporting to my immediate superiors at SEAC HQ, and I took the precaution, as always now, of keeping the Director in London informed as well.

What had happened when Department M established its forward base, as we saw it, in Colombo, was that our official designation had changed to Department M, Field Division, and we'd been seconded, on a temporary basis, to the Army Intelligence wing of SEAC.

In certain ways, this meant that we were serving two masters instead of one, and it increased the paper work enormously. But it also allowed us a good deal of room for maneuver, and I took advantage of this. Added to the fact that our stock was still so high, in view of the continuing success of Strand's mission, the end result was one whereby I could more or less do as I pleased.

I'd been cautious in exercising this power. I didn't want to stick my neck out too far and get it chopped off. So that now, when I really needed to use my position, I had some leeway for a very considerable clout.

I've said that I knew right from the start I'd have to get very high level authorization for our demands. In effect, I knew that I'd have to go and make out my case with Mountbatten in person.

At this stage in the war, with the planning for his Burmese offensive at its height, there wouldn't normally have been any question of a comparatively junior colonel obtaining a private audience at his own request.

So it's some measure of my own self-confidence at the time, as well as the Department's high reputation, that I felt quite convinced I'd be granted what I asked for.

After several abortive requests through normal channels, backed up by a suitably teasing extract from our digest of Strand's report, I framed a final memorandum direct to Mountbatten himself. I knew how to see that it would reach his desk, on top of the pile too.

We were an Intelligence unit, remember. We had ways and means of cajoling and bribing our material into the right hands—and the right drawers. In this case it was a staff captain who owed Brundall a favor through the transfer of some information in our own diplomatic bag to Whitehall. It had saved the captain time, and perhaps his commission, and he was properly grateful. He made sure that Mountbatten saw my memo.

After that, it was easy. Mountbatten was like an old pike, in his way, voracious and curious. I knew how to hook his interest. I baited my news with a spice of technology and I had him between the gills.

I was summoned for an immediate meeting at SEAC HQ. I had my uniform pressed, and I packed my leather attaché case, and I took the train up from Colombo to Kandy.

In those days, there were two ways you could go, by rail or by road. For all I know, there's a service by helicopter now, or a chair lift. In 1944 it was a choice between a three-hour bumping drive up the mountain in the back seat of an army Morris or a four-hour slow jog on the wooden seats of a Victorian carriage hauled by a steam engine.

174

I chose the train. I like driving, but I didn't want to have to concentrate, and those unfenced hairpins needed attention. I could have gone in style, of course, with a brace of outriders on motorbikes, and a booted chauffeur.

But I didn't want to make that kind of splash. I knew the Supremo wouldn't like it, and besides, I wasn't in the mood for small talk with some conscript from Birmingham. I wanted to be alone with my thoughts.

So I waited on the sweltering platform amid all the goats and baskets, and I clambered up the jittery steps into the frail carriage with the rest of the crowd, and I found a space by the window and ran the blind half down against the glare.

There was the whistle, and the release of steam, and then the clank and surge of the couplings, and the old engine was on its way. The smell was pretty unbelievable, and the noise was nearly as bad. I expect that a journey on the Indian railways is still a fairly bone-jolting affair, but in those days it was a trauma for the senses.

You had to be used to it, and, of course, I was. I'd ridden those old bullock-catchers since I was a boy, when my father was posted to Madras. They were part of the whole nostalgia of childhood for me.

Nowadays, you'd get much the same experience on the London underground, from what they tell me. The aroma of curry, and the trick and lilt of Urdu or Hindustani. There's a proper place for everything, though, and I don't have any taste for the style of Calcutta on the Piccadilly Line.

On the mountains up to Kandy, it was different. It felt right to be brushing mothers in dark saris and young men in their English duck suits. This was British India, and the heartland of the greatest empire the world had ever known.

It was what we were fighting for. I thought about that as I ran the blind up in the cooler air as we climbed. They'd made a muck of the whole thing, in more ways than one, but there might be something left still. It was a good country, and it ought to be properly ruled.

It was four and a half hours, that day, before the train arrived in Kandy. I was drinking my third glass of mint tea when we came around the last bend, and I saw the artificial lake there away to my left.

The engine announced its approach with a long, shrill hoot, and the passengers began to grope and scuffle for all their belongings. I sat very still, waiting for it. And then, there it was, the Dalada Maligawa, the famous Temple of the Tooth, serene and profound at the lake's far edge, ringed by the flowering hibiscus and frangipani, and spreading its own reflection like a magic carpet over the water.

I'd seen it before, several times. But I never ceased to be amazed by this first lyrical glimpse as it swam into view from the train, almost as if it had been gently poled forward like a great sacrificial barge.

It was going to be just that, I thought, if the Japanese had their way. It was a fitting place, perhaps, to assassinate a prince of the royal blood. Every year, on the tenth day of the festival, the holy relic, the tooth allegedly taken from the flames of the Buddha's funeral pyre, was placed in a special traveling casket and was paraded on the back of a sacred elephant through the streets of Kandy. This had happened for centuries, to the accompaniment of enormous pageantry, but the tooth had never before been taken out of its casket and shown to a layman.

It was a very great honor, and a fitting one, I thought, for the allied commander and the king's relation. No matter that the relic itself was rumored to be a fake, and not even human bone tissue. No matter that the original, anyway, had been stolen by the Portuguese in the seventeenth century. It was still a great honor.

For Mountbatten to be assassinated—shot down on the steps of the temple by a bullet from a secret camera-gun— would be an appalling blow to British prestige.

I shuddered. It seemed cold suddenly in the train, and not just from the air of the mountains. The carriage was empty now, and I was the last to go.

I lifted down my attaché case from the wooden overhead rack and hoisted it in my hand. It felt heavy, and not just, I felt, with the weight of the files I'd packed inside. As I walked

176

along the corridor, I was carrying more than a bundle of army papers.

I was carrying the fate of Lord Louis Mountbatten, and perhaps the outcome of the war in the East, in my one dangling, miserable right hand.

I know now what I didn't know then. It makes a difference. I've read Strand's diary, and the secret reports by Su Lin and Jimmy Fong.

Operation Chameleon was a great success, and then it was a great failure. And here was the man who dreamed up the whole scheme, walking along the station at Kandy, in the cool air, and kicking a dog out of his way, and refusing alms to a beggar, and in mortal fear that what he was going to say and do would distort the future, and abort what he wanted.

It was a hard moment. I found a beat-up 1920s taxi, though, and a smiling, effusive Singhalese driver, and I was on my way out of the old capital toward the new one, the shabby prefabricated wooden city in the grounds of a rubber plantation that the British Army, in their wisdom, had seized and translated into the HQ of their Southeast Asia military empire.

The driver had the canvas hood rolled down, and I sat high on the buttoned seat, with my arm along the windscreen, and enjoyed the wind. I was going to meet the man on whom the whole drive of my military life for the last four years was about to hinge and pivot.

I took a deep breath and rubbed the palms of my hands. They were wet with sweat.

The interview was easier than I expected. It began with something of an anticlimax. I arrived at the gates of the Supremo's HQ a little ahead of time, but I decided to be driven in and wait rather than hang about.

A sentry inspected my pass and waved the car through, and we ground over well-swept fine gravel between rows of azaleas. The house had been built for a plantation owner at the turn of the century, and it had all the white marble sumptuousness of late Victorian pride.

There were pillars, and a long flight of steps flanked by urns. It was all very grand, and daunting, if you were susceptible to that sort of thing. There was the usual high-level staff receptionist too, with her hair in a bun and her sleeves rolled up.

That was a trick they all learned from Mountbatten himself. It was thought to suggest efficiency and a no-nonsense attitude. In fact, it tended to increase the number of mosquito-bitten arms, and I noted, with satisfaction, that this particular prim little hussy was no exception.

"You're early," she said, stating the obvious.

I agreed. There was the thin, high whir of a fan and the faint scent of some American perfume. I felt a slight sense of nausea.

"He's watching a film. You could stand at the back and watch," the receptionist suggested.

So I found myself choking back a desire to retch and instead tiptoeing through a huge mahogany doorway into a long gallery lined with oils of British dignitaries in gold frames. A number of them seemed to frown down at me for being late as I glanced around the room.

It had been converted, rather bizarrely, into a temporary cinema. Curtains had been partially drawn over the tall classical window bays, and a group of what looked like eighteenth-century drawing-room chairs had been arranged in concentric circles facing an unrolled screen.

A number of senior officers in full uniform were disposed in these chairs watching the film. Easily recognizable, even from behind and at some distance, were the long crossed legs of Mountbatten himself, extended in front of him in the middle of the front row as he lolled back in elegant relaxation to enjoy his beloved Chaplin.

It was *City Lights*, and I'd arrived in time for the last reels when the tramp won't reveal his identity to the girl he's saved from blindness by paying for her eye operations. I'm sure you know the film. It's a poignant moment.

Mountbatten demonstrated his style the moment the film was over and someone started to draw the curtains. He was on his feet, long and rangy, in immaculate tropical kit, and he came straight up to me as I stood by the door.

"Sorry, Colonel," he said. "I hope you haven't been waiting long."

It was impressive. He knew exactly who I was, or he took the risk of being wrong for the sake of the high reward of being right. It was typical of his methods, as we were all coming to know.

He was shaking hands with officers as they left, smiling beside a potted palm, nodding, and occasionally putting in a word of greeting. He was absolutely at ease, and in command. I began to feel, at first hand, what Yoshida had intuitively realized.

Mountbatten had charisma. He was able to combine a sort of casual naturalness with the grace of a visiting monarch or a famous film star. I was a little dazed, and absorbing this, when I felt his hand on my shoulder.

"We'll stay here," he was saying. "It's a cool place to talk."

The room had emptied, except for a handful of unobtrusive aides. There was a stenographer, and a young soldier with the flap of a pistol holster open, and a man in civilian clothes who might have been a doctor.

I'd been motioned to a chair, all white brocade and rococo curves. It felt stiff and unyielding. A bad sign, I thought. It was very much like having an audience with royalty, except for that incongruous note of the unrolled cinema screen.

Mountbatten had taken another chair, a more comfortable one, it seemed to me in my paranoia, and the stage was apparently set for our interview. I noticed suddenly that we seemed to be alone. I had a sense that the acolytes had withdrawn to a short distance, beyond some invisible line.

"Awfully nice chap," Mountbatten was saying. "He made a film for Edwina and me as a wedding present, you know."

He managed to make it sound as if Chaplin had just left the room, and we were talking about my first impressions of him, as two old friends. It was a royal knack, I thought, and Charles I had had it, and Henry V too, perhaps. It was the sort of charm that men will die for.

"He's a little too sentimental for your generation, I imagine. But his time will come again."

He'd sensed my lack of warmth, I felt, and I shivered. There was something uncanny about his perception.

"Colonel," he was saying, and I saw now that he was moving me inexorably forward through the various stages he'd already planned, "I want to congratulate you in person on the success of your work so far with your agent in Singapore."

"Thank you," I said, flushing, I'm sure, "very much, sir."

He'd had his briefing, and he'd got the facts at his fingertips. He took me through the several heads under which he approved of the operation, and they were all sound, if somewhat flatteringly put. I had no doubt that I was being given some kind of treatment now. I was on my guard.

"So, Colonel," he said at last, "you now want me to withdraw your excellent Major Strand and employ him locally to uproot some Japanese agent here in Kandy."

I took a risk. I felt fairly sure that he was testing my initiative.

"No, sir," I said boldly. "I could withdraw Major Strand on my own authority."

For a moment I thought the ornate cut-glass chandelier above my head would fall and crush me to the floor. I was contradicting Almighty God.

There was silence. Mountbatten was looking at me with that long head of his slightly to one side, as if he were training a gun.

I rushed on. There was nothing else to do.

"I need your authority to prevent the intervention of the Navy in the business of landing Major Strand from the Japanese submarine, sir," I said.

I'd meant to be smooth, and to use cunning, and it had all come out rough, and straight from the heart. I felt a moment's panic, a fractional sense of ruin. And then I saw that Mountbatten was laughing.

"You know, Colonel," he said, and he was letting his tongue flick the top of his palate in a sort of elegant mannerism he had, "I spent the first twenty-one months of this wretched war in a destroyer. I was sunk off Crete in 1941."

180

He was shaking his finger in the air, in a parody of emphasis, or refusal.

"And you're asking me to instruct the whole of the British Navy to put their feet up and let an enemy vessel sail blithely through their blockade. Now is it on? I ask myself. Now is it really on?"

I could see that he didn't want an answer. He'd already designed his next two speeches in his mind, and he didn't want any interruption.

"You can thank your lucky stars, Colonel," he was saying, leaning forward and frowning at me, "that my ship was sunk by a Stuka. And not a bloody submarine."

Outside, on the gravel, there was the sound of a squad presenting arms. I had a curious sense of distance from the world of present hostilities, as if we were talking together in Aldershot, or in Simla in the 1920s. It was all too calm, too much in the tone of Edwardian summers.

I watched Mountbatten as he talked. He looked tall, even when sprawling, as he now did, in a chair. He would always make a clear target, wherever he was. In a crowd it was hard to believe that a dedicated assassin could miss him. He would stand out like a beacon.

I wondered if I was going to persuade him to do what I wanted.

As it happened, I didn't have to. He'd already made up his mind. I don't know why. I suspect it may simply have been the cloak-and-dagger aspect of the operation that took his fancy.

He was a great reader of detective stories, and he'd been a friend, before the war, of Agatha Christie. He'd even suggested the plot for *The Murder of Roger Ackroyd* to her. He had a taste for any kind of mystery, particularly one with a spice of action.

And then perhaps—I've sometimes wondered this in recent years—he was anxious to meet Strand in person. He was fascinated by the danger, and the double life, that Strand had been leading.

At any rate, he'd decided, and he told me there and then. But he gave another explanation, and I have to set it down.

"You're not married, Colonel," he said, making it a question.

"No," I said.

It was 1947 before Mary and I even met, and the wedding took place when Churchill came back to power in the 1950s. I was a bachelor for a long time, in the war and after.

"It makes a difference," Mountbatten said.

I nodded.

"You see the future in more everyday terms," he added. "Children and grandchildren."

There was an awkward pause.

"That sort of thing."

He had risen now, a hard-edged man, like the prow of a longboat.

"The Navy will make it easy for your chap to land," he concluded. "You have my word. I just hope he completes the job."

He shook my hand, and I left. I saw him many times again after that in films and on television, but never again in the flesh. It was hard flesh that he had. I remember the feel of the bones in his cold fingers. It was as if he'd hauled himself, that moment, from the icy, broken waves of the Mediterranean around his dying ship.

It was as if he were already there again, blown to smithereens as he trailed those fingers in the Irish water from the side of his cabin cruiser.

I've remembered that meeting over the years, and what he said. It does make a difference. To be married, I mean. It makes a considerable difference. Even at the age of sixty-nine it makes a difference.

In the last analysis, though, and he knew this himself, the old warrior, there comes a time when you have to walk down the ramp and into the water alone, and there isn't anything else to do except grit your teeth and accept the bombardment for what it is, the final test of a man.

It was Strand who taught us that, in his way. And the hundred thousand who died pressing grenades to their bellies on Okinawa, without surrendering. They, too.

19

It was the smell of boot polish that reminded me this morning. I've always enjoyed brushing my own shoes, even when I had a batman as a young officer in India. It's the business of rolling your sleeves up, and getting the box of cloths and tins out, and drawing a stool forward on the floor. It helps the mind to feel efficient.

I was cleaning my riding boots on the steps of the dairy, hearing Mary behind me in the kitchen making coffee. And suddenly the wrinkles in my forearms had gone and I was five thousand miles and thirty-five years away.

Vonnegut was there under the swinging oil lamp, in his blue Guernsey sweater, with his American frown. There was the sound of the wind from the ocean, and a loose pane of glass was rattling in the window.

I had my own sweater eased up to the elbows, and the squat round brush was poised in my fist. I had one black shoe off and the other on my foot. Over all that space and time, the dull odor of Cherry Blossom was just the same.

It had seemed a strange thing to Vonnegut. He was calmer than I was, perhaps, or he had less imagination. He'd laughed, anyway, when I took the brushes out of my suitcase.

"Colonel," he said, "I don't imagine that Major Strand will be noticing how your boots look in the darkness."

"It clears the thoughts," I told him. "It keeps the nerves cool. And besides, I like my shoes clean, and we have some time to waste."

Vonnegut never liked wasting time. Billiards was one of the civilized rituals of life, and he saw the point. Shoe cleaning was something to be left for servants, and it didn't amuse him.

He was standing staring out the window, although there was nothing to see. It occurred to me that he was considering going out for a walk. Even a swim. He was nervous, all right. More than I was.

"They won't be here for another hour. Why don't you make us a pot of tea," I suggested.

For a moment he didn't seem to have heard. I was beginning to get annoyed by his mixture of tension and distance. He was less good company in the field than at home, and I was sorry I'd had to bring him.

"That's an order, Major," I said very quietly.

It had been the same for the last three hours. We'd arrived at the rendezvous early, driving over the mountains in the Sunbeam Talbot. I'd known it might be a rough journey, and I'd left a good margin for delay.

As it happened, I'd overestimated, and we'd reached the village and then found the cottage at the edge of the bay with plenty of time in reserve. I was pleased about this, and I'd brought the means to fill in my time. I could relax and be ready for whatever might happen when Strand came ashore.

Vonnegut hadn't appreciated my caution. He was a man for the last-minute spurt, oozing energy on the final stretch to the tape. It was coming out of him now like ticking from a burst sofa. He was starting to look the worse for wear.

We'd discussed who was to come at some length. I could have sent Brundall or Clark, and stayed behind in Colombo. Technically, that might have been the secure thing to do. If anything were to go wrong, and it all turned into a shooting match, the man who ought to survive, in terms of the operation's future, was me.

But that wasn't really the essence. I couldn't resist the

184

chance of briefing Strand in person. This was the climax of my whole coup, and I had to savor it at first hand.

Unfortunately, although I could order Clark and Brundall to stay behind, and with good reason, I had ultimately no authority to do the same with Vonnegut. I had rank to command him in action, but the power to secure or deny his presence at any vital conference lay in the hands of the men in Washington.

As long as the dollars flowed in to finance us, and they were still doing so, the Americans were going to insist on having a finger in the pie. In practice, this meant, quite simply, that Vonnegut was able to insist on access to any documents he chose. He could also demand, as of right, a seat at any meetings he chose.

So he'd come with me, taking his turn with the driving, making the conversation I was now starting to become so very bored with about his family in Houston. A little of American home life goes a long way, I'd learned.

I dipped my brush in the soft black cake of the polish and smeared a new layer on the toe cap. I tried to force my mind away from this drafty little room and back over the circumstances that had brought me to it.

I began to brush with slow, even strokes, listening to the chink of china as Vonnegut sullenly made the tea in the chipped white cups we'd found under the drainboard. Like all sequestered houses for these operations, this one was badly furnished.

The signals to Jimmy Fong, agreeing to what Strand had asked for, had been rapidly dispatched after my return from the visit to Mountbatten at Kandy. Further signals had soon confirmed the date the submarine would be aiming to make its landfall, and we'd suggested a suitable point on the eastern coast.

At first there had been talk of running the submarine down the western coast, so that Strand would have an easier route over the mountains, but the navy experts insisted that this would enormously increase the chances of accident.

As it was, in those days, with asdic as highly developed as it had become, it only needed a trigger-happy or misinformed destroyer captain and the Japanese submarine could be depth-charged to smithereens.

The Navy were prepared to offer some reasonable guarantee of noninterference along the coast south of Trincomalee, but nowhere else. I accepted their offer. It was the best we could get.

So we sorted out a quiet little bay with the help of a friendly captain in the Merchant Navy, and the navigation instructions were duly signaled through. By now, the possibilities of error were becoming considerable, and I was worried that the submarine might end up landing Strand several hundred miles off course in either direction.

We'd found the fisherman's cottage through a local contact in opium smuggling. It had been used regularly to take in loads of raw poppies off junks from Bangkok, and it had the advantage of a powerful searchlight that could be manhandled onto an outcrop of rock and shone directly out to sea.

According to our contact, who was rich enough to be trusted in this, it could be seen for miles. As soon as we'd arrived, I'd made sure the searchlight was working, and we'd got it run out and fixed in position.

The rules for making contact were simple. The rendezvous time was nine o'clock, and we were going to switch on the beam five minutes before the hour. If the submarine was there, it would signal back, and in due course a dinghy would come ashore and land Strand in the bay.

In the event of no signal being received from the submarine, we would wait for an hour and then repeat our signal. This process would be continued until contact was finally made.

Such was the plan. It made no allowance, of course, as is the custom with such plans, for the possibility of the submarine failing to arrive at all. It was tacitly assumed that at some, in fact unspecified, time, the patience of the home team would be exhausted, and the mission would, as it were, be suspended.

So there we were, Vonnegut and I, waiting. I finished brushing my left shoe and put it back on. I glanced at my watch. It was a quarter to nine. Vonnegut was draining his cup of tea. The loose pane was still rattling in the window.

"Let's go," I said.

Outside, the wind hit us with some force as we walked along the headland. I was glad we'd decided on civilian clothes, and the Guernsey sweaters.

Beside the light we kneeled together, staring out to sea. I glanced again at my watch and decided we'd give them a beam.

"Switch on, Major," I said.

I was prepared to have Vonnegut with me, but I was determined that he was going to do the dirty work, even if it was only a matter of turning on a searchlight.

I heard the click of the switch and saw the long beam spear out across the waves. There was a long silence while I counted out the seconds. Twenty, thirty, fifty. One minute. Two, three, four.

"Switch off, Major," I said.

There was a moment of utter blackness. I was dazzled by having stared into the beam, and it took a little time for my eyes to refocus. It was Vonnegut who spoke first.

"Sweet holy Christ," he said softly. "They're there, Colonel."

I felt a lump come in my throat. Against all the odds, it had worked. There was a tiny dot, far out to sea, blinking to us.

It was Strand, after three years, returning in triumph to the bosom that had nourished him. But this time there was a difference. The fangs were out. The viper had arrived for the kill.

Vonnegut was ahead of me, racing for the beach. He had his automatic out, and I'm sure the safety catch was off. I did the same for mine, legging it over the pebbles and then the wet sand. I wasn't expecting trouble, but you never knew.

Vonnegut, I'm sure, had anticipated some sort of substitute for Strand, who would assassinate us on the spot. In a curious way, his paranoia was justified. But, like all Dallas paranoia, it was allayed too easily by an English accent. The moment he heard Strand speak, he felt safe.

Now he was down on one knee, behind a rock, the barrel of

his gun aligned in the direction of the submarine. He couldn't see anything, of course, but he was alert for the slightest sound.

I knelt beside him, panting. He was very fit, and he'd outrun me by several yards. I smelled the faint odor of something he'd used to drown his body odor, and then I let my other senses merge into a single-minded concentration of hearing.

They would be using special oars, of course, and they wouldn't speak. I imagined two men would row the dinghy, for speed, and in case of ambush, and Strand would be ready to wade the last few yards on foot.

In the event, that's exactly what happened. They were even quieter than we thought they'd be, and the first noise I heard was the swish of water on moving legs. Vonnegut heard the same, and he had his torch on in his left hand and his gun still leveled in his right.

The beam splayed over the water, catching and passing the single wading man and moving over to focus on the withdrawing rubber boat. There were two men in it, one rowing, fast and skillfully, with long, low, silent strokes, the blades curving and slicing in flat arcs across the waves. The other man was crouched facing us, his finger on the trigger of a submachine gun. The beam hovered on his face, intent and still, and I felt his discipline, even across those twenty yards of water.

He was waiting for the first sign of trouble before he fired. He didn't blink, or shout, or smile. He just sat very still, a difficult, compact target, with his hands ready, if necessary, to pump out bullets until he died.

Then the torch moved, and I saw the wading man again, the water down to his ankles now, his hands over his head supporting a suitcase to keep it dry. I hadn't seen him for many, many months, but the face hadn't changed. It was Strand all right.

"Put out the light," I said. "It's Strand."

We rose together from behind the rock, and Vonnegut slipped the torch back in his pocket as Strand approached over the shingle. He was a dim outline now in the sudden darkness, a swish of clothes and a crunch of pebbles.

I stepped forward, leaving Vonnegut a pace behind.

188

"Major Strand," I said, extending my hand, "welcome home."

He'd put his case down, incongruously it seemed, as if we were meeting at a railway station.

"Good evening, Colonel," he was saying, and I felt the cold, strong pressure of his fingers in mine. "It's been a long time."

"Let's go up to the house," said Vonnegut.

He was reaching to pick up Strand's suitcase, but Strand had already taken it and was walking ahead along the beach. They'd fed him well, I remember thinking. He looked just as athletic as he'd done in Clapham.

In the little stone-flagged kitchen, under the still-swinging oil lamp, I made the introductions.

"Major Vonnegut," I said. "Of U.S. Army Intelligence. Major Strand."

They didn't like each other. I could feel that at once. Strand was annoyed to see Vonnegut there at all. He wanted to be alone with me. Vonnegut sensed that Strand was contemptuous of him and wasn't going to disguise it. He was right.

"I see," said Strand. "I'm working for Uncle Sam now."

"Dead right, buddy," said Vonnegut. "You are."

Their voices met and clashed. I marveled at how Strand managed to sound so nastily public school. He couldn't have spoken a word of English for two and a half years. The very edge of his vowels made Vonnegut slide from his usual drawl to a curt Yankee shortness.

I decided that I had to take matters in hand. There was a job to be done, and we needed a facade of good manners. I didn't like Vonnegut's presence any more than Strand did, but it had to be accepted.

"Sit down, both of you," I said in my best parade-ground style.

I went and stood facing them with my back to the sink. I was angry, and I let it show.

"Look, gentlemen," I said very crisply, "there will be no bickering and no disagreements. Strand, I want you to realize that Major Vonnegut is an essential part of this operation, and a valued and trusted colleague. Vonnegut, you will accept the fact that Major Strand is riding point in this unit, and in that position is entitled to whatever license of speech or manner the exceptional pressures on his nerves may demand. Is that clear?"

It was very clear, and they both shut up. We got down to business. For the first hour, as we sipped tea and listened to the wind, Strand went over the main details of the Japanese assassination plan as he'd already, more briefly, conveyed them through Jimmy Fong.

"The basic points are these," he concluded. "One, it's a *kamikaze* operation. I'm not expected to return. Two, there's a backup. Someone locally is in place to provide me with support and pick up the pieces if anything goes wrong."

"But not to make the kill," said Vonnegut thoughtfully. "I mean, if you get caught."

"I don't know," said Strand. "In theory, no. He's not employed on that basis. But in practice, who can tell? They've stiffened my own resolution by insisting that it's entirely up to me. But it may be that this local lad is more lethal than I've been given to understand."

"I'm sure he is," I said. "It seems certain to me that they're banking on a second assassination attempt if yours goes wrong. The local man may be even more ready for a suicide shot than you are."

Strand was looking at me. There was a slight smile on his face.

"You bet he is," he said.

He was a good actor, all right. I'll say that for him. It even made Vonnegut snort with laughter for a moment.

"They really believe you'll do it," he said, making it a question. "I mean, they really believe a guy would sacrifice all chance of survival to get a close-up shot?"

"They're desperate now," said Strand, stroking his nails. "The Japanese Army is full of young soldiers who would do this without thinking. It's a question of the economic use of manpower. One certain casualty will be thought a small price for the death of the British commander in chief. Makes a curious kind of sense, you know."

190

He was very cool, very English, that night. He was playing with Vonnegut in his way, taking even bigger risks than he needed to. It was a clever, deadly performance.

"Look," he said, later on, opening his case. "It's a fiendish instrument they've invented."

He showed us the adapted camera he'd been given. I hoisted the heavy metal in my hand. It had a long silencer, designed to be screwed on like a telephoto lens. The barrel was fitted inside the leather sides of an old Zeiss Ikon case. You pressed a button, as if to adjust the focus, and a butt and trigger mechanism dropped through a hole in the base. You could fire, with a soft plop, slam up the butt, and appear to be taking pictures again.

"It works all right," said Strand. "Believe you me. I've used it in target practice. There's a bit more noise than one might like, ideally, but I doubt if anyone would notice in the midst of the loyal cheering."

It impressed us both. With one of those, an unsuspected man could get within yards of the Supremo. He'd have a good chance of making a kill, even if he had to arrange his getaway. If he was willing to forget about that, his hopes of a successful shot would have to be rated as high as nine out of ten.

"Supposing someone else had one of these," I said slowly. "The local man at Kandy, I mean. We'd have a hell of a problem."

Strand was shaking his head.

"It's unlikely," he said. "This thing was a highly complex, one-off job, from what I hear. But I take your point. The mole has got to be dug up and eliminated."

"The only question," I said, "is how."

Strand pursed his lips. He elaborated the situation. The Japanese, with characteristic ingenuity, had more or less made him self-sufficient. He was carrying a false passport in the name of San Chin Hu, a Chinese photographer working from an address in Colombo. He had a set of business cards, a file of sample prints, boxes of unused film.

Most important of all, he had the camera-gun and several rounds of ammunition. As far as could be seen, he wasn't, except in an emergency, going to need any support from the local agent at all.

"He'll be watching me," Strand explained. "If he thinks I need help, he'll show his face. If he thinks I'm doing fine, he'll keep out of sight."

Vonnegut was unscrewing the cap of a bottle. He took a quick swig and passed it to me. I glanced at the label. Wild Turkey. It was good stuff, raw and warming in the throat. I took another pull and passed it to Strand.

"So there's no basic plan for contact," Vonnegut said.

"None," said Strand.

There was a silence, and we listened to the loose pane, rattling, rattling, irritatingly, in the window.

"Jesus," said Vonnegut.

"I'll sniff around," said Strand. "I may be lucky. He may appear any time. He may have some last-minute orders for me from Singapore."

"He may," I said. "But he may not. You're going to have to send out some kind of distress signal."

Strand nodded.

"I know," he said. "He'll respond, of course. But only if he's sure it's vital. And that means waiting until the last possible moment."

He got up and went to the kitchen cupboard, opening doors, looking for something.

"Are there any biscuits?" he said, and then found a tin, and turned, munching. "I know it's a risk," he said. "But there's only one time we're sure to get him. And that's when I'm there at the Temple of the Tooth, waiting to fire. He's bound to be watching. He'll show his face if I signal some problem with the working of the camera. He'll know how to put it right, and fast, at the last minute."

It was awe-inspiring, looking back. He was buying himself a free run right up to the moment he was planning to make the kill.

I watched him brushing crumbs off his drying blue suit. He was twisting the British and American Intelligence services around his little finger, and there wasn't a damn thing to be done about it.

Oh, yes, you were clever, Strand. Very clever. And never more so than that night in the fisherman's cottage on the coast south of Trincomalee. You were the perfect salesman, with your case of samples there on the worn teak table in front of you.

You and your mole. You and your local mole, deep in the earth, biding his time to show his snout and help you to the kill.

That was the man in all our thoughts that night as we finished the Wild Turkey and let you go. That was the man who stood behind you and threw his shadow along your path when we dropped you off on the road home toward Colombo. That was the man who watched over your destiny now as you reached out for your final triumph outside the Temple at Kandy.

I would see you again. But only briefly. It felt like our last meeting as I watched you walk away in the dusty blur of the head lamps.

It felt like the end of something. In a way, it was. Our final encounter, only five days later, was a kind of aftermath. It added nothing. It only took away.

"That sure is one helluva cool guy," said Vonnegut as we drove back through the mountains. "Let's hope we can find his local contact."

"It won't be easy," I said.

"No," agreed Vonnegut. "It won't."

The sun was rising over to our right, through a bank of dense screw pines. It was Wednesday, July 19, 1944, and the sun would rise only four more times before the end of the festival.

20

It was the ninth day when Strand made his final preparations. They didn't involve the loading of his false camera with a clip of ammunition. They never had. The Zeiss Ikon had been devised as a red herring right from the start.

The real assassination plan was very different and appallingly simple. It was one that required patience, and a certain tact, and unusual coolness of nerve. But Strand, as we know, had all these.

I know from his diary how he'd had to exercise these qualities. He walked along beside the lake that night and reached the temple in the darkness. The air was heavy, he tells us, as in so many Buddhist temples, with the smell of long-melted candle wax and the stale aftermath of incense.

Several of the priests, in their saffron robes, had already noticed the quiet young Chinese with the box of camera equipment, and one or two had nodded to him as he came in. They'd seen him many times over the days of the festival, and they were used to his reverential presence in the temple.

At first, he'd seemed just like all the other tourists, humping the square box of his camera, and the flashlight, and the awkward tripod. There were so many strangers in the town for the Perahera.

They'd had visits from snake charmers, gazing in faked awe at the votive stones in their bowls, drawing the sleek rubbery skin of the trained pythons through their skillful fingers. They'd had visits from astrologers, pouring cards between their dark palms or rattling old bones in their narrow cedarwood boxes.

Dancers would pass through to enjoy a moment's coolness after their fierce gyrations to the beat of the local drums. Jugglers would squat in silence before the golden idols, watching the twisted arms of the Buddha as if to learn some secret of balance from his poise.

The temple had lain on its muddy ground beside the lake for two hundred years, and it had seen many holy visitors and many secular ones. Its wooden floors, and its robed guardians, the priests, were well aware of the varieties of human nature and the broad range of reasons for men's attendance at sacred places.

Usually, they came out of base motives. They came from vulgar curiosity, or to ask for some boon or favor in return for the promise of better behavior or larger contributions to the temple's coffers.

Even the priests were often venal or conniving, wanting some extra sign of attention they might carry away as proof of their special sanctity. It was rare to come across a genuine face, a man who was there in a fine humility of spirit, or in search of some real peace of mind or some insight into the truths of the world.

Most visitors came only once. They made their pilgrimage, or asked their questions, and that was the end of it. The little Chinese with the huge camera was different.

The first day he took pictures, and went all over the temple to find good places to photograph from. The monks indulged him, and were helpful. They didn't expect to see him again.

But he came back. He gave them sepia photographs he'd taken, some of them very elegant, and he asked them many questions, not only about the temple but about the nature of the world and the state of the soul. He was searching for something.

Every day he came to the temple and prayed. Sometimes he would stay for hours on his knees before a smoky image or at the foot of the steps up to the balcony where the sacred tooth was kept in its casket.

They'd let him go into the little square room where it was laid in state, waiting for the procession. He'd taken snapshots of it from several angles. He'd admired, and stood in silence. They respected his sense of wonder and his evident emotion.

It was real enough. I know that now, as I read over Strand's account of those many visits in his diary. He was looking for something important in his visits to the temple, and not just for the best way to accomplish his mission. There was that as well, of course, but his motives ran under and behind this.

He had to be sure of himself, and to know his reasons for what he was going to do. It mattered to him, as the meaning of life matters to a man dying of cancer.

Strand knew he would never return to Singapore alive. He would either succeed in his mission, and eventually be captured and executed as a spy; or he would fail, and he would die. He was ready for that, and he'd made arrangements.

In the little bamboo villa he'd rented across the lake, he had a bare space prepared on the upper floor. There on the wall he'd hung the *kakemono* Yoshida had brought for him from Osaka, a thin scroll in *sumi-ee* with a house under a mountain and a river running by to the left.

On the mat below the scroll he had a narrow vase, and he changed the three lines of the flowers every day. The sword was there, too, and the fold of tissue paper, and the white kimono he would wear, but for the moment all those were laid away in a chest of drawers.

He went quietly through the long darkness of the temple now. Outside there was the feverish climactic beat of a drummer, and a troupe of Kandyan dancers practicing by torchlight on the temple steps. The monks were unconcerned. They watched Strand walk along, with measured, religious pace, beside the statues. They soon lost interest, turning back to the whirling excitements of the dance. He'd chosen a good moment for what he had to do.

He thought about it, so he tells us in his diary, as he climbed the eighteen steps to the square room where the relic was kept. He knew that the method of assassination that he'd chosen was the right one, as he'd always known, from the moment he and Yoshida had first discussed it in Singapore.

The camera-gun was a false lead. It was beautiful, in its way. It might even have worked if Strand had got close enough for a shot. It certainly sounded persuasive, and Vonnegut, for one, in his dry memoir, still believes it might have been lethal, in the right hands.

But it wasn't, from the very beginning, the weapon Strand intended to use. He had more than photographic equipment and cartridges in that ancient suitcase he was carrying when he came off the submarine. He had the means to construct a bomb.

At the top of the steps, with his equipment in his hands, Strand paused. Ahead of him were the tall, heavy doors that marked the locked Shrine of the Tooth. They were never opened except by one of the temple priests, with a special set of keys. Normally, the tooth would have been inaccessible.

However, as Strand in his careful researches had discovered, for the nine days prior to the sacred procession, the tooth lay in state in a small private room to the left of the shrine. It was released from its seven concentric caskets and placed on a bed of velvet inside a single golden case like a small beehive.

Priests and visitors who were unusually privileged were allowed—as Strand himself had been—to enter the little room and adore the golden case in quiet isolation. No one had noticed the pad of wax that Strand had slipped into the door lock.

Now, as he glanced rapidly down in the darkness, he made sure that he was unobserved. He tried the key he'd had made. It turned, very smoothly, and with a swift step he was inside the room.

He unlocked the suitcase. Inside, there was an adapted hand grenade with a length of tape holding down the trigger in place of the usual pin. There was also a lead weight with a small ring in the top, a length of adhesive tape, and a pair of nail scissors. He stood for a moment, listening, with the suitcase in his hand. There was the casket, the little golden beehive, on its carved table in the middle of the room. Outside, he could hear the beat of drums. Inside the temple, nothing.

He went forward and laid his hands on the lid. I can guess the way he must have felt. He must have steeled himself even to finger the cold metal of the exterior. No one except a Buddhist monk was supposed to have done that for eight hundred years. It was a kind of sacrilege, a vandalism.

"Forgive me," he says he breathed, half aloud, in the gloom.

He was offering what he had in penance. He had already crossed his own final bridge. There was no going back. He would die, one way or another, in the next twenty-four hours. His life was a sacrifice.

So he gritted his teeth, there in the darkness, and he lifted the lid and laid it aside. After that, each further step was a logical sequence of the one before.

The tooth was nested in a cushion of velvet in a tiny jade bowl. With both hands, as if performing some ritual, Strand picked up the bowl and laid it down on the table. Then he took a lacquer box from his pocket and shook the tooth into it.

With the scissors, Strand cut a length of adhesive tape and attached one end of the tape to the small ring in the lead weight. Then he took up the domed lid of the beehive casket and stuck the other end of the tape to the central point of its inner side.

With more pieces of tape he made a system of secure crisscrosses and then inspected the result. It looked fine. The weight hung like the clapper of a bell two inches below the bottom of the dome.

Unwinding the restraining tape on the hand grenade, Strand kept the trigger down with his thumb and slid the mechanism onto the base of the casket. Then slowly, very slowly, he allowed the lead weight under the dome to settle down into position, and slid out, stage by stage, his down-pressing thumb.

Then he secured the lid. The bomb was ready. When the lid was lifted in the presence of the Lord Admiral, the weight would be pulled out of position and the grenade would be detonated.

It was a savage, elegant plan. The very act of revelation, the very ritual of honor, were themselves to become the agents of destruction. Both as a practical device and as a symbolic gesture, the consequences would resound around the world.

It was the night Strand planted his bomb that we heard the news. I was reading in bed, the final volume of *The Tale of Genji*. It was my second time through. Clark was pale with fever, and he sat down on the edge of the bed, without asking, before he spoke. His voice was very quiet, as if he thought someone might overhear.

So very many times, I remember thinking, it was Clark who bore the ill tidings. He was the gods' messenger, the prophet of doom. The reading lamp shone down on his knotted hands now, and they were trembling.

"He's a traitor," he said.

That was all he could say for a long time. I tilted his face up and stared into his eyes. Then I swung my legs down to the floor and went over to the chest of drawers and poured him a stiff measure of Haig.

We sat together on the edge of the bed, and he gulped the Scotch, and the story came out in full.

I wonder, when I look now at the fatal letter here in the file, how ruthless men acquire their Achilles' heels. We all have them. Even Hitler, we know now, had a soft spot for his pet Alsatian, and Admiral Onishi showed his tender side with his evening primroses.

It was Japanese of Strand to be hard, and he was hard like a jewel is, more hard than any man I've known. But he had his weakness, if weakness it was. He admired loyalty, and that meant he admired loyalty in others.

Ogawa had been an officer in the Kempei Tai, as he was himself. They'd knelt in Ogawa's flat together and drunk tea and examined sword guards.

It wasn't a *kamikaze* operation. It didn't have to be. Ogawa was a senior, experienced officer. He could still be invaluable to the Kempei Tai in another posting. He had to survive.

So the plan to sneak him underground had arisen. An arrangement with another brothel, perhaps. The diary is curiously reticent about the details. It may, after all, have been Strand's initiative.

Alas, the pull of Su Lin's memory was too strong for security in the long run. It revealed the truth, and brought about Strand's downfall.

We can reconstruct the circumstances fairly easily from the dry report that Jimmy Fong sent out to us over the radio. It's filled in very well by Su Lin's own account, as she gave it later on.

The fat major with the cow-catcher teeth arriving in the middle of the night. The interview in the back room, Su Lin reclining under her beige shawl on the ottoman.

"I have a letter for you."

Su Lin cagey, Su Lin closing her eyes a shade.

"Yes, Major."

The fat major's eyes running up and down her bare thigh. His gloved hand on his sword hilt.

"From a dead hero," he says, back very straight.

"Show me," Su Lin says.

She goes to the other side of the room with it, her long spine only an offer now. She reads quickly. She jumps, as she would inevitably jump, to the wrong conclusion.

"My dear one," the letter says. "I want you to know I kept this picture with me until I died. We had fine times together, in other days. I am dead now, and my soul has gone to the Warrior's Shrine. I shall wait there for you, like a spring swallow for its mate. I bear no ill will to the living, least of all to you."

Of course, he signed it, with a rich flourish, it seems to me, examining the ink here under the camellias in the conservatory. With a flare of real grace, at the end.

The photograph is here too. Of Su Lin, naked to the waist, with high heels, and a whip in her hand. It's pinned to the back of the letter now, as perhaps it was then.

I see her turning in the House of Happiness, very grand suddenly, and upright, drawing the thin lacy strip of silk around her shoulders, a kind of widow in her bite of grief.

"Thank you," she says.

"He died on Guam," the major says. "Very brave. Fighting to the last."

"We were going to be married," Su Lin volunteers.

She sees the windmills at Thurne, their sails turning in a high wind, the smoke coming from the chimneys of thatched cottages, men in red coats on horseback following foxes over dikes. Tears form in her eyes and she feels her shoulders quiver.

The fat major smiles, a cynical smile.

"Doubtless," he agrees.

He comes forward, reaches out an arm to fondle her breast. She ducks aside neatly, knowing how to do this, knowing how to avoid any trouble.

"So sorry, Major," she says with a coy, carefully affected leer. "I'm expecting a visitor. Your colonel."

The fat major is nonplussed. He doesn't believe her, but he daren't risk it. He nods, he fingers his sword hilt, he goes.

I imagine her then alone amidst the erotic, ramshackle decor of their first encounter. Walking aimlessly to and fro, picking up ornaments and putting them down. Touching herself gently, and remembering.

Falling, perhaps, on the bed or the sofa, in a tremor, and then a tempest, of weeping. Michael, Michael, Michael, she thinks. Oh, Michael, my poor Michael, to die so far from home. To die like a Japanese, in a foreign uniform. And no one to know.

She picks up the letter again, goes over the dull, formal phrasing, the flattened expressions of emotion he would know were certain to pass the sharp eyes of the military censor. It doesn't sound like the Michael she knew, and of course it wouldn't.

The tears come again. She fingers the ink of the signature, the flowing *kanji* for Kato Ogawa, the name he would still have to use if the letter were ever to reach her. She turns the letter over, glances at the photograph of herself.

Some time passes. The diamond wristwatch ticks on her wrist. In another room, a colleague simulates the ascending scale of erotic abandon. The photograph begins to tremble in her hand.

Su Lin gets up. She goes over to a little lacquer cabinet and unlocks a drawer marked with her name. She takes out a bundle of blue letters tied with a ribbon. Unfolding one of these, she inspects a signature. She compares it minutely with the signature on the letter the fat major has brought.

"Ogawa," she says aloud.

She studies the photograph. It reminds her of one she had posed for long ago. Something about the hair, the dress. It was taken before she knew Michael. By Kato. Yes, by Kato, like so many other pictures of her.

Michael had several. He liked them. He found them erotic, ingenious. Yes, but this one was different. It was coming back to her. She remembered now.

The small, neat figure of Kato Ogawa with a piece of film and a cigarette lighter in his hand.

"My masterpiece," he was saying, laughing. "I want there to be only one of these. My own."

The dark celluloid curling, and the foul smell, as he burned the original negative.

It must have taken her hours to accept the consequences. The signature was Ogawa's own. The picture was one of which only he had a copy. The letter had an odd reference to bearing no ill will to the living. It all added up to a clear conclusion.

Ogawa had not been killed by Michael Strand. He had somehow been smuggled out of Singapore, alive, and had survived to fight and die in the Japanese defense of Guam.

It sank in, at last. Su Lin put on her coat, and she went around to see Jimmy Fong, ringing his bell at two o'clock in the morning and rousing him from a dream of lurid ecstasy beside the snoring bulk of his heavy wife.

Between them, they went over the whole of her story. They talked over low cups of spiced tea until dawn. They assessed and calculated. They came to a firm decision. There was only one thing to do.

So Jimmy Fong passed on the evidence over the radio to

Clark at nine o'clock that night, and reserved his judgment. He didn't need to.

It was only an hour before Vonnegut learned that Strand had disappeared from his bare hotel. There was little need for deduction, little time for crying over milk spilled. I had to act.

21

You get a rough ride in a jeep. We'd bounced up the winding mountain road to Kandy in the middle of the night, and our bodies were crying out with fatigue in the small hours when we swung past the Temple of the Tooth over to our left.

Brundall had been at the wheel, with Vonnegut up front. Vonnegut was doing his General Patton act that day, with a baseball cap over his eyes and a lot of chewing gum in his jaws.

In the back seat were Clark and I, lurching against each other on all the bends. Clark had a faint odor of diarrhea about him, or I thought he had, and the contacts didn't improve my temper.

I was worse than irritable by the time we unbent our legs in the muddy square at Kandy at five o'clock in the morning. The police had been alerted, and there was a bleary-eyed young Indian sergeant out to greet us.

He managed a fairly extravagant salute parody, the sort of thing you used to see in Giles cartoons, and then we were all trooping after him down a curry-smelling corridor into his crammed office behind the National Bank of Malaya.

There were other policemen, all wearing turbans, and a general air of hectic submissiveness.

"Very difficult problem you have here, Colonel," the sergeant was saying. "There is a most numerous Chinese population currently in Kandy. Many people, you see, are coming for the festival."

He said this as if we might not have heard of the festival. Clark had his head in his hands. He looked very sick.

"You are wanting the lavatory accommodation, perhaps," the young sergeant suggested. "My colleague will show you where to go."

Vonnegut leaned back on a crowded rolltop desk and chewed his gum. Brundall tried to look wide-awake and keen. There was a brief silence, broken by a lewd flushing, and then a sheepish Clark reappeared and settled onto a walnut stool in a corner.

I began to feel my sense of the surreal getting out of hand. There was too little sense of menace and urgency, combined with too much traditional imperial sloth. I took a deep breath. After all, it was early in the morning.

"You've checked all the hotels," I said, for the sake of something to say.

"Most certainly we have checked the hotels, Colonel," the sergeant agreed. "Unfortunately, very many people are accommodating themselves in private rooms. With friends, you see. And some are sleeping out of doors in this excellent weather we are having. Some people, too, are moving from one place of accommodation to another. Very difficult, therefore, to be sure of where everyone is."

I saw his point. There were probably tens of thousands of temporary visitors in the Kandy area, and he had a staff of nine policemen to check them over. It would have been hard enough to get hold of anyone living quite openly. Someone trying to keep out of sight had a perfect opportunity.

"You've circulated Strand's description," I suggested.

This time the sergeant allowed himself a thin smile.

"Now, Colonel," he said, shaking his head, "you are knowing as well as I do, I think, how all Chinese are looking the same to our people. This is not an easy matter."

"But a Chinese in a smart Western suit," I persisted. "With a lot of camera equipment. There can't be a hundred of those around."

"Four or five," the sergeant said, reaching for a crumpled yellow file. "Here are their names and descriptions."

I leafed through the flimsy pages. The faces that stared up at mine were all equally inscrutable. But none of them was Michael Strand's. I handed the file back.

"You've done very well, Sergeant," I said, rising to my feet. "This is a difficult assignment. You understand, however," I added, frowning down on him, "this is a matter affecting the future of the British Empire. His Majesty the King is personally concerned with the life and safe conduct of his viceroy, Lord Louis Mountbatten. He will be suitably grateful for any special help you and your hardworking men can provide."

Vonnegut was yawning. But it was worth laying it on thick. I could feel the sergeant swelling with importance.

"It's up to you, Sergeant," I ended. "Now tell me where I can find some breakfast and use a telephone."

It wasn't easy. Word had gone ahead to the Hotel Suisse to expect a party of four first thing in the morning, but the night porter emerged from a dark cubbyhole in his pajamas.

"Breakfast," he repeated, rubbing his eyes.

It was obvious that the best we could get for the next hour and a half would be some ersatz coffee and a plate of Crawford's biscuits. I installed myself in the main lounge, a desolation of lonely rattan and potted palms, and we made our dispositions.

"There's nothing for it but luck and keeping our eyes open," I said. "When Molly gets here on the nine o'clock train with Walpole and Billington that will make seven of us who know Strand by sight. Seven pairs of eyes. That's all we've got between us and a bullet in Louis Mountbatten's brain."

The biscuits arrived, a forlorn row on a flowered plate, and a tall silver pot of coffee to wash them down. The porter hovered, and I shooed him away with a handful of rupees.

"For the moment," I said, as I poured a brown stream of the stuff into each of our exiguous cups, "I want you, Brundall, to take the quarter between the temple and the mountains. Clark, you'll have the rest, from here to the station and the square.

206

Just use your eyes and look at faces. And report back here at ten-thirty. When the others arrive, we can make the areas smaller."

I chewed a ridiculous ginger biscuit, stale and with a hint of mold. I must have been very tired.

"Vonnegut," I said, "I want you to go everywhere. Forget about faces. Just ask questions about photographers."

"We've got to find the bastard," said Vonnegut.

I looked at my watch. It was very quiet in the huge lounge, and our voices were echoing in the Victorian Buddhist ceiling.

"Look," I said. "It's going to get easier as it gets more dangerous. There's no point in kidding ourselves. Put yourselves into Strand's shoes. What would you do all day today?"

"I'd lie very low at home and rest," said Brundall. "But it doesn't follow that Strand will. He may have some plan to get himself into a good position for the shot."

"Let's hope so," I said. "It gives us a better chance of setting eyes on him. But remember: if we don't, the crucial time is going to be shortly before and after the climax of the festival. When Mountbatten's here, and in public view, he's bound to show his face to make the kill."

"It's too dangerous," Clark put in. "At ten o'clock tonight, when they open the casket and show the tooth, the temple and the grounds will be milling with a crowd of perhaps a hundred thousand people. There's a full moon, but it won't make every face in the crowd shine crystal-clear. Nor will the torches. He'll be able to skulk very close in complete darkness. And make his getaway in darkness too."

"It's worse than that," said Vonnegut quietly. "It's a *kamikaze* operation, remember. He won't be bothering about his getaway. He'll come in close, and he'll go on shooting until we stop him."

It was like the defense of Singapore all over again. Our guns were all facing out to sea, expecting a naval attack. And the enemy was poised to come south by land, through the jungle.

We were going to be looking for a man trying to kill Mountbatten with a camera-gun, while the danger lay, all the

207

time, inside the sacred beehive that was going to be raised and opened in the C-in-C's face, a Pandora's box of lethal horror, on the steps of the temple.

"There's one last thing," I said, finishing my fourth cup. "I've got to phone Mountbatten's HQ and warn him to stand well back from any photographers."

But I didn't have much faith in my chances. When I did get through to his HQ at last, at half-past eight, squatting on a high splintery stool behind a folding V-door in the hotel reception, there was no one to receive my warning except a frozen-voiced Yorkshire corporal.

Later in the day, I got an interview, but not with the great man himself. The war was making demands that day, and then he had to dress for the festival. It was a mean, nut-faced little brigadier I was seen by, and he spent his time paring his nails while he listened.

"Old boy," he said when I'd finished, "you know what Louis's like. He doesn't scare easily. I'll do what I can."

I doubt if he did. I doubt, anyway, if anyone or anything would have altered Mountbatten's public style. He'd have gone out there as he did, whatever the risks. I admire that. He had guts.

So the tenth day of the Perahera wore on. The sun came out, and a lot of people walked in it and enjoyed the air and the spectacle. The astrologers told their fortunes, and the snake charmers played with their pythons, and the sellers of betel nuts and little sweet cakes and strange teas and juices all made their profits and pleased their clients.

The crowds were everywhere, and through the crowds, red-eyed and vigilant, walked Molly Jenkins, fat and waddling, with her knitting under her arm; and Corporal Walpole, stolid and frowning; and Billington, still with his terrible acne and his proneness to mosquito bites and itching; and Brundall, like a fox-hunting car salesman; and Vonnegut, like Eisenhower; and Major Clark, sick with nausea and consumed with a lurid bitterness of spirit and an aching need for vengeance.

And all day Michael Strand sat cross-legged at home in his villa, in front of his *tokonoma*, meditating in his white robe. In the distance, across the lake, he heard the sound of the festival. And he knew that the hour would soon come. He had only to stay indoors and wait.

At twelve o'clock we held a conference. I had a back room at the Hotel Suisse now, with a grotesque neo-Elizabethan sideboard and a sluggish overhead fan that seemed to be just on the edge of strike action. It was supposed to be cool in the mountains, but we were all feeling the heat.

I spent my time pacing up and down with a rhinoceros-hide fly whisk and trying to control my temper with Vonnegut.

"There's one thing going for us," he kept on saying. "He doesn't know we're on his tail."

Molly was knitting. She consulted some abstruse pattern.

"I wonder," she murmured. "He certainly seems to be keeping out of sight."

She seemed to be about to add something else when Brundall arrived, late and breathless. I poured him a tumbler of iced wine. We had a bucket of the stuff, awful but cooling.

"Look," I said, as I'd said before. "I'm assuming there's no local agent. It was all a red herring. But he can't know that we know that."

I paused.

"As John says," I went on, using Vonnegut's Christian name for the first time, "we may well assume he doesn't know we're on his tail. That may help us. But, unfortunately, it won't help us until the last few minutes. He's going to keep out of sight. He'll have made his final preparations. He'll be resting, and he'll be calming his mind. It's the Japanese way."

They all knew it as well as I did. We had to go on searching, but we knew it was just a waste of time. It was keeping our nerves from breaking, that was all.

We were all trained, even Walpole and Billington, in the classic school. We'd done our courses on patience and vigilance, on how to avoid any signs of cracking under tension. At the High Tor weekends in the Lake District, we'd all been watched for days being bored and irritated, searching for nonexistent needles in haystacks.

We knew how to keep ourselves fit and attentive. But it was

harder out here on the ground, surrounded by jostling Indians and dizzy from lack of sleep. We were growing restive, and we wanted blood.

It was Clark, the vengeful Clark, who drew the first signs. The day had worn on till six o'clock, and we had four hours left before Mountbatten was due to arrive. I'd been trying a last telephone call to his HQ, sweating in the glass box that stank, for some reason, of stale creosote.

No one had had any luck, or any inspiration. Three Chinese had been brought in for investigation, all sullen and fearful, expecting this fiery young English colonel to order their thumbnails to be torn away or their testicles crushed.

I was in the mood for that. They were totally unhelpful, apparently not having seen any of their fellow countrymen since the festival started. One was running a laundry, one seemed to be selling copra, and one was a kind of pimp for his sister.

I sent them away and finished *The Tale of Genji* with my feet up on a bead stool and a glass of lemon barley water to keep me cool. It had been a heavy afternoon, as well as a slow one. I was short of ideas, and I never liked that.

I'd taken walks myself, shoving my way through the dense, foul-smelling crowds, and wishing I was away from it all and back in Sussex, beside the sea. I'd just had a telegram, by special messenger from the Director of Military Intelligence in Kandy, to say that my mother had gone into hospital for an emergency operation.

It wasn't helping my mood. She recovered that time, and she saw the end of the war, and the return of Churchill in the early fifties too, but I didn't know all this would happen that sultry day on the streets of Kandy. I used my boots and my stick like an old imperialist.

I went out along the lake and stood watching the temple shimmer in the haze. It rose, roof over roof, above a canopy of hibiscus and oleander trees. Dark wood over orange and purple blossom, over white and brown faces, torrents of white faces. I remember blinking, and finding myself swaying slightly in the sun.

I'd nearly fainted. I walked on, past the rows of elegant villas behind their screens of bushes, azalea and guelder rose. I kept my eyes on the people I passed. They stared back, some with insolence, a few with pride.

A man tried to sell me a box of beads. An old woman wanted to tell my fortune. A boy ran beside me with a three-legged dog, begging. I was clammy with sweat. It was the kind of British India I knew too well.

I was tired of it, that day. I wanted something less colorful, less idle, less promiscuous. I wanted something that was working, and not on perpetual holiday. I wanted something that was economical and controlled.

So I got back to the hotel at a low ebb. I took a bath in a huge, diseased old galvanized bath, with feet like dolphins and a pair of elephantine brass taps that groaned and belched forth steam and trickles.

I felt better after it, but still very tense. I went downstairs and ordered some tea, and I was in that stinking upright coffin trying to phone when I saw Clark through the glass.

He was walking beside a thin, terrified-looking girl, his hands gripping her forearm. Behind him, excited and jubilant, there strode our Indian sergeant, swatting his thighs with a cane. They provided, it occurred to me, an image of resplendent sexual provision on the sad Victorian tiles.

I felt like a voyeur at a brothel as I watched the girl being dragged through the heavy mahogany double doors into our lonely back room. She was protesting, in what must have been loud Hindi, and the sergeant was mingling reassurance, I suppose, with blunt threats.

I saw him pause to harangue an appalled clerk at the desk and to smile at an ancient lady with a lorgnette on a swaying cane rocker. Then he too followed Clark through the doors, and the hall was buzzing with shocked inquiry.

I came out of my box and glared around. There was an immediate, alert silence. Then all eyes bored lasciviously, or in prim horror, into my receding back as I myself strode through the doors into the back room. They were all clearly expecting the worst.

It's strange how it was. Even after almost four years of war,

211

there was little change in the life of Kandy. You just didn't see young native girls being dragged protesting into barred rooms by British soldiers.

I made a mental note to apologize when I'd sorted out what was going on.

Clark's shirt was wet with sweat. He was panting with rage, and he was under a tremendous excitement. He turned to face me.

"Strand's had her," he said roughly.

The sergeant coughed. This was rather too strong for his Bombay mind.

"This is apparently what the young lady seems to be indicating," he said modestly.

I looked at the girl, cowering now on the horsehair sofa, her thin sari pasted with sweat over her teen-age breasts. She had huge date-brown eyes, and they ran like weasels over the floor, hunting for a means of escape.

I sat down facing her on a hard chair.

"Look here, Clark," I said, "I don't want her roughly used. You'll remember your manners. You're an English gentleman, for my purposes. Now let's hear the full story," I said.

It seemed that the girl, who lived locally and claimed to have been a virgin, was filling a pitcher with water from the river when she was taken and, as it were, biblically known by a Chinese man.

He'd abused her apparently from behind as well as in front, and he'd taken his time about it, filling her mouth with a rag to stop her screams. The girl said she'd never seen the man before. She had no idea who he was or where he lived. He'd left her on the riverbank and pulled up his trousers and run away. At the point of climax, and the girl had volunteered and repeated this information, according to the sergeant, the man had mouthed a single foreign word. It had sounded, the girl said, like Dan's eye.

"*Banzai*," I said.

"Exactly," said Clark triumphantly. "It was Strand all right. One last orgasm," he added, "to clear himself before the kill."

It was all too plausible. It was just the kind of thing that Strand would have done. I went through the details again with the girl, talking to her as gently as I could under the dry fan, offering her tea, and then brandy. She refused both, but she stuck to her story.

I sent the sergeant to pick up the girl's mother and father, to check the background. As it happens, it was sound. They were poor but honest people, and it seemed likely it really had been the girl's first sexual experience.

I went down with the girl myself to examine the place on the riverbank where the assault had taken place. It was a lonely, muddy spot, and there were signs of a sort of struggle in the vegetation at the point the girl identified. They could have been caused by a rape.

I searched around in the reeds, the girl watching, with her thin hands at her neck, the little glass bracelets tinkling on her wrists. I envied Strand as I watched her. He had chosen well.

I found nothing. He'd been careful. There were no clues, no bits of paper or even fragments of clothing.

I questioned the girl again and again as we walked back, but she had no ideas. The sun began to set, and the torches were lit all along the banks of the river, and the drums began to beat for the climax of the festival.

I passed the grove where the sacred elephants were standing in the shade, lifting and dropping their enormous feet, flapping their huge ears to ward off the flies, waiting to take their positions in the procession by torchlight to the gates of the temple, where the admiral, Lord Louis Mountbatten, would arrive by open car to be greeted and honored, and to be shown, as the first layman in history, the holy tooth in its casket of gold.

I wiped the sweat from my brow and let the girl go.

It was Clark who voiced the full horror of the situation when I got back to the hotel.

"He'll keep indoors now, for sure," he said, with brutal Yorkshire shrewdness. "He's taken his one big risk, and he's had his last little bit of fun. He'll know that he's burned his boats. He's shown his hand, in his true colors."

Brundall was whittling a pencil to a fine point with a razor blade. He paused, holding the sliver of thin metal in the air, between finger and thumb.

"You mean . . ." he said slowly, then paused. "Yes," he said. "You mean that he'll assume that he's been rumbled. He's given us the clue of the rape, handed it up to us, as it were, on a plate. So that means he's decided to behave, from now on, as if we know who he really is."

There was a long silence.

"You're right," said Vonnegut. "You sure are right."

"So we're finished, sir," said Corporal Walpole. "We'll never find him."

22

Nobody thought we would. Except perhaps for Vonnegut, we were all disillusioned. It seemed that our chances of finding Strand before he made his assassination attempt were close to minimal.

When I look back now, and realize that we did find him, and lose him again, I see that it must be hard to convey the curious flexibility of those last hours, the sense of time as elastic, elongated for a moment, as if it would never stop, and then twanging to, very fast, with a ping, and a stinging sensation.

We found him, yes. At last we did find him. But it was after we'd all gone out for our last, hopeless reconnoitering.

At six o'clock I'd assembled my weary troops in the back room, and we'd gone over the public plan for the evening's celebrations.

They were going to be grandiose and sumptuous. Our own, more private, involvement was, alas, to be a touch more squalid. Amidst all the official gold braid and white ducks, Department M was not going to parade in full army fig.

Vonnegut suggested that our only hope of success lay in some concession to the arts of disguise. So we started, each of us, to work out our own versions of fancy dress. Brundall was going to be seen as a Singhalese porter. Clark opted for an Indian fakir, complete with turban, though without any public bed of nails.

Vonnegut was going to go the whole hog and turn himself out as a dancer. For myself, I decided on English tweeds, as if a local planter of loyal disposition who'd come out to cheer the royal.

As for Molly, Walpole and Billington, to be honest, I don't remember. I have a suspicion that Molly wore something puce, and flowing, and it rather suited her buxom spread.

Having reviewed our disguises, I summarized the expected movement of the evening, with its advantages for us, and its perils.

The fifty sacred elephants were to walk in state along the mango-lined main avenue to the gates of the temple, and then up through the groves of oleanders to the steps.

A huge crowd would obviously be lining the route, and would move and surge as the elephants did, with all the flexibility and unpredictable fullness and rush of a great river in spate. There would be light, from torches and from the full moon, but it would only serve to increase the uneasy balance of shadow in the general darkness.

At the steps of the temple, the procession would pause and wait for the arrival of the guest of honor. Mountbatten would have been driven in an open Rolls around the other side of the lake, and his car would arrive, in theory, a few moments after the last of the elephants.

The High Priest would step out at the top of the temple steps carrying the sacred casket in his arms. At the foot of the steps, in the midst of the milling crowd, he would lift the lid and reveal the sacred relic to the royal visitor.

It would be the first time in history this had happened, and everyone was expecting the whole uncontrollable crowd to be craning its collective neck to get a good view. There would be people all over—up trees, on the temple steps, on the backs of mules and elephants and motorcars.

The police would be doing their best to control them, but it would be an impossible job. In the immediate vicinity of the C-in-C, a company of armed soldiers would maintain a cordon of safety, but it would be a narrow one, a protection against knives and blows rather than bullets.

216

When the casket had been opened, the official plan was to close it again and to pass it to the priest riding on the sacred temple elephant, which would carry it in procession around the circumference of the lake, and eventually back, for safe-keeping, to the temple itself. The whole procession, there and back, would last about three hours.

Throughout this time, there would be an enormous crowd. But Mountbatten himself would only be present in public for about fifteen minutes, there at the foot of the temple steps.

Afterward, he would make a brief progress through the streets of Kandy and would then be taken to the Town Hall for an official cocktail party and banquet. Indoors, he would probably be fairly safe.

So, at any rate, I judged. From the information we had available about the camera-gun, one could presume the period of maximum danger would last only about five minutes, while the priest was actually in view and carrying the casket down the steps.

Up to that point, attention would be turned away from Mountbatten toward the priest, and the assassin would have his best opportunity.

Our plans were laid accordingly. All seven of us would follow the procession with the sacred elephants. At the temple, Brundall and Clark would be at the top of the steps, under the overhanging roof. Vonnegut would be behind Mountbatten's car; Walpole and Billington would be near the sacred elephant. I would be stationed, with Molly, at the bottom of the steps.

At the slightest sign of trouble, from Strand or from anyone else, Vonnegut would fire his pistol in the air, and we would assume that Mountbatten would take some instant evasive action. It was a doubtful precaution, but, as Clark said, it was better than nothing.

So there we were, all in civilian or fancy dress clothes, with our faces blackened and our eyes open, slinking through doorways and pushing through the crowd, in the steaming wake of the great, slow elephants as they plodded in their massive, caparisoned glory toward the temple.

It was a scene of voluptuous decadence.

I remember thinking of T. E. Lawrence, that grim scene in *The Seven Pillars of Wisdom* where he goes in disguise behind the Turkish lines, and they take him prisoner.

It was a kind of uncanny anticipation. We did take Strand prisoner, our own Lawrence in disguise, and we were ready to put him to the same torment as the Turks put Lawrence, too.

It happened fast. I was alone, avoiding being trampled on, it seemed, for much of the time. And then I was back with the whole old team in London, except that now they were gathered at my shoulder in Kandy.

Brundall had one arm in a stranglehold, and Vonnegut had his pistol leveled. It was Clark who made the introductions.

"Prisoner for you, sir," he said fatuously.

I remember staring at Strand for a long time, not knowing what to do, or what, for a moment, might happen next. He looked boyish, and naughty, in a way that seemed to make light of the strange tragedy we were wading into the depths of.

Then Vonnegut was plucking at my buttoned sleeve. I went aside with him, angry at his insistence.

"There's something wrong," he said, nodding at Strand. "He's far too goddamned sure of himself."

I heard the incessant beat of the drums, almost an African tribal noise, it seemed, but with a sort of eerie quality too in the darkness. I tried to see Vonnegut's face. I couldn't. He was just a barren outline, a two-dimensional cutout of a man.

"We got him beside the temple," Vonnegut said. "I found an old monk who'd seen him around, and he pointed him out to me."

I looked across at Strand, a slim, contained form, with Clark's revolver in his ribs. It seemed impossible.

"Well done, Major," I said. "For a time I thought that he'd beaten us. You got the gun, I assume?"

"Of course," said Vonnegut. "He was carrying the camera, with the gun in place, and a box of shells in his briefcase."

"Then what are you worried about?" I asked. "We've drawn his teeth, surely?"

Vonnegut was silent for a moment.

"I wonder," he said.

The drums were loud now. They were drumming for the kill.

"He knows something we don't," said Vonnegut. "He has an accomplice, maybe."

I felt very tired suddenly. A sense of déjà vu overcame me, sharply, like a cloud of rain.

"So what do you want to do?" I asked.

I asked, but I knew. There was only one thing to do, in the circumstances, and I knew that Vonnegut, with all his American logic, would require it of me. I waited for him to formulate the precise words, and I watched his embarrassment.

Then I let him off the hook.

"Let's go back to the police station," I said. "It'll give us time to think."

We did allow for some forms of torture, in the interests of information, when the stakes were high; that was always known. In Intelligence work, it was never spoken of, except in the quieter, passing jargons of the time as perhaps "a little sweetener" or "a touch of ointment for the wound."

It was another, coarser phrase that Clark used as we stood in the dripping cellar of the police station with Strand bound in a chair and Vonnegut slapping the blade of his penknife open and shut. They made a fine medieval pair that night, in their Ku-Klux Klan robes, with their blackened faces.

I took my time making up my mind, and I watched Strand there, silent and absorbed in his own dreams, in his chair.

Finally, Vonnegut was the one to fear. There was no solution to his bare American need. He had to turn over every stone.

I looked at Strand again, and I felt a slow despair sinking through my bones.

"Loosen his hands," I said.

I went over to a corner and picked up the electric iron. We were going to have to go through the motions.

There was only a single hard-backed chair, and we had Strand in that, loosely fastened. We were just about to start.

Clark was standing back, with his head on one side, like a man arranging someone for his portrait, and Vonnegut had come over to help me unscrew the plug.

"It's against the regulations, Colonel," said Strand conversationally.

"Fucking shut up," said Clark.

His nerves were bad. We were all watching Strand, and then suddenly none of us were.

The explosion seemed to rock the walls of the building. It was more like an earthquake, at that distance, a kind of shaking feeling rather than a loud sound.

None of us took it in for a second. It was a distraction, and a curious, unexpected one. It gave Strand all the time he needed.

He must have been counting steadily in his head. He knew just how much time he had to hold on for, how much of his beleaguered vitality he had to try to conserve.

He took it all in one lump, and he gathered his forces and flung himself up and through the window into the yard, naked except for his underpants.

It gave him a better chance. There were plenty of people dressed like that in the heat. He was fifty yards away, running with a steady stride across the square, before we, stumbling against one another in the doorway, were out and onto his track.

Vonnegut got a shot off, two-handed, down on his knees under the POLICE light. But Strand was zigzagging, and Vonnegut missed.

"Fucking cocksucker," Vonnegut was saying, years before we knew that Texans used that sort of language.

Then we were all running hard. Through the town, ducking past stragglers, trying to keep our eyes on Strand in the crowd.

It was no good. We lost him before he reached the gates of the temple compound.

We struggled up through the confused crowd. No one seemed to know what had happened. There was a bustle and shouting of confused accounts, but the word "bomb" seemed to occur in all of them.

"Christ," I remember Vonnegut saying. "Where the Christ did he get a bomb?"

At the temple steps we realized what had happened. A huge chunk of the building had been blown apart, and the steps were littered with bits of wood and rubble, and the dreadful, torn remnants of human flesh.

I spoke to a soldier, his submachine gun at the ready. I had my military pass, thank heaven, and he told me what I wanted to know.

"Mountbatten's okay," he said. "Oh, yes, I'm sure. It looked like the golden beehive thing that priest was bringing down just blew up in his face. The C-in-C was thrown back against the car, but he's okay."

A few yards away, I heard the sudden rasping whir of an outboard motor starting. Vonnegut, over to my left, was shouting.

"It's Strand," he was saying. "He's there. In the boat."

I ran down to the lakeside. A small motorboat was hurtling across the water in the moonlight. There were the sounds of several shots, a ragged burst of submachine-gun fire.

But the aim was erratic. The boat kept on, and suddenly it was there at the other side, moored at a small jetty, and a dim, naked-looking figure was running from it toward a villa with a FOR SALE notice in the garden.

"Let's go," said Clark at my elbow.

I ran with him along the side of the lake. Suddenly he stopped. There was a parked car with the ignition key in the lock.

I got up on the running board as Clark clawed the wheel and fiddled with the huge, swordlike hand brake outside the door.

It was an old, old car, but it would still go. We began to chug around the lake in what I later discovered was a 1916 Mercedes.

23

So there was Strand, running up the lawn toward the French doors of the villa, feeling the moist grass under his toes for the last time.

Michael Strand. He'll always be that to me. He had a Japanese name, of course, and he might have liked to be known by it in England as he was in Japan for a while, until the end of the war, when MacArthur took over and the Americans had their will.

I'll write it once, before I finish, but it's a hard name, and it flows badly in English. It's best, I think, that he stands in the main story as Michael Strand, our magnolia tree.

He was running then, with a few strides to go to the cool verandah, and a little time, only a very little, to do what he had to do. The moon was shining in a long, pale swath across the lawn, and he looked back once, maybe, and saw the moored boat, and the cold steel of the water, and, far away, in the glimmer of torchlight and smoke, the ruin of the Temple of the Tooth.

I see him struggling now, very tired physically, as he works at the handles of the doors. Panting, he lifts his knee, forces. The doors open, and he goes in, to the gathered, held warmth of the house. He wastes no time downstairs amidst the baroque hired clutter of someone else's furniture.

He hasn't the energy or the appetite for such passing trivialities as admiring chairs. He goes up the bare treads of the wooden stairs, two at a time, his hand light on the curling banister. He takes two strides, and the inner door is there.

Beyond it, the loose world of the summer festival, with all its fortunes and oleanders, its torches and prurience, has contracted to the wooden death chamber of Michael Strand, the narrow pot in which the magnolia tree will die.

Many men have wondered, and some have written, about why Strand should have done what he did in the next five minutes, in the isolation and piety of his own room. Some have believed, and Vonnegut is one, that he thought his mission had failed, and he took the only way he knew to atone for his shame.

It may be so. I knew myself that Mountbatten was still alive when I spoke to the soldier, and that Strand had missed his chance. He may well have questioned someone himself, as he ran, and heard the news. It's possible, and it's even likely, to a European mind.

There has to be some reason, some overbearing pressure, to the Puritan conscience to account for a man taking his own life. I wonder, though. He was running very fast, and we were hard on his heels.

He hadn't very much time to hear the news, and none at all to verify it. He could see the building blown to smithereens, and the blood and confusion everywhere. He was very tired, and weakened by what he'd been through, and, besides all that, he was pretty crazy in his last weeks.

He wasn't the Michael Strand he'd once been. He'd lost his caution, it seems to me. The pressure of all those years in the bottom drawer, in the undergrowth, in the skin of one or another alias he must lose at will, had begun to decay his identity, his power, at heart, to remain himself.

There was something that had to burst. It was too much for him, for anyone. So he lost his wits, in a way. He nearly broke Su Lin's hand in the mangle at the House of Happiness; he showed his face too much to the monks; he took an Indian virgin beside the river.

He flaunted himself, he must have done, to Vonnegut, at

the steps of the temple. He was very mad by then. He was full of the sin of Pride. He thought he could do what he liked; he could fool the whole world, in his own way, and forever.

I'm not a man for psychiatry, for the cheap solutions of your Harley Street impresarios. It doesn't do to be clever about the brain. But, for all that, and with reservations, I think that Michael Strand was a man who wanted to die.

At the end, he did. He was crying out for help, for a way to cope with the burden the world—I mean, Yoshida—had given to him. He couldn't bear it alone any more. He'd reached his limits, the way we all do.

So he started to make mistakes. He began to lay his trail of little errors, to pave his own way to the tiny room in which he'd be bound to do what he did. He had to justify his desire to give it all up. He had to be wrong; he had to fail.

So he made it easy for himself. He didn't care, you see, at the end, if Mountbatten was alive or dead. With the top part of his brain he could feel that he might have won, that he'd done what he'd lived to do. With the bottom part, he was all a burning need, now, to be gone, to be shut of it all, to be part of the turning mold.

He didn't know this, of course. He had no more idea than the moth that goes to the flame. When he opened the door of his bedroom and walked across the floor to the chest of drawers, he was thinking only of a simple military necessity.

We were on his tracks, and he knew that he couldn't hope to escape our torments if we took him alive. There were things in his brain, if we prized them out, that would subvert the work of the Kempei Tai for a generation.

He was very strong, and he wasn't afraid, I'm sure of that. There are risks, though, that an agent in the field can never take. You have never any right to suppose you can hold your brain unbroken in the face of the ultimate sanctions. You have to remove the key from your tempters.

So he had to die, or we'd have opened his head like a tin can. That's the way that Major Clark saw it, and he was right. We all were, in our way. There were fragments of all these reasons, and others buried, too, in what Strand did.

224

It's the thing itself that stays and blights the mind. Tonight, five thousand miles away in Shropshire, the blinding rain comes down outside my window and irons down the creases. It's flattened out, the memory, to a barren plain of absences, and refusals.

I see him go to his upper drawer, and slide it open, and lift out the *tanto* in its fold of tissue. I see him turn and draw down the laundered white kimono from the single raw hook on the back of the door. This is the one he'd never worn before, the one he'd kept aside for the final hour.

He drops his underpants, kicks them aside. Naked now, he breathes very deeply, then slips his arms into the wide, hanging sleeves. He knots the *obi* at his waist, the loose, easy knot he will soon unloosen.

There are so many, such beautiful, representations of it, perhaps most movingly of all in the noble scene from the *Chushingura*. I once saw Minoshawa play it out for twenty minutes at the old Kabuki Theater in the *Ginza*.

For Strand, there were fewer minutes, and more stresses. It wasn't a play for him, an act of will in front of a still, attentive audience, on a wide, lovely stage in a great theater in his own adopted country. It was reality, the final reality.

He must have thought of others, as I would have done. Perhaps he remembered Taki Zenzaburo, who gave orders to fire on the foreign troops at Kobe in 1868. Perhaps he remembered the brothers Sakon and Naiki, who tried to kill Iyeyasu.

I see him kneeling, his mind focusing now into the slender corridor where the delicate steering toward the incision has to begin. He lets the images in the *sumi-ee* drift away, renouncing the world. He sifts out the three branches in the *ikebana*, discarding his last flowers.

He lays the scabbard aside, sheathing the rippling blade in the crisp papers. There must be only a little blood. It must be done well. He loosens the knot at his waist, leaning back on his heels.

He begins to hear the great sea, watching the waves turn and curl in the dulled, exquisite silver along the *kashira*.

Downstairs, he hears the breaking of glass, the shattering

window of the drawing room he had locked behind him. He hears footsteps, voices. But it doesn't matter now. His mind is balanced at the point in front of the altar.

There is no going back.

He feels the blade rise and arc of its own accord, reaching out its narrow beak for the exact spot, a little to the left of his navel.

This is how it was, but it wasn't what was in Clark's or Vonnegut's mind as our ancient Mercedes ground to a halt outside the long verandah and we all ran for the front door. We'd had a noisy journey around the lake, but a stylish one: Clark with his arms high at the wheel, I beside him in the rigid leather passenger seat, and Vonnegut, Al Capone-wise, on the running board. He'd caught up with us, in a tight sprint, at the edge of the compound, and I'd run the window down and put out an arm to help him up.

There were torches, torches everywhere, it seemed, and the endless undertone of the tom-toms behind the florid roar of the heavy engine. Faces had gone by, and legs and arms twisted in the last contortions of the devil-dancing. And then we were out under the trees, on the curve of the road.

We'd moved faster there, with Clark ramming his foot down on the worn accelerator, and Vonnegut hanging on with his head laid in against my window. The lake had been glittering off and on to our left all the way, and we'd watched the moon, silver as an old salver, beside a swatch of clouds.

We'd spoken little. Each of us, no doubt, had his own thoughts, and his own fears. It was a short journey, anyway, and there was never any question of where we were going. Clark, the eagle-eyed Clark, had noted down the only villa with a FOR SALE sign at the gate.

"There it is," he said, and then we were swinging in, past the low, overhanging branch of a Spanish wisteria. It was a small wood-built villa, dark under overgrown vegetation, but it had its air of expensive charm, a little bewildered to be so run-down.

You might have thought there was no time for this kind of

idle speculation, but there's always time in moments of fast action. It's as if the brain moves quicker, the senses are all more alert. You can do what you have to do and still fill in the background.

So I was smelling the deep odor of something rotten beside the wall, feeling a stitch in my waist, hearing the remote yowl of a kind of singing, all this overlaid on the chill, smooth grooving of molded woodwork as I groped at the front door for the lock and handle.

It wouldn't turn. I felt Vonnegut at my shoulder, pressing hard, and then cursing, and then Clark was calling from around the corner of the house.

"Over here."

We pushed our way, as he'd done, through a bank of shrubbery, something prickly tearing at my tweed jacket, feet sinking in earth. Clark had a brick in his hand; I can see him now, dedicated and symbolic, Roman almost in his white robe, the man poised to hurl the first stone.

Then there was the crash and the splintering, glass flying in all directions, and the French window was an open wooden frame. Clark was reaching through, fumbling the catch aside, throwing the window back.

I followed him through. I had my revolver out and cocked now, and I knew Vonnegut behind me had a pistol, but Clark was unarmed. He was brave as a lion that night, our vengeful little Yorkshire tyke.

I couldn't see for a moment in the dimness of the room. I stumbled over something, a chair maybe, or a low table, and I felt a sharp pain in my ankle.

"Strand," I heard Clark call, ahead of me, blundering but still on his feet. "It's no good. Surrender, you bugger."

They were both very foulmouthed that night, he and Vonnegut. Unusually so, not like themselves. I'd seen it before. The stress of emotion often brought it out, this dirty talking, as if the mouth had to ratify the coarsening of the physical fibers, their crude readiness to use their force for violent ends.

There was no reply. It was pointless talk, the kind there often is to steel the resolution. I came to my knees, and then there was a flood of light. Vonnegut had found the switch. We were in some kind of reception room. A marble floor, potted palms. The traditional double-leaf arches above the doorway.

Clark was a tall, white target in one corner, a sitting duck for anyone there to kill. But the room was empty except for ourselves.

"Upstairs," I heard Vonnegut saying. "I'll lead the way."

He was through the door, crouched low, his pistol nosing ahead like a rat's snout. I went after him along the wall, dipping and weaving as I came through into the hall. It was empty, too, so far as I could tell, but the light was vague here, and no one seemed to be interested in looking for another switch.

I heard Clark behind me, tripping over something and cursing. I remember thinking that if Strand had wanted to he could have picked us off at his leisure by the noise alone. It wasn't a classic mopping-up operation, not by any means.

Then Vonnegut was climbing the stairs, a lean, low shape in the mixed light from the moon and the reception-room light. I stubbed my foot on a tread, and then I was after him, with Clark at my back.

Everything was slowing down now, even more. I remember reaching the landing an age later, as it seemed, seeing Vonnegut hesitating in slow motion, as if in mid-stride, not knowing which to choose of the four or five doors.

I don't know why I chose the one I did, or why it turned out to be the bathroom. But it was. All white tiles, and the hanging chain of the lavatory saying PULL. I saw this in a blaze of light when I touched the switch.

Vonnegut had found one locked. I saw him wrench at the handle as I came back to the landing. Clark had drawn a blank on a bedroom. I saw his white ghostly shape looming back toward me.

"He's in here," said Vonnegut. "For sure."

He shot the lock off with his pistol, and the noise seemed to expand and fill the whole house. Then we were all on our knees, the door open, staring at piled-up furniture and old musty picture frames.

Clark was the first to try the right room. It was locked too, of course, and he used his shoulder. The hard wood of the door bounced him back, and then Vonnegut had his gun down again.

"Take care," I said. "This is the one."

It was all happening, I suppose, incredibly quickly. I doubt if we'd been in the house for more than fifty seconds. But there seemed to be time for leisured reflection now. I'd seen, with a quick step back and a flash of the switch, that the fifth room was empty. So either Strand had escaped through a back door or he was here in this room.

Somehow we all thought he was there in the room. Our later accounts agree on that much. But we had our own ideas about what we'd find when we broke the door.

I know from Vonnegut's memoirs that he suspected some kind of bomb. He writes that he warned us all to keep back when he shot the lock off, but I don't recall him speaking. Nor does Clark, for that matter.

But we were all very keyed up. We saw, perhaps, what we wanted to see, and we heard, no doubt, only what we needed to hear. I know that Clark was imagining Strand in there with a gun leveled, and a full magazine to rip us all apart when we came in through the door.

In view of this, he was very brave when he stepped forward, unarmed as he was, and went in first with his bare hands. I stepped after him and had the switch on and Clark thrown aside all in a single movement, I remember.

Vonnegut must have been somewhere behind me. But I didn't think of Vonnegut. I thought only of what we'd found, as I'd known we would.

You know what it was. He was at right angles to us, from the door. He'd made the incision as we came in through the window, I estimate, and he'd managed to turn the blade and move it across in the classic fashion.

He was rocking on his heels as he squatted facing the scroll on the wall. His hand was rigid on the hilt, and his head was bowed. He was making no sound, as I remember.

I suppose we made a frozen tableau for a second or two. But

there was no applause from the unseen audience. Just the slither of feet, and then Clark saying, "Oh, my God," and the sound of his vomiting in the corner.

Vonnegut was beside me. I lifted Strand's head, and I held his face in my hands. I looked into his eyes for what seemed like a long time.

"He'll live," I heard Vonnegut saying. "I'll get a doctor."

Then I put the barrel of my revolver into Strand's mouth and pulled the trigger.

24

You see, he might have betrayed me. He would surely have known that himself, even with the sword in his side. He might have smiled a little, or said something involuntarily, through the pain. He was too far gone then to be in control. So would anyone have been, in the last stages of *seppuku*.

Vonnegut thought that he might survive. He keeps on saying so whenever he has occasion to go into print or onto some television program on the subject. He retains his taste for publicity, despite his arthritis.

Strand was dead already, though, or as good as, when I put my gun in his mouth. It's all there in the official autopsy reports. I did no more than put the poor man out of his misery, as you'd kill a rabbit with myxomatosis, or shoot a lamed horse.

That's what the British Army decided, and they were right. He couldn't have lived long enough to be interrogated, and he wouldn't have given much, at any rate, under any official pressures. Not that those were what Vonnegut had in mind. He had his thoughts on the thumbscrews and the rack.

Well, Vonnegut was right, of course. Poor Vonnegut. He'll have a heart attack in his wheelchair when he hears the news.

You were right all the time, my dear Vonnegut, in what you suspected, and what you never quite dared, for fear of libel, to say. You were right, and you were wrong. I didn't shoot Michael Strand to keep his mouth shut. And I didn't shoot him out of simple compassion either.

I was his *kaishaku*. I ought to have been there behind him with a long *katana*, ready to sever his head at a single stroke when he drove the blade in. He deserved that. We all deserve that, *in extremis*.

It's out now, on the table. It's why I began the book, the need to confess, to set the record straight at last, and the need grows. I've seen it before, a dozen times, with interrogators, the slow trickle of the victim's confession broadening to a steady gush.

I feel it now in myself, for the unseen interrogators, for my readers, for history, for Clark, and for Vonnegut. I want them all to know now, to see who managed the whole operation, at all levels, who held the strings of their fate and their glory in his own hands.

It wasn't Strand, not entirely. It wasn't Yoshida, either, though he was the one who broached the matter in words for the first time, as early as 1936. We were in the old Imperial Hotel, drinking gin fizzes and discussing the Roehm purge.

He was a real one for the Germans, Yoshida. He couldn't see that the way Hitler got rid of the SA leaders was any kind of betrayal. Treachery begets treachery, I remember him saying. You have to beat it with its own weapons.

It led us on to treason, and we knocked the ball about for a while through most of the famous cases. Yoshida knew my views on the way England was going, and the concept hung in the air a little when we came to the present day. There was nothing specific said, but I saw later on why he'd brought the subject up.

So it wasn't entirely a shock when Michael Strand appeared in my life that crucial morning in 1941. I'd almost been expecting somebody. What Strand proposed, though, was a simpler affair, by far, than what we evolved together.

It wasn't in Michael Strand's imagination to run his future for three years as a double agent. He wanted information only, when he first approached me; at best he hoped for an accomplice inside the Army's Intelligence Department.

The dream that planted the magnolia tree was mine. It could never have flowered in its pot without my planning and my administration. It needed the care of tender and loving hands.

I gave it that. I needed Michael Strand. He needed me. We made a fine team. We were like a good head on a strong pair of shoulders. I had the dreams and the ideas. Strand had the will and the muscle to put them into action.

It's cold now, without the gas heater on. The cylinder's exhausted, and I haven't the strength left to go down and drag another one up the stairs from the cellar. It helps in a way, to be cold. It keeps the mind clear, and it gives the will to press on, and finish.

I can hear an owl outside, hunting, sometimes, as I pause in my typing. He'll be looking for mice down by the oak wood that was once my father's tennis court. So much has changed, so very much. But not the owls hunting in the twilight. Thank God they can never take that away.

It's nearly twelve. Mary will be putting down her Agatha Christie and smoothing the pillow. She'll know I'm not coming to bed for a while yet. She'll lie awake with the covers up, hearing the typewriter, the heavy machine gun of the words rattling over the page, and after a few minutes she'll reach up and switch the light off, and she'll turn over on her side and try to sleep.

It's hard to be seventy, and still in love with someone, and unsatisfied. It's hard too to have kept a secret for thirty-five years, and to have to break it open, and to make it clear, for strangers.

Treason, they'll say. High treason. The sort of thing that put William Joyce in front of the firing squad, though I'll say this, he should never have gone. He died for his principles, like a man of honor. And besides, he was Irish.

Irish, yes. Like the unknown man who turned the dial of his

radio on the hill and killed Mountbatten in the bay. The unknown man who set me writing ten months ago. The unknown man with a guilty secret like my own. What kind of betrayal was his, I wonder.

No, they'll not say betrayal, though, at the Rotary Club, or the Church Carnival, when it comes. We've had too many causes here in Shropshire to see things as clear as that. There are families down the road who have ancestors who turned their coats for Cromwell, and again for Charles II.

But that was a long time ago. And both were English. I read the other day that Errol Flynn's supposed to have been a spy for the Nazis. Errol Flynn. The man who won the war for the United States of America in *Objective Burma*.

It's hard to believe, and I see that David Niven denies it was possible. We need our friends to say that. I wonder if Peter Losely-Campbell will deny the report of my treason when he hears the news over his vodka and orange juice in the bar at the Savile?

I rather fancy he may. Poor gullible Peter. The best sort of English gentleman. He'll not want to think his old golfing companion was a former enemy agent. It won't seem proper to him.

They're all too bloody narrow-minded, when it comes down to it, the English. And the nicest ones are the worst of the lot, in some ways. They can't see beyond the lines of sycamores at the ends of their noses.

But it isn't lines of sycamores anymore, and it hasn't been for a long time. It isn't church bazaars and growing cabbages and the forelocks being tugged to the squire and the parson. I drove a tram in the General Strike, in 1926. I knew it was changing, even then.

We had to renew the faith. It wasn't going to be enough to give the working classes more money. They wanted blood and pride. Hitler saw that, I'll say that for him. I'd never have gone in line with the Nazis, even before I knew what they did to the Jews, but at least they diagnosed the problem.

The Romans were wrong. The people need more than bread and circuses. They need a sense of belonging to something transcending the banal concerns of their everyday lives. They need a sense of a just society in which they share some part.

It mustn't be what the Russians tried, that empty materialism of leveling down. It has to have history on its side. We've lacked a renaissance of the old values, the accepted hierarchies of responsible position, and we've lacked any kind of organization, or model, to give us this. It's been gone since the 1930s.

Only the Japanese were able to stop the rot. They saw the dangers, and they held the structures. The *samurai* became their officer class, and they nearly won the war. They'd be fighting still—some of them are, in the islands, for that matter, in Guam and the Philippines—if the emperor hadn't told them to stop.

The ones who did stop had the skill to shift their place. The officer class, those who were left of them, became the captains of industry, and they've nearly won the peace.

The British Empire's come home to roost in Haslemere and Notting Hill Gate, and what's it done for its loyal subjects? Pensioned them off with a melting bundle of pound notes and a few hollyhocks in the Home Counties. Or dragged them penniless and disillusioned out of the slums of Calcutta into the Babylon of Bristol.

We have to learn. It's not too late, maybe, still, if we try. We're an island nation, just like the Japanese. We rely on our foreign trade to be rich. We have the remains of an old, formal society. We're a race of warriors, with a special pride and a reticence of our own.

In the 1890s the Japanese had the wit and the humility to learn from ourselves. They bought our clothes and our ships. They learned how to build a fleet that would smash the Russian navy at the Battle of Tsushima Straits, in 1905.

They transformed themselves, and they remained a great civilization. The greatest civilization the world has ever known, in my opinion. Capable, at its best, of producing the *inro* of Joko and the metalwork of the Goto family.

What have we got to put against that? A few landscapes by Constable and a handful of derivative Latin plays by a Stratford actor. You can keep them, for my money.

It was no treason in the 1940s to want to ally oneself with people like the Japanese. When the choice was Hirohito, the embodied descendant of two thousand years of unbroken respect, and stammering George VI, who only became king because his brother fell in love with a Yankee divorcée, what sensible man could be in doubt?

With the Japanese as our friends we could have divided up the trade of the world. We could have set common, decent social standards from Zanzibar to Hawaii. We could have held off the creeping American democracies and the crude Russian vulgarisms.

As it is, we won the war, and we lost the battle. The worst people have taken over, just as surely as if they'd fought for what, in fact, they've stolen and spoiled. Our ideals and our hopes.

Oh, yes, I'm letting rip now, I know. I've gone a long way from Michael Strand, and Lord Louis Mountbatten, to make my justification. I was a traitor, they may say. But at least they'll know my reasons.

The children will, anyway, and Mary. At least they'll read the story the way I've written it, if no one else does. Poor John. It won't be easy to hear his father spoken of as a traitor. It doesn't matter, perhaps, about the reasons. Not in public. The very word has a cold ring.

They'll take my name, perhaps, and make it a synonym for a kind of treason. Like Lord Haw Haw and Guy Burgess. It's a strange bag to be with. I don't have much time for the others. They never really set their necks in the noose.

Apart from Quisling. There was a man who gave his name to a thing, as exactly as the Earl of Sandwich did. I remember reading about Quisling when he stood before the firing squad.

All his life he'd done what he believed to be right for Norway. All his life he'd lived according to the principles of mathematics. As he stood facing the guns, he took time to calculate the weight of his body and the probable velocity and impact pressure of the bullets.

He was able to balance himself with such precise care that his body remained in a standing position when he died.

236

That must be a metaphor for how it should be. To end one's life still upright, triumphing over the enemy in the very moment of annihilation, and on one's own terms.

I would like it to be so with me. If anyone cares. If anyone, apart from Clark and Vonnegut and perhaps poor torpid Molly, still cares. In my bad moments I've wondered about that. In a way it may be the worst outcome of all.

To have been a traitor, and to have confessed, and to have justified one's treason to the last letter, and to find that at the last, thirty-five years later, there's no one left alive who has any interest, one way or another.

It was an old war, the children will say. Who fought against who in the war, Grandpa? Was that in the first war, or the second? Were the Japanese on our side? Let's march on Sunday against the National Front. Those old struggles are of little importance now.

I wonder. The official files are open. I couldn't have told the story without their help. I needed Strand's diary, and the memoranda. It's public knowledge, most of it, mere history.

I couldn't be prosecuted now, I don't suppose, even if there were any evidence to bring me to trial with. It may even be that this last chapter will seem like an old man's ravings, the delusions of an addled, scandal-hungry brain.

It may be. But it doesn't matter, really. It isn't the common crowd I'm writing for, I know that in my heart. It isn't Vonnegut or Clark, either. It's you, Strand. You, in whatever warriors' heaven you decorate with the sword wound still there in your side.

The wound from this sword I have here tonight on my desk. The blade unsheathed on the puce blotter. The faint line of the *hamon* a little darker, it seems, in the artificial light, than the softer steel of the ground.

I could use it, Strand, as you did. I could open those loose tweeds and put it into the dry folds of skin in my ancient belly. I can't have very long to live, whatever I do. It would close our score, and with more honor, if I choose my own time.

You see, I know what the real treason was. I say that you went crazy, that you had a death wish at the end. But at least

237

you planted the bomb, and you planted it well enough to explode. You made your bid.

Warped as you may have been, after years in the double service of sly masters, at least you got your shot in at the enemy, and you died on the battlefield. You have your place in the fields of glory.

It was up to me after you died. It was up to me even before you died, when I say I thought you were mad. I was the unseen accomplice in place to kill. I had my chance, or I could have made one. It only needed what I never had when it came to the point—the *kamikaze* spirit. The willingness to die.

I betrayed you, Strand. I could have shot Mountbatten there in his cinema, with my service revolver. It needed only the guts. He was only a yard away. I could have forced an interview, on security grounds, and shot him that very night in the hospital bed after the bomb.

You knew, as well as I did, that I never would. So did Yoshida, when I interviewed him in the prisoner-of-war camp. I saw his lip curl, in a kind of contempt, and with a kind of sympathy too. He knew, as you knew, that men have their different qualities.

I was the head that planned; you were the hand that slew. It doesn't make it any easier tonight, knowing that. Knowing that I might never have broken down inside my head, under pressure, as you did. Knowing that I was the stronger one in mind, you in will.

It's the courage of the will that matters most; we both know that. It's what we were fighting for, idealists as we both were. We wanted an England where moral fiber was what it used to be, where men were still prepared to be absolute for what they believed.

You died exemplifying that. I lived denying it. Until now. So after thirty-five years, the truth's out. It's out for the public, here in my story. And it's out for you and me in these last paragraphs.

I've drawn the curtains. I can't see much, the moon's gone behind a cloud. I know what's out there, though, every shrub

238

and tree down the hill as far as the river. I could name them, one by one.

I don't feel quite as cold as I did. Only the sword feels cold, here on my skin. I might be playing a game, I don't know really. I might be going to sheathe it again, and rise, and switch the light off, and go to bed.

I could even get up early and burn the manuscript. Or I could get my shotgun and do it that way. It would be easier, and it might, after all, not really be so much less Japanese.

I hear the owl, still hunting. I know only one thing. That I have to finish typing and leave these papers ready for John to find in the morning. That I have to clear the space in front of the *tokonoma*. That I have to put my kimono on. That I have to sheathe the blade in tissues. That I have to try.

Ave atque vale, Magonojo Teruo. You showed me the way.